W9-AUO-629

WHAT WAS MINE

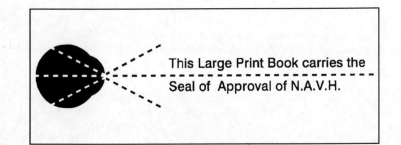

This Large Print Book carries the
Seal of Approval of N.A.V.H.

WHAT WAS MINE

HELEN KLEIN ROSS

THORNDIKE PRESS
A part of Gale, Cengage Learning

GALE
CENGAGE Learning·

Farmington Hills, Mich • San Francisco • New York • Waterville, Maine
Meriden, Conn • Mason, Ohio • Chicago

GALE
CENGAGE Learning®

Thorndike Press® Large Print Women's Fiction.
The text of this Large Print edition is unabridged.
Other aspects of the book may vary from the original edition.
Set in 16 pt. Plantin.

LIBRARY OF CONGRESS CATALOGING-IN-PUBLICATION DATA

Names: Ross, Helen Klein, author.
Title: What Was Mine / Helen Klein Ross.
Description: Large print edition. | Waterville, Maine : Thorndike Press Large Print, 2016. | © 2016 | Series: Thorndike Press large print women's fiction
Identifiers: LCCN 2015050439| ISBN 9781410489111 (hardback) | ISBN 1410489116 (hardcover)
Subjects: LCSH: Mothers and daughters—Fiction. | Kidnapping—Fiction. | Deception—Fiction. | Family secrets—Fiction. | Life change events—Fiction. | Large type books. | Domestic fiction. | Psychological fiction. | BISAC: FICTION / Contemporary Women.
Classification: LCC PS3618.O845263 W47 2016b | DDC 813/.6—dc23
LC record available at http://lccn.loc.gov/2015050439

Published in 2016 by arrangement with Gallery Books, an imprint of Simon & Schuster, Inc.

Printed in Mexico
1 2 3 4 5 6 7 20 19 18 17 16

For my mother, Margaret Whelan Klein
and in memory of her mother,
Helen Callaghan Whelan

OLDE CELTIC LULLABY

Fhuair mi lorg and eich's a phairc
Fhuair mi lorg na h-eal' air an t-snàmh
Fhuair mi lorg na bà 'sa pholl
Cha d'fhuair mi lorg mo chubhrachain

I found tracks of the horse in grass on the
  hill
I found tracks of the swan on the shore of
  the pond
I found tracks of the cow in the daffodils
But I found no trace of my fragrant wee
  one

■ ■ ■ ■

PART ONE

■ ■ ■ ■

I looked around, as anyone would, for its mother. Nothing was there. What did I know about lambs? Should I pick it up? Carry it . . . where?

— ANNE STEVENSON, "THE ENIGMA"

1
LUCY

Kidnap. Parse the word. It ought to mean lying down with baby goats. Words can be so misleading.

I can't tell my story straight. I have to tell it in circles, like rings of a tree that signify the passage of time.

Shall I start with how badly I wanted a child?

I did try to have a baby the conventional way, although Warren and I didn't pursue parenthood in the first years of our marriage. When we married, I was twenty-five, he was twenty-six. We thought we had all the time in the world.

At first, we devoted ourselves to our respective careers. He: jostling ahead of other associates at a consulting firm; I: spending long, fluorescent hours at an ad agency searching for selling propositions unique enough to propel me from a drywall cubicle to a windowed office.

After three years, Warren had secured a place toward the top of his "class" and I had been promoted from a cubicle to an office with a small but undeniable window. My name was etched in a metal bar affixed to the door, and sometimes, finding myself alone in the corridor, I'd polish the bar with the end of a sleeve, shining it as if it were a medal, which indeed it was.

We lived in the city, which in that part of the world, in that century, meant Manhattan. We rented half of the top floor of a narrow brownstone only blocks away from the Central Park Zoo. East Sixty-Fourth Street was a perfect location in which to raise a child, I'd think on early-morning runs under the zoo's clock tower. It marked the half hour with musical chimes and the twirl of bronze goats and bears and kangaroos. Perhaps it still does. I'd sometimes stop running to take in the show and imagine watching it someday with a baby in a jogging stroller. But we weren't ready for babies, not yet. We couldn't have a baby in that apartment. It was a fifth-floor walk-up and I couldn't imagine being pregnant and walking up five flights of stairs several times a day. And no way could we make 540 square feet include life with an infant, or the well-appointed life with an infant we projected on mental screens constantly running the movie of our future selves.

The suburbs were a better place to raise a baby, Warren insisted. He was from the Bronx, but spoke authoritatively. I had my doubts, having grown up in a suburb, but was eventually swayed by the abundance of space and natural light we discovered answering ads for houses for sale outside the city. Space and light were things we couldn't afford in the heating-up market of 1982 Manhattan real estate. I assumed space and light were prerequisites for a happy childhood. But that was before I had a child.

What made us ready to have a baby was that we both turned thirty and Warren lost his dad. We stopped feeling like kids ourselves and started wanting to have them. Also, ridiculous as it sounds now — Prince Charles and Lady Di had just had a baby, which added to the zeitgeist of procreation.

We started to shop for houses in Westchester, but one train trip to Bronxville convinced Warren to switch our sights to New Jersey. "Everyone on the Metro-North platform wears the same raincoat," he said. This surprised me. In fact, Warren wore the same raincoat they did, and the same ties, too: dark-colored silks striped or specked by rows of tiny geometrics. But I understood then, as I hadn't before, that he wanted to be seen as a man who marched to a different tune. This should have been a warning to me.

We bought an updated colonial in Upper Montclair, paying extra because the yard was just inside the preferred school zone. We celebrated the signed contract with a champagne-soaked dinner in Manhattan and took the subway back to our apartment, which now seemed even smaller. We began that night pursuing parenthood with purpose and exuberance. How freeing it felt to let what we called my Frisbee idle inside its pink plastic clamshell as we made love without it. Soon we were happily trying new things on our new king-size mattress in our new king-size bedroom in New Jersey. We had a goal and this suited both of us. We were goal-oriented people, it was one of the traits that had attracted us to each other in college. We'd met at Cornell, in a co-ed dorm, a new housing option where sexes were segregated by floor. There was a snack machine in the basement and all I first saw of Warren was his blond hair tinged green by its neon light. We were both taking breaks from all-night cram sessions. He kicked the machine into releasing a package of corn chips for me. Seven years later, we married.

We assumed that having a baby would simply be a matter of trying. In fact, we'd gotten pregnant before without trying. I'd been "in trouble" with Warren during our senior year of college. It wasn't a question for either of us whether or not I should keep it. We didn't have money for a baby then, nor the inclination. He'd borrowed money from a friend who gave him the name of a doctor. It was 1975, abortion had only recently been legalized, and it still took care to find a doctor who wouldn't kill you along with your unwanted baby. I was grateful to Warren for making the arrangements, but we were both surprised that, in the days leading up to my appointment, I began to wonder if I'd be able to go through with it. My second thoughts didn't come from fear of the doctor or from my being religious, though I'd been raised a Catholic. I'd chuffed off religion while still learning it from the nuns in convent school. My change of heart about having an abortion came from a growing sense that something human was flourishing inside me and that I did not wish to assert dominion over the life of this other, no matter how small and nascent its stage of development. I'd been mesmerized as a child by photos of an embryo in *Life* magazine. The thing inside me had lips and toes and a brain.

"It's not a baby, it's a lima bean," Warren protested, pointing to a drawing in his premed roommate's biology text. But I couldn't think of what I was carrying, no matter how small, as something inanimate, a disposable object.

Yet — what else could I do? I couldn't take care of a baby and knew I wouldn't be able to give birth to one and open my arms and give it away. I wasn't that generous. I apologized to it for what I was planning to do. I spoke to it silently, words that I passed from my brain through my heart. "Come back in a few years," I whispered again and again.

Then, the day before my appointment, the baby came out of its own accord. There was blood in the toilet. It didn't look like a baby, it looked like a clot, but I knew what it was and left it for Warren to see when he came over. We stared at it silently for a while, then flushed it together, his fingers curled over mine on the handle. As the swirl of red disappeared into white porcelain, I felt a cavern of sadness open up in me, which didn't make sense, as what happened was the very thing we meant to have happened, only now we could cancel the expensive appointment.

■ ■ ■ ■

After some months of trying, Warren and I were both surprised that zealous effort hadn't resulted in my getting pregnant again. I faithfully popped vitamins, gave up alcohol and sushi, swam strengthening laps at a health club before getting on the bus to work. Sometimes I'd feel a twinge deep inside when we made love, and be certain it was the feel of a baby being implanted. Afterward, I'd will myself not to move on the bed, so as not to dislodge the bud of our baby. But month after month, my body betrayed me.

Books advised buying certain equipment and soon our bedroom resembled a chemistry lab: graph paper, colored pencils, a thermometer to take my temperature before I got up. Our experiments failed, though we didn't know why — they always proved successful on paper. I began to fear something I never shared with Warren — that our lost baby had somehow warned others off me, spreading word that I was a hostile environment.

After a year, we went to a fertility clinic and soon became fluent in its harsh language: harvested eggs, assisted hatching, embryo selection. The whole thing was ugly and complicated and hard on us both. Warren had to work himself up to giving me injections, which he learned how to do on an orange in shot class. I'd lower my pants and curl against him on the bed, closing my eyes and bracing myself for the jab. The first time he did it, the shot took so long in coming, I looked behind me to see what was the matter.

After two tries at the clinic, Warren insisted we stop going because insurance wouldn't pay anymore. Without insurance, the treatments were prohibitively expensive, more than we had put down on the house. Warren wouldn't consider adoption. He said he didn't want to inherit someone else's problems. Problems are just as likely to happen to kids you give birth to, I told him, reminding him that plenty of people had problems with kids they hadn't adopted. Agencies screen for health problems, I assured him. But Warren wouldn't listen.

Dealing with infertility means you're always poised at a fork in the road, staring down two paths: life with a baby or life without. Warren was already setting off on the life without, accommodating himself to childlessness, acquiring fantasies that having babies precluded: exotic vacations, vintage convertibles — but these things stirred no desire in me.

I was reminded countless times in the course of each day of my inability to accomplish what came easily to others. Things I'd barely noticed before now seemed fraught with accusation. Childproof caps. Family-size cereal. Car windows boasting *Baby on Board*!

Some mornings before work, I'd stare out our front window, a bay window which I'd come to think of as pregnant, and see people in suits walking children to bus stops, children they ignored or tugged at impatiently. One mother dragged her toddler on a leash, jerking him from objects that caught his attention. So many people had children they didn't deserve. Every day in the papers, newborns turned up in garbage dumps or parents left babies to care for themselves. One father grew so impatient getting his kids ready for school, he took a gun out of his sock drawer and shot them.

As years went by and our childlessness continued, I tortured myself with how many images the word "barren" could conjure: a dried-up field burned brown by the sun. A frozen tundra. A dust bowl or desert where nothing can grow.

A friend at the office suggested visualization, to which she attributed her house in Southampton. *Picture it,* she said, *and it will come true.* Why not? I thought. I had nothing to lose. I outfitted the spare bedroom with a crib, pine rocker, a cheerful border of ducks on the wall. I'd sit in the rocker and close my eyes, imagining a small weight in my arms, rocking back and forth, back and forth, as if I could rock myself to where I wanted to go.

When Warren left me, I was thirty-five, the age grandmothers died in the Middle Ages.

2
WARREN

Trying to get Lucy pregnant was fun at first, but soon the sex was like a part-time job. There were certain days, even hours we had to clock in. If one of us had to stay late at the office, we had to borrow an apartment. There wasn't even the pretense of romance about it. It got so that even when we were in the middle of things, Lucy had her eye on the clock, worrying we wouldn't make deadline. "Hurry up," she said once, which had the opposite effect than the one she'd intended.

Once we got started at the clinic, I had to do my part in a room marked *Collections,* a closet, really. I tried to relax in a fake leather recliner with a paper pad spread over the seat, watching TV, whichever porn video I'd picked out of the box, trying to ignore sounds of other guys waiting their turns outside the door. Needless to say, I preferred giving at home, but we lived in New Jersey.

The clinic was in midtown Manhattan. Which meant that, to get to the lab in time — sperm is only viable for about an hour — I had to drive like mad, hoping there was no tunnel traffic, with a baggie taped to my abs, under a down vest to keep it at body temperature. This was before they figured out how to freeze it.

The worst thing was having to give her injections. There was a reason I went into business instead of to med school. I'd hated needles since I was a kid. I'll never forget the first time I had to give her a shot. She was kneeling on the bed, waiting, her trusting butt in my face. I was holding the syringe, when I turned and saw our shadows huge on the wall. I looked like a monster about to knife her. I hurried to do what I had to do with the needle before she looked up and saw that monster, too.

At a certain point, I realized a baby wasn't going to happen for us. But I couldn't get Lucy to see it. And nobody but me was willing to put an end to the quest. Everyone else had a vested interest in keeping our hopes up. The leader of our counseling group at the clinic worked for the makers of Pergonal, one of the biggest infertility drugs at the time. The drugs made her look pregnant. Her breasts got engorged. She put on an extra ten pounds, not her fault, and began to waddle because the drugs hyperstimulated her uterus, making walking painful for her. Walking! Forget sex. We'd stopped having it if it wasn't on schedule.

I tried to reason with Lucy: We shouldn't go on. We should resign ourselves to the fact we weren't having a baby. She was enough for me. It made me sad I wasn't enough for her.

I didn't realize how crazy the baby thing was making her until one night, I came home from a business trip and saw she'd turned the guest room into a nursery. Completely outfitted: crib, rocker, even a border of ducks on the wall. When I saw those ducks — in permanent paper, not tester strips you can peel — it was like a cold hand slapping my face, waking me up, making me see how far out of control things had gotten.

Lucy and I stayed technically married for a year after that, but we'd already separated, at least in my mind. By then, she wanted only one thing from me and I couldn't give it to her. I met Sasha at work. She was a new hire and I fell for her the first time I saw her in the elevator. I'm not proud of that. But we've been married now for twenty-one years. I have to say it was a relief to be with someone with whom I didn't share a giant problem. We had two kids right away. I put that pressure on. She's ten years younger than Lucy, but one thing I learned going to all those fertility classes — putting off kids, for women, is like Russian roulette. The older the eggs, the higher the chances of problems.

Lucy and I didn't keep up, but I ran into her at our twenty-fifth college reunion. It was good to see her again. She had her daughter with her. Cute kid, doing cartwheels on the quad. Lucy said she was adopted. That was over ten years ago. We didn't keep in touch.

3
LUCY

After Warren left, I toyed with the notion of sperm donors and even called for the literature. But my sister put me off the idea. Cheryl's a nurse. She said my baby could have hundreds of siblings. I imagined the sperm donor as a Pied Piper, followed by midgets who looked just like himself. I didn't want to do that to a child. In my experience, one sibling is plenty.

I looked into adoption, but this was the late 1980s. The irony was, now that I'd separated from my spouse who didn't want to adopt, I couldn't adopt because I was single. I couldn't get approval, unless I went to China, but I'd read up on Chinese adoptions — their process took years. My best bet was to do a private adoption. Private adoptions were beginning to be popular, mostly in the Midwest. I got an art director at work to help me place an ad in the *Kansas City Star*. I liked the idea of a baby from

Kansas. I began to dream of a house twirling in air, bringing a baby to me.

Loving Professional Seeks to Mother Your Baby. But none of the girls wanted to consider a single mom, which is what they themselves would have been. "They all want a home like in the sitcom *Family Ties,*" said a lawyer I called. "I'm sorry," he added, but I didn't feel apology from him, only haste in dismissing me. I called numbers in ads placed by girls themselves, seeking homes for their babies. It traumatized me, how roundly I failed auditions again and again. I wouldn't get anywhere telling the truth, I realized. I decided to fake a spouse and ran another ad: *Loving Couple Wants to Give Your Baby a Beautiful Home.* I got calls this time, but soon discovered that the process of adoption involved too much paperwork, too many inspections to pull off this kind of deception.

Did I want to foster an older child? If so, I could probably bring one home right away, someone told me. Part of me wished I was bighearted enough to take in an older child who needed mothering. But I wasn't that generous. I wanted a baby. My heart was set on having a baby, not a child too old to be beautiful in the way that all babies are beautiful. I wished it were otherwise.

It seemed everyone I knew was having babies. I attended shower after shower for coworkers and friends, even hosted one myself, for the art director who'd helped me place the ads in Kansas. I went all out — it was a big deal to ask people to schlepp out to New Jersey and I wanted to make the commute worth their while. Instead of napkins by the plates, I folded cloth diapers. I filled party bags for each of the guests, with jars of gourmet pickles. I spent a shocking amount on cheese to go with the theme: Tetilla, a Spanish cheese in the shape of a breast. During Baby Bingo, one of the guests en route to the bathroom mistakenly opened the door to the nursery and soon the entire party was gathered at its threshold, faces agog, silent, and I saw myself as they did: a woman stocking up for a baby I'd never have. For the first time, I realized, as they did, as Warren had tried to convince me — I wasn't ever going to have a baby. I just wasn't.

Once the party was over, and I walked the celebrant to her car carrying shopping bags full of loot and the hat made of the ribbons in which they'd been wrapped, I spent the rest of the weekend in bed, mourning the baby I'd lost, the marriage I'd forsaken in futile pursuit of parenthood. The baby I might have had (I'd felt it was a boy) would be fourteen years old then and I imagined, with tenderness, the crack in his voice, new hair on his smooth face. He'd be four years older than Cheryl's Jake and I imagined them together, Jake looking up to his older cousin, the same way Cheryl used to look up to me. Now it was like Cheryl thought I didn't know anything anymore. Once she had babies, it was like she stopped being sisters with me, and became sisters with our mother instead. At family gatherings, they talked in corners, exchanging stories, secret language, as if they were members of a club that I couldn't get into.

By Monday morning, I was myself again — or rather, I acted like myself: made myself get out of bed, take a shower, put on a smart outfit, take the commuter bus to the city, and throw myself into my work. Soon I was the go-to copywriter for fast turnaround: brochures, print ads, TV spots. I practically grabbed pink pages off the top of the pile of job requisites, whereas before, like most creatives, I'd hidden when traffic people came around trying to get me to accept assignments. No job was too much for me to take on. To meet deadlines, I'd sometimes stay overnight at the office, tap, tap, tapping at my Kaypro computer. I came to be one of the copywriters in highest demand, one of the first to be called upon when the agency pitched accounts. I redirected my fervor for a baby into a passion for work, creating campaigns for clients who were like babies themselves in their constant demands, their inability to separate their own needs from that of the person gratifying them.

And that is how I took my first trip to IKEA. The store in Elizabeth had just opened, it was only the second IKEA store in this country.

An account man drove us out to do research — driving is never left to creatives. The parking lot was crowded, though it was midweek and I recall thinking how well the new campaign must be working. Yet, the brand manager was already seeking to replace it. He'd invited the agency I worked for to pitch the account.

It was only May, but we were having a heat wave. We had to walk a long way from the car, in hot sun. The heels of my shoes kept sticking to the tar of the parking lot and I stopped a few times to extricate them. When a wall of glass doors opened up to admit us, a wave of happiness washed over me, which at first I attributed to air-conditioning.

A woman in a red apron greeted us cheerfully, handing us bright yellow bags for our shopping convenience. The yellow bags were enormous, the size of trash bags — but they weren't big enough to hold furniture. I was confused. Wasn't IKEA a furniture store? *Furnish Your Life* was the tag line. Yes, there was furniture — lots of it — but there were little things to buy, too: candles, bottle openers, fridge magnets, measuring cups, clocks, all designed in practical but unexpected ways which made ordinary household items seem exotic. I followed the group into a forest of floor lamps, but soon wandered away, drawn by the room displays. I was mesmerized by dioramas of family life. A white canvas sectional around a giant TV screen showed the commercial the brand manager hated. Blond dining rooms, dark book-lined studies, eat-in kitchens with groceries on the counter — all appeared to be lived in by happy people who had just stepped away. I meandered through room after room of intentional disarray gleaming with possibility. A childlike optimism invaded me. This seemed a place where nothing bad could happen.

I spent the next few weeks holed up in my office with my art director, working to come up with campaign ideas that would make others fall in love with the place, as I had. Our presentation got a standing ovation, but we didn't get the account, after all. The agency of record retained it. But I found myself going back to the store. Not just once, but again and again. I went there on summer Fridays as others went to the beach. Sometimes I'd pack a sandwich from home and eat it on a wooden bench by the entry, observing the comings and goings of people who would enter empty-handed but leave with so much that red-aproned helpers had to assist them out of the store. Or, I'd stand by the Ball Room and watch children playing soundlessly behind glass. The Ball Room was like a giant aquarium: instead of water, a sea of brightly colored foam balls in which kids were jumping, diving, mutely laughing in the swell. Basically, it was a babysitting service, a clever marketing move, as it freed parents to concentrate on filling their carts.

Sometimes I'd go to the café, where menu items were Swedish, and linger over meatballs and lingonberry juice, transfixed by the motions of mothers around me, admiring their skill at keeping both trays and babies aloft. They moved in pairs, combining broods of small children, seating them at tables laden with food, fencing them in

31

with large shiny carts overflowing with the fixtures of family life. I imagined their good fortune wafting to me, borne in the mingle of scents from their trays. I pictured myself in their midst, dandling a baby on my knee as I joined in their discussions, weighing in on the advantages of wood cribs versus metal, classical versus pop songs for musical mobiles, at what age to take a binky away.

The press has it all wrong. It was not premeditated.

4
LUCY

The agency had summer hours: every other Friday off.

August 10, 1990, was an off Friday for me. I convinced myself, as I sometimes did before pointing the car toward IKEA, that I needed to buy something there. The heat was unbearable, air conditioners were taxing operational systems all over the East Coast, and there were rumors that the strain would cause a blackout. I needed candles and IKEA sold them — perhaps sells them still — in handy boxes of many for a bargain price.

There I was, innocently trawling the aisles, empty yellow bag slung over my shoulder. (I always took a bag from a greeter when I came in, so as to look shopperly.) I was trying to remember where candles were, when I came upon a baby sitting alone in a cart. Not sitting, exactly. The baby was too young to sit. She was slumped in a plastic infant carrier which was the same yellow as the bags. The carrier was attached to the seat of the shopping cart, as was common in the days before car seats became portable. The baby was in a fallen-over position that looked extremely uncomfortable. Her eyes were open and wide and blue. She was staring at me and my skin prickled all over. Her face looked exactly like the one on the cover of a picture book I'd loved as a child: *Baby's First Christmas.* Whenever I thought of having a baby, hers was the baby's face I'd imagined. She was a girl, I knew. Her sunsuit was pink. She looked at me wonderingly, as if trying to work out where she'd seen me before. When she smiled a gummy grin, I felt a sea swell under my breastbone.

No one else was around. The baby was alone in the long, empty aisle. Her eyes were bright with expectation. A wisp of blond stood at the top of her head. It was as if the cart was a spaceship that had landed, bringing her to me.

"How old is she?" asked a passing shopper who was pregnant and pushing a cart full of wicker. She gazed at the baby with admiration and I welled with an inexplicable pride.

"Two months," I said, without thinking,

beaming idiotically, as if the baby were mine.

"Two months? She's enormous!" and I guessed that I had grossly miscalculated.

Now the baby was listing further in the seat, held by straps, but not very tightly. There was a chance she could fall. I saw that the woman expected me to prop her up.

I can honestly say that my only intention in reaching into the cart was to right the baby. But as soon as my palms pressed against her doughy arms, I felt a force so strong I can still feel the bind in my chest. Her skin was cold. She had goose bumps. She was dressed for heat, not for air-conditioning, wearing a lacy bib, but no shirt. The folds of her neck were slick with drool, making her susceptible to drafts. She could catch pneumonia!

As I straightened her in the seat, she gazed at me with what looked to be gratitude. I inhaled a sweet scent from the down on her scalp and a flow of something warm started through me.

The pregnant woman leaned on her cart and pushed away.

How could someone leave a baby alone in a shopping cart? Anyone might come along and take her, someone who might do her harm. I couldn't just leave her there.

I decided to take her to the front of the store, to one of the cashiers. As soon as the cart began to move, the baby brightened and looked around, pumping her bare feet as if to help propel us on the little journey we'd embarked on together. The cart glided easily, almost of its own accord, down one aisle and up another, toward the bank of cash registers at the front of the store.

Then, it was moving away from the registers, toward the exit sign, four vivid red letters lurid in their suggestiveness to me. I told myself: I was only taking her outside for a minute, to get her out of the cold. She could catch a chill. A deathly chill. The air outside would warm her up.

And then, we were within inches of the exit doors, when alarms went off, and I do what I always do when I panic — I froze. A tumult sounded, electronic bells were banging and bonging, and the baby began to cry as a woman in uniform hurried toward us. I felt a sudden distance from my own body, as if I were watching myself on a movie screen, wondering how the picture would turn out.

The woman smelled like jasmine, which, oddly, was the name on the badge over her breast: *Jasmine, Security.* But her eyes

36

weren't accusing, they were apologetic.

"Guess your baby forgot to pay for this," she said, smiling as she leaned into the cart and wriggled a rubber duck from inside the baby's sunsuit. She squeaked the toy, which made the baby stop crying, and waved us into the bright, waiting world.

My ears were throbbing with the sound of my own heart as I unstrapped the baby. I lifted her cautiously out of the cart. She was heavier than I thought she would be. Talcum, a scent I hadn't inhaled in years, came to me as I pressed her soft weight to my chest. Rubbing her back in circles to keep her calm, a motion resurrected from years of babysitting, I dropped my chin on her back (a possessive gesture I noticed often in mothers) and walked quickly — but not too quickly — through outer doors which opened automatically to release us. Us! Oh, the enormity implied by that diminutive word, how exhilarated I was by its sudden insinuation into my consciousness.

The heat of the unconditioned air was a shocking contrast to the cool inside the store and this moving from the comfort of one place to the shock of another brought to mind the process of birth, which I'd often imagined — though not in this way.

5

JASMINE

I even apologized to her. God forgive me. It never crossed my mind she was a kidnapper. It was my first job as security. It was a sophisticated system, state of the art they'd invested in because they were afraid of high shrinkage — retail for shoplifting — because of the area. I was told the system was sensitive. They were still getting the kinks out. I was supposed to check bags of anybody who set off the alarm, but the lady didn't have any bags. I saw the duck in the baby's clothes. It had a sticker. Stickers were always falling off one thing and onto another, and sure enough, the duck was marked SHOWR CRTN. I sent them on their way.

The security cam hadn't worked that day. Some electronic had failed. We didn't know it until the next day when the FBI requested tapes. There was no footage to identify her and I couldn't remember anything about her except she was white. If only I'd detained her for a minute, things could have been different, is what I kept telling myself for years.

6
MARILYN

How many times have I relived that terrible day, the day of the "event," as Tom, my ex, called it almost as soon as it happened, distancing himself from it, or trying to, as if it had impaled some other family, some far-flung unlucky family you read about in the news.

Luck had always been with us before. We both had good jobs, or what I thought was good in those days, when career and financial success were still paramount. Tom was a lawyer on Wall Street and I'd just been promoted to sales manager at AT&T, a top-ten company for working mothers. We'd recently renovated a colonial in Cranford, in a good school district. The mortgage was already half paid down.

Of course, luckiest of all, we had a new baby. A wondrous, perfect baby girl, Natalie. Tom thought she was named for his mother, but secretly, I'd named her after the secretary to my first boss, a girl whose carriage and delicate facial structure I found so beguiling that my breath stopped each time I had to approach my boss's desk.

That morning, I overslept the alarm. I was tempted to leave out this detail later, in the recountings I made to the police and the press. I thought it made me sound lazy and was afraid this detail — a lackadaisical mother! — might prejudice people against me and reduce the urgency of the search. But I didn't hold back even this morsel of memory, in case it was an important piece to the puzzle. I was already beginning to apprehend the connectedness of the universe.

At 7:58 a.m. the phone rang, pulling me out of a dream. I remember the time because I was shocked to see the numbers on the Dream Machine clock switching over, dropping from 7:57 to an impossible 7:58, with a soft click, well past the time I'd usually be getting Natalie up and changed and fed and ready for Charu to dress her in whatever outfit I'd laid out on the bathinette.

What was the dream, a policewoman wanted to know, but how could I remember? I didn't put much stock in dreams in those days and didn't see what dreams had to do

41

with the nightmare of the reality that had descended upon us.

Still groggy from sleep, I reached for the phone, knocking over a wineglass that was on the nightstand. I never could get that red stain out of the carpet, though I scrubbed it with every product imaginable. When we put the house on the market a year later, I pulled the bed over, to hide it.

I couldn't tell who had called, at first. The snooze alarm was going off and the buzzer was so loud I couldn't hear whoever was on the other end of the line. At first, I thought it must be Tom calling from the office, but he'd still be on the 7:49, his car phone out of his reach, embedded in the dashboard of his new car parked at the lot. The only way he'd be able to call from a train would have been from a cell phone which he didn't have, practically no one had one in those days, no one but me. The company had given it to me the month before. AT&T had just started a policy of letting new mothers work off premise. My last month on maternity leave, an IT guy had come out to the house to set me up with a company computer, fax machine, even a cellular phone, a new compact model the company was coming out with and touting because it weighed less than a pound. I could test-drive it for

R&D, he said.

I thought maybe the caller was Tom's mother. She sometimes called at odd hours and maybe they were putting off their drive up from Virginia. They were due to drive up that weekend, to meet the baby. It was already Friday! They'd be there the next day and there was still lots to do to get the house ready for them. I'd wanted to give them the master bedroom, but Tom felt that wasn't necessary, they could stay in the room we both used as an office. That room was fine, but its bathroom needed a few things: a shower curtain, a bath mat, a hanging shelf for toiletries. I planned to run out after a meeting, to go shopping at Conran's, which was a few blocks away from the AT&T office on Forty-Eighth where I worked.

When I heard Charu's voice, my heart sank. If Charu was calling, it meant that she wouldn't be coming at 8:30 like she usually did. Without a babysitter, I was in trouble — or so I thought, then still unaware of what real trouble was. Without a babysitter, I couldn't go into the office, I wouldn't be able to deliver the report I was due to present at the meeting that afternoon. My boss had chosen me to present it in his stead and I'd been up until 2 a.m. the night before, rearranging slides and rehearsing words I had memorized, words meant to sound spontaneous, but which I didn't dare trust to spontaneity, because the thought of public speaking sent shivers down the back of my legs. Little did I know that my preparation that night was readying me to speak on television, for the first time.

As I was talking to Charu, Natalie woke up. I could hear her on the monitor, the little song she used to sing to herself upon waking. I knew exactly how long that song would last — three minutes. Three minutes would give me just enough time to call the office and say I wasn't coming in. I dreaded making that call. The report was important. If I delivered it well, it could mean I'd get the new account I'd been angling for. But of course, by the end of the day, my career wouldn't matter to me anymore.

I hung up with Charu. I wasn't angry with her, as some news reports said I was. How could I be angry? It wasn't her fault that her son was sick and she couldn't come in. I was frustrated with myself for having no backup to call. I supposed I could call in a sitting service, but I worried about leaving a four-month-old baby in the care of someone I hadn't met. Of course, later, I wished with all of my heart that I'd called in that service.

I left a message with the group secretary saying I wouldn't be in. My boss wouldn't be happy, but what could I do? Bring a four-month-old in and hope she wouldn't roll off the table when I made the presentation? Now I hear the company has day care on-site, but that was a distant dream in 1990.

I still ache to remember how distracted I was with Natalie that morning which turned out to be the last I'd spend with her for twenty-one years. I look back at my old, unseeing self lifting my baby out of the crib, thinking not of her, but of the consequences of having to take care of her, and wish I could reach back and shake myself into consciousness.

If I could grab back a minute of my life, it would be when I laid her on the vinyl mat of the changing table, raining talcum on her as she gurgled and kicked in the moment before I put on her last diaper. I'd look at her, really look at her as I buttoned the straps of her new sunsuit, inhaling her sweet scalp as I took my daughter into my arms for what would be the last time in her baby-hood. I'd give her my full attention, instead of what I was thinking of instead: of the report due at work, the visit from Tom's parents the next day. No. If I could take

45

back any minute, of course, it would be when I turned my back on her in the store. That's the minute I'd go back to, and change.

I worked at home that morning at the dining room table, Natalie happy in her swing beside me. She loved to go back and forth in that swing. Battery-operated swings had just come out. Tom and I called it our time machine, because putting her in it gave us at least twenty minutes to do whatever we had to do. We assumed we had all the time in the world with her. She'd sit in that swing with a beatific expression, listening to an electronic version of "It's a Small World." Her eyes fixed on some odd object of fascination: a knob on a cabinet, a water stain on the baseboard. She'd assume a half smile, then list to one side, a position that looked uncomfortable but didn't seem to bother her. She'd frown when I'd right her and soon she'd be happily listing again, her lids drooping lower and lower until she passed out, as if drunk.

While she swung in this seemingly trance-like state, I sat at the table beside her, trying to tune out the Muzak, working up final numbers for the presentation, before I faxed them. It was bad enough I wasn't going to be there. I didn't want the numbers to be wrong, which would make me look even worse.

Natalie went down for a nap around ten, but when she woke up she was fussy and I did what I always could count on to soothe her: strap her into the car seat and go for a drive. I needed to go out anyway, to shop for the hall bath before Tom's parents arrived the next day.

IKEA had just opened and I'd wanted to go for their inaugural sale, but I hadn't been able to figure out how to get there. This was before they made a special exit off the highway for it. The area wasn't developed yet, the store was hidden away on some hard-to-find back road. When I found myself driving past it, I thought: This is my lucky day.

7
CHARU

If I came to work that day, the terrible thing wouldn't happen. Always, I feel sorry for this. But my son was just six and sick with a fever too easily passed to a four-month-old baby. I could not bring him with me. My sister usually took care of Ranni when he had to stay home, but Vina was back in my country to stay by our mum. Our father was ill and our mum needed a daughter to help her with him.

My husband was on day shift at the factory, but even if he had been home, he couldn't take care of a sick child. He is a man who can't even take care of his sick self.

Marilyn called me at lunchtime, as I was trying to get Ranni to take some soup, and I could not hear what she was saying. Her crying was strong and her words came in and out so that I knew she was somewhere not home, calling on the cell phone that was a new kind of phone in those days. At first, I thought she wanted to talk about if I can come in the next day, but instead she was asking if Natalie was with me. These words made me feel afraid right away. Because if Marilyn's baby is not with Marilyn, where did she go?

Next, a police lady is on the phone asking me questions: who I am, where do I live, how many children do I have? She wanted to know can she come over to where I was right away. I didn't want her to come over because it is Friday and Saturday is cleanup day, so the house isn't looking too good, but I know I cannot say no to this question. I was glad I got my special visa already.

I took out this visa and left it on the table so when the police came, they could know without asking, that I was legal, nothing to bother about once they see the baby I don't have.

I believe this thing would never happen when I take care of Natalie. Because taking care of a baby is my job and my job was important to me, to my family. But Marilyn's job is not taking care of a baby. Her job was an office job. That day she was trying to do a good job, like me.

Sometimes a baby is better off with someone who is paid to take care.

8
MARILYN

I took Natalie from the car seat and snapped her into the Snugli and hurried across the parking lot to get us both out of the blistering heat. August in New Jersey can feel like a furnace, hotter even than summer here in San Mateo, where the heat is broken by breezes from the bay.

I'd heard that IKEA had child care onsite, and as soon as I went through the entrance doors, I saw the Ball Room. But Natalie was too small to leave there. She was just four months old, she couldn't even sit up yet. Beyond the Ball Room were rows of bright red shopping carts fitted together. I found one with an infant seat in it, and took her out of the Snugli, and I ache to remember how happy I was to unburden myself of my baby's weight.

I knew I didn't have much time for shopping. I could depend on Natalie to remain quiet for only so long. I checked my watch:

12:30. I remember thinking the presentation would start in an hour without me.

I rolled Natalie through the wide aisles and she looked around with great interest, taken by the colorful displays: bright aluminum cookware, animal-shaped oven mitts, pastel-colored dishware. We passed a tower of toasters and her little legs pumped and I stopped to let her look at herself, to see if she was recognizing herself in their reflection; recognizing herself in a mirror would be a milestone in her development. She seemed to see herself in one of them, but I couldn't be sure. As I started moving the cart, Natalie's face in the reflection began to crumple and I knew she was about to cry. I reached for a rubber duck from a lineup of them on a shelf and gave it to her. She promptly sucked on its head. Is it clean? I wondered and decided it was. Every item around us glistened, looked newly emerged from shrink-wrap.

Then, I saw what I'd come for — shower curtains. They hung, colorful drops of cloth rippling in gusts of air from the ceiling vents. As I reached up to feel one, the bag on my shoulder rang. My cell phone! It was big as a brick, easy to retrieve even in the jumble of the big bag full of things I packed whenever I went out with the baby.

There was no readout screen, but I knew the call was from the office. Only my office called this number. I pulled up the antenna to answer the call. The voice of my boss was hard to hear through the static, but his impatience came through loud and clear. Something in the presentation was wrong. There was a number missing in one of the slides. And suddenly I was back in the office, where I should have been. Did I know . . . ? What? I couldn't hear his question, only his irritation.

"Hello?" I said again and again, inching forward to close the distance between us, trying to mollify him, to reassure that I'd always be there, able to supply him with what was needed.

9
MARILYN

Nothing seemed wrong at first. I pressed the button to disconnect the call, but my mind didn't return right away, I was still at the office, focused on what I had said, what I should have said instead. An alarm went off in a distant part of the store, which jolted me back into consciousness — only later did I realize what that alarm meant.

I saw I had walked away from my baby.

I'd walked away from my baby! My scalp went cold. I hurried to where I had left her. The cart was gone. The cartless aisle, its vast emptiness, registered like a body blow. I stared and stared at where the cart should be, where I had left Natalie, looking away, then back again, thinking my eyes were playing a trick, that she was actually there.

Maybe I'd misremembered the aisle. I rounded the corner to the next aisle, the next. She wasn't there, or there, or there. My hands went to my throat. I felt a stinging behind my eyes.

Could the cart have rolled? Could someone in a hurry, not paying attention, have taken my cart and Natalie by mistake? My stomach lurched higher and higher. I pictured my baby being spirited away in the arms of a stranger.

Don't jump to conclusions, I told myself. Someone, seeing the cart unattended, had probably wheeled her up to the front. Any moment I'd hear the PA system saying, *Would the parent of an infant please report to security?* And just then, the intercom system did click on: *Attention, shoppers.* But the announcement was about a sale on countertops.

My mind sped up and this is what I recall happening next, though of course it couldn't have happened this way: I see myself running up and down aisles which stretch into eternity. There is literally no one else in the store; though, of course, that wasn't so. There is just me, the clip, clip, clip of my heels, faster and faster as realization sets in. My hand keeps returning to the empty Snugli flapping against my breast. Each time I touch it, I hope the baby will somehow be there. I hurry toward cash registers, and suddenly there are the people, lines of them. Faces turn toward me and I look to see if anyone is carrying a baby. No one is. I become aware of faces looking at me in disapproval and several mouths are saying things but the only sound I can hear is someone screaming something unintelligible. Then, I realize that person is me.

I stop and try to gather myself, for Natalie's sake. I try to assume the look of the nice, normal woman I'd been a few minutes ago when I walked into the store. I didn't yet know I'd never be that woman again.

I speak loudly, but slowly, enunciating carefully, so there will be no mistaking the words I must say:

Somebody. Help me. My baby. Is. Gone.

10
LUCY

If she had cried, I would have taken her back into the store. But she didn't cry, not at first.

Pressing her to my shoulder, I shimmied between parked cars, trying to find my Nissan. Blood pumped in my ears. The parking lot seemed to have tripled in size as I searched, weaving in and out between great hunks of metal, holding the baby tight to me as if shielding her from danger, as if a parked car, unattended, might suddenly rear up and roll into us.

I didn't yet think I was taking the baby. To the extent that I was thinking, I had in my mind I was only borrowing her. I meant to keep her for just a little while, then bring her back, return her as if nothing had happened. Of course that now sounds ridiculous, even to me.

When I reached my car, I shifted the baby to my hip to free a hand to retrieve my keys from my purse. This required effort of balance and a painful pull of my midsection and I marveled that motherhood was physically demanding, like an athletic event I hadn't been trained for. I opened the back door and gently unfolded the baby onto the seat. I stood staring down at her. How perfect she was: her heart-shaped face, her long lashes. The lovely pink nails of her plump little toes. She lay on her back, staring at me, her eyes glowing with wisdom and recognition, as if we shared a secret from the rest of the world.

A siren wailed in the distance. My knees trembled. Then her hands started working as if she were wringing them, as if she, too, were thinking: What to do? What to do?

"That's illegal, you know." My heart flung itself against my ribs. I turned and looked up to see an older woman peering over half-rims chained to her neck. "A baby that small should be in a car seat." She didn't wait for a response and my insides went liquid as her straight back receded out of my sight. What if she meant to report me?

I couldn't just stand there. I had to do something. There were beach towels folded on the backseat. I gently dried the baby's neck and chest with a towel, and dabbed at the bib to dry the wet cotton against her skin. Then I picked her up, along with the towels, closed the back door with my hip, and opened the door on the front passenger side. I made a nest of the towels on the seat, and carefully laid her down, like an egg.

I faced her so her head was farthest away from the door. I thought that was safest, in case of an accident. But I wouldn't have an accident. I'd drive very slowly. I'd drive with more caution than I'd ever driven with before.

I secured her small body with seat belts, reinforcing those restraints with bungees I'd kept in the trunk. While I was doing this, the baby smiled and kicked her plump arms and legs, as if forgiving the restraints, knowing they were for her own good, showing me they weren't too restrictive.

I shut the door gently twice, to make sure it secured, then slipped around to the other side, into the driver's seat. It took forever to buckle my seat belt. My hands were shaking. The siren wailed louder. I couldn't feel my fingers, as if they'd stopped being attached to my hands, but I managed to exert enough control over them to turn the key and start up the engine. I eased the sedan cautiously forward, my foot resting lightly on the pedal, my right arm extended to keep the baby from falling onto the floor, although there was no way she could have fallen given the web I'd constructed, all those crossings and recrossings.

I didn't turn on the air-conditioning, not wanting chilled air to blow on her. I opened the windows instead. Sweat trickled down the back of my neck, but my insides were ice. Slowly, I backed the car out of the parking spot. I had never been so conscious of the presence of another being — her soft weight next to me on the seat, her head on a pillow of terry cloth, her wide eyes considering her new surrounds.

As I pulled onto the highway, the siren grew louder and my throat constricted. Perhaps the siren scared her, too, or she sensed my terror. She started to cry, whimpering at first, then erupting in wails, kicking the armrest to emphasize her displeasure.

"We'll be there soon, baby," I assured her, stroking her cheek with my guarding right hand, although I had no idea where we were going. My only thought was to get us out of the vicinity. I pressed my foot a little harder on the pedal. I was driving toward home, but didn't mean to take her there. Taking her home would have been stealing her and stealing a baby wasn't what I meant to do. I'd never stolen anything in my life. I'd never broken the law. I never even pulled warning tags off mattresses!

As cars passed on both sides (I was the only car on the road not exceeding the speed limit) it felt as if time had stopped for everyone on the planet except for the baby and me, and as in a fairy tale, we'd been granted the chance to temporarily live outside the continuum of it.

I had an odd sensation of being behind the wheel, and not. I alternated between points of view — looking out at traffic in front of me, through the windshield, and alternately, seeing the traffic from high above, my little blue car headed for — some disaster, a sudden drop-off, some unavoidable cliff. My ears hummed as I took us farther and farther away, into the unknowable.

Then, something strange happened. I heard the calming voice of my Scottish grandmother, singing. It was a song in Gaelic she'd sung to me as a child and I realized the voice I heard was my own. I hadn't sung the song in decades but it was as if it had been at the tip of my tongue all along, waiting for a baby to receive it. The words came easily, though I didn't know I remembered them:

Fhuair mi lorg and eich's a phairc

Fhuair mi lorg na h-eal' air an t-snàmh

The song quieted her. I took my eyes from the road to see how the baby was faring. She was admiring her tiny fists, opening and closing them as if trying to catch the words in the air.

Then, I was looking for someplace to pull over. I wanted time to think. Also, I wanted to talk to her. At that point, I thought our time together would be temporary and I wanted to make the most of the moments we had left. But where could we go? The Garden State was a busy artery. I couldn't veer off the road, onto a shoulder, without a police car or Good Samaritan stopping to investigate. I wished the car could lift into the hills that rose from the highway, taking us into secluded swells of green where we could enjoy the time allotted to us, in private.

It is hard to find solitude in the suburbs. This surprises city dwellers, who imagine counterparts in the suburbs lead a solitary, sylvan existence, but it couldn't be further from the truth. Suburbs are built on a bedrock of belief in the bettering aspects of community: *community* parks, *community* pools, *community* beaches and halls and grounds. Almost no provision is made for private withdrawal, even behind the doors

61

of your home. Neighbors think nothing of ringing a bell without notice, as do purveyors of everything, and hawkers of religion or political candidates.

Where was I going? I couldn't think straight. It was as if a jackhammer was drilling into my brain. But when I saw signs for Maplewood, I suddenly knew. I nosed the car off the highway and onto an exit that led to a hidden trailhead where Warren had once brought me. He'd liked to walk. He'd had many pairs of shoes (perhaps he still does) each suited to a different sort of walking: a pair for hiking rocks, a pair for walking flatlands, a pair for climbing hills. He'd counted 119 trails in New Jersey and had set out to do every one. The one he liked best led to a waterfall and he'd taken me there several times. There was a back entrance to a trail you'd never know was there. I turned off into a covert indent by the side of the road, parked, and, after gently unraveling the belts around her, took the baby out of the car.

It was blisteringly hot in the sun, and I shielded her head with my hand until we reached the dark shelter of trees, and the temperature grew cooler by many degrees. I held the baby on my hip, securing her with both arms, as I navigated bumps in the trail, glad I'd gone out that morning wearing sensible shoes. I hoped a place I remembered was still there: a grove of pines around a redwood table. I crested a hill, and my heart leapt — the table was still there.

The air was heavy with sweetness as I sat with the baby on a sturdy bench at the table. I took a few deep breaths, to make my heart stop beating so fast. Then I began to talk to her. I didn't speak gibberish as I've heard mothers do. I spoke in words that revealed my heart while she regarded me with a wise, sympathetic expression, like a friend who knows you need someone to listen. I talked to her of the majesty of nature, pointing out the beauty of birdsong, the slices of blue between boughs that rose like arms of giant sentries guarding us from the rest of the world. I told her how much I wanted a baby. I said what a beautiful baby she was. I confessed that I longed to keep her, but assured her I was bringing her back to her mother. I couldn't endure the thought of her mother's sorrow. I told the baby I was sorry I couldn't keep her, and when I said this, she began to fuss and I wondered if perhaps she was telling me something: that she wanted me to keep her, not to bring her back. I thought of the baby Warren and I had lost and wondered if possibly, impossibly, that baby was this baby, redirected to me. Perhaps her mother was mean to her, inept, or cruel, or otherwise unfit. But the baby's fat, healthy cheeks and neatly ironed lace bib assured me that was wishful thinking on my part. She began to cry. A small, restrained whimper. I picked her up and stood swaying back and forth over the soft carpet of fallen pine needles. I sang to her. This seemed to console her. There was an echoing chorus of birds singing sad songs, as if in solidarity. I waited until she fell asleep on my shoulder, until her breathing was raspy and regular. Then, I carried her, stepping carefully to avoid rocks in the path, back to the car.

I laid the baby, still sleeping, on the front seat, nestled her in the impression she'd made in the towels. I secured her again with the belts and the bungees.

With a heavy heart, I closed the passenger door, walked to the other side of the car, and slid behind the wheel. Our journey together was over. It was time to bring her back.

The key glittered as I held it above the ignition and maybe it was this flash of brightness in the dim car that pierced my brain fog, returning me to my senses. How could I bring her back? Walk in the store and look for *Returns*? I'd be arrested as soon as I walked through the doors. The baby's disappearance must be a news story by now. Had the woman with half-glasses taken note of my license plate? Had the police traced the number? Was I being hunted already, my name on the news? My hand went for the knob of the radio, but I decided not to turn it on. Not only because the baby was sleeping and I didn't want the noise to wake her. I didn't want to hear news about the baby's disappearance. I didn't want to hear the name I hadn't named her. This would make the fact that I'd taken her real.

When I was in school, a nun read us a story about a soldier on a train. I don't remember who wrote it, but the narrative has stuck with me all of these years. The soldier has gotten leave to visit his sick wife and receives a telegram just before he boards. He knows it's bad news, but he doesn't open the envelope. He spends the trip talking people's ears off about his wife — how beautiful she is, how kind, generous — all the while feeling the unopened telegram in his pocket, knowing as soon as he opens it, she'll be gone. It was like that, for me, in that moment. I wanted to isolate myself from reports of what I had done, extending time, being outside of it, beyond the point where laws of our universe obtain, pretending for as long as I could that the small being on the seat beside me was mine.

Without consciously deciding to do so, I drove the rest of the way home to Montclair. Where else could I go? I would figure out what to do, once I got there. I cruised past signs for the Oranges, then for Bloomfield. Sweat trickled down my neck. It was so hot in the car that my shirt stuck to my back. Beads had formed on the baby's temples and upper lip, but she continued to sleep peacefully on the seat beside me. I reopened the windows, letting cool air rush in.

The only time I took my hand away from the baby, besides opening the window, was driving up my own driveway, to press the button on the remote to open the garage. When the garage door went down behind us, shutting us off from the bright, exposing midafternoon light, it felt like we'd entered the safety of Ali Baba's cave.

I put my head down on the steering wheel and wept. I was physically spent, as if I had just run a marathon. I sat there, needing time to gather my strength, to figure out what I should do next. I cried quietly, not wanting to wake the baby, not wanting her to know my distress. Her little arms were a halo around her head.

I struggled with whether or not to take her into the house. Taking her into the house seemed a crossing almost as momentous as taking her out of the store. Somehow, staying in the car with her seemed not as damning to me as taking her into the house. If I'd been caught with her in the car, I could say I had found her somewhere and was returning her, *Just trying to do the right thing, Officer* — but no. I couldn't lie about not having taken her out of the store. *Jasmine, Security* would surely recognize me. I'd say I'd taken her out of the store for her own good — it was freezing in there and she'd been dangerously cold — and now I was on my way to bring her back. The lapse in time could be explained by . . . my lack of a sense of direction — I had just gotten lost. Anyone who knew me — coworkers, my ex-husband — would confirm that I had a terrible sense of direction. As long as I was in the car with the baby, I was still in transit, destination unknown, intentions improvable. But once I took her out of the car and brought her over the threshold, well, then my intentions would be undeniable.

The car grew hot and airless. The baby

woke up. There were beads of sweat on her upper lip. I bent toward her and she studied my face as if trying to place it. Then, she smiled in recognition. My chest flooded, as if a dam had been broken. Her smile turned to a grimace. Then came a stench. She began to cry and suddenly the complications of my dilemma faded away. I knew what to do next. It became very simple. The baby needed something. I needed to do something for her. And I acted on what would guide my actions for the rest of my life: giving her what she needed. What she needed now was a new diaper. What I should do next became clear. And that is the reality of taking care of a small child — there is so much they need from moment to moment, so many decisions to make on their behalf in the course of each day, that you rarely have time to stand back and consider the big picture, which is something I succeeded in ignoring for years.

I got out of the car and went around to her side of it. I opened the door and unstrapped her from the seat. I took her into my arms and walked, without doubt or question, through the passageway that led from the garage to the kitchen door. But as I stepped from cement to linoleum, a queasiness came over me. My feet were acting

out a decision the rest of me hadn't agreed
to yet.

11
MARILYN

Store security called the police and I called Tom and a storm of blue uniforms made real what was impossible — my baby had been kidnapped.

They took me to a room in the back of the store. A door opened and the store stopped being shiny aisles of colorful merchandise and turned into grim, gray surrounds. The room was airless. There were no windows. I felt as if I were unable to breathe. A detective asked questions: When did I realize my baby was missing? When had I last seen her? Had I ever lost her before? My mind was already crowding with horrible visions. You can't imagine what it's like to be tortured by thoughts of what is happening to your child as you are being grilled as if you are a criminal, while whoever took her is being allowed to get farther and farther away.

I know now that questioning a lost child's

parents as if they are the kidnappers is standard procedure, but I didn't know it then and it was agony to be made to account for every minute of my day to an angry-looking detective who'd sat me in a room separated from Tom, who was being asked the same questions, to see if our answers matched. At a certain point, I stopped talking, stopped being able to understand what was being asked of me. Voices went too soft to hear, then came at me deafeningly loud. I had to focus on lips to get the meaning of words.

They dusted the rubber duck — the last thing I gave my baby — for prints. A man in a white coat, wearing plastic gloves, pushed long Q-tips into our mouths and swabbed saliva off the duck, to match DNA with the samples they got from the Q-tips, to confirm that Tom and I were her parents. They said most abductions involve a biological parent, and this about sent me over the edge, because even in my agitated state, I knew they were referring to abductions that happen when parents have separated and Tom and I were still together, which should have been obvious to them.

Then the press showed up. So many people with notepads and mics wanting to talk to us. We were told it was best to give an exclusive, that would get us the most airtime for our plea. We chose Connie Chung because our lawyer said that CBS had the biggest audience. We wanted to spread the word as fast as we could. This was before social media, before AMBER Alerts. We were told that most abducted children who come home are returned to their parents within twenty-four hours. The alternative was unthinkable.

How I regretted not having a better photo of Natalie. Babies change fast. The picture we had of her at two months looked nothing like how she looked at four months. But this was before digital. People didn't snap away at their babies like they do today. I'd made appointments at Olan Mills Studios, but had canceled them because things always came up at work. I could have sent her with Charu, but I wanted to bring her to the studio myself. I didn't want my sitter to do it. We had plenty of time for a session, I thought. The Christmas-card deadline was still weeks away.

That TV appearance! I'll never forget the horror of it. Lights shining on us bright as kliegs as we sat there trying to look like good parents, not crazy, having to plead for mercy from the monster who took our baby, hoping the monster was watching Connie Chung.

12
LUCY

It felt as if I were walking into someone else's house, so different did it seem with a baby inside it. The air was strangely charged. The light in the kitchen seemed brighter, sharper. Objects I saw every day acquired new luster, new clarity. The toaster gleamed, vivid in its dark corner. Pastel Fiestaware deepened to the colors of rainbows. Little painted teapots danced on the walls. The house was no different, yet everything had changed. It felt both larger and smaller, shape-shifting around the baby's presence, her small weight on my shoulder somehow expanded to fill up the space. The narrow corridor widened as I brought her to the nursery. Its windows were street-facing, and once there, I pulled the blinds shut. Not because I was afraid some neighbor might drop by unexpectedly. I barely knew who my neighbors were; I spent most of my waking hours at work in Manhattan. I took the precaution because I didn't want to risk the chance that anyone — landscaper, postman, salesman — might peep in and see me walking around, suddenly endowed with a baby.

Gently, carefully, I took her from my shoulder and laid her down on the changing table. She looked around, taking in the mobiles, the stars on the ceiling, the ducks on the wall, the sconces, which were in the shape of sheep, smiling as if in appreciation of the decorating efforts I'd made on her behalf. For years, I'd imagined a baby in that outfitted room. In my mind, she had long been a presence there. But now I realized that tending to a baby was different from imagining one. How vulnerable, how trusting she was in my care, and how little I knew about taking care of her. Changing a diaper, which I'd done only a few times as a sitter, now loomed as a terrifying prospect. What formidable responsibility. My ignorance could cause her injury, perhaps even death! What if I made the diaper too tight, cutting off her blood supply? What if I missed a spot with the cream and she got infected? How much more was at stake when the baby was yours. Holding her with one hand to keep her from rolling off the table, with the other I tore into the package of disposable diapers on the shelf below. In my nervousness, I dropped the first diaper. How far from my reach it looked on the floor. Rather than bend down, which would require removing my steadying hand from the baby, I retrieved another from the package. I saw that the diaper was too small for her. *For babies up to ten pounds,* said the packaging. I unsnapped the crotch of her sunsuit, which was now stained brown from the seepage, unpeeled the sticky tabs of tape at the sides of her diaper and marveled that such a tiny, sweet-looking body could have produced such a mess. But I didn't find the foulness offensive, which was strange because I didn't have a strong stomach for that kind of thing. I hadn't been able to deal with my mother's incontinence at the end. My sister had rolled her eyes at my squeamishness. But she was a nurse.

"What the heck did your mother feed you?" I wondered. Saying "your mother" made me flinch, but she didn't notice. She seemed intent on grabbing a cloth star from the mobile I'd hung above the table. It played "It's a Small World." The song made her smile. I rewound it and she pumped her tiny fists to the music as a colorful galaxy twirled above her head.

I was afraid the wipes had gone dry, but when I broke the seal on the plastic, I was glad to feel that the cloths, though years old, were still soft and wet. She smiled as I cleaned her, gurgling a little, kicking free, glad to feel the fresh air. I checked the old diaper, expecting it to be marked with a size, but all that was on it were decorative animal prints. Not even the name of the company that made it! I rolled it up and slid it and its contents into a step-on metal can and reached to a shelf where I'd stacked some cloth diapers. Once, in a focus group for Pampers, I'd heard that cloth diapers were the better, more comfortable option. But how to turn a cloth rectangle into a diaper? I reached for a book. The answer was on — I'll never forget — page 137 of *Dr. Spock's Baby and Child Care,* the trusted bible by which my mother had raised Cheryl and me. Well, not her edition. That had gone to my sister when she'd had her first baby.

Folding a diaper looked easy in the simple line drawings explaining the process. But I had to lay the baby down on the braided rug while I practiced folding and folding the cloth into shapes that seemed as complicated as origami. No wonder disposable diapers had taken over the market. Lying on her back, she gurgled with happiness at her half nakedness — or perhaps it was amusement at my dilemma. I turned her onto her tummy so I could arrange the cloth over her, according to drawings. She extended her arms and legs and arched her back and I stopped folding and watched her, her perfect, plump, splendid body, seemingly preparing for flight. Even then, I thought her a magnificent creature, capable of anything.

In the end, I couldn't stick pins near her. I opened the plastic duck ends of the diaper pins, but was alarmed by how big the needle exposed was. How could I be sure it wouldn't break free and lacerate her? I resorted to wrapping the diaper with packing tape. Heavy-duty, clear, dependable tape with no sharp edges or potential to maim. The baby looked like a precious package prepared for shipment by a sender who'd never shipped a package before. Which, in a way, she was. It was the devil to get the diaper off a few hours later. I used a sewing scissors, the one from my grandmother, the sharpest scissors I owned. I warmed the blades first in hot water from the bathroom faucet so the steel wouldn't feel cold against her skin, then pushed the blades forward, millimeter by slow millimeter, until the diaper fell open and the baby kicked happily free again.

To know what to feed her, I had to find

out how old she was. According to Spock, age could be determined by a baby's weight and whether or not she had teeth. I took her to a scale to weigh her. I didn't have a baby scale, so, holding her, I stood on my bath scale and subtracted my weight. She was just under fifteen pounds. Holding her on my hip, I washed my hand in the sink, then gently probed her gums for protrusions. There was a tiny bump in her upper gum and my forefinger slid smoothly, up and down, as I felt for others. There weren't any others. She drooled and sucked at my finger until I removed it from her mouth. I studied the chart. She was four or five months old, I discovered. No wonder the wicker-pushing woman in the store had been so surprised! There were Similac cans that I'd long kept stacked behind boxes of pasta in the pantry. I checked the expiration dates. The cans were still good. I opened one, grateful for modern preservatives.

The baby was happy in my care, and I began to wonder. If she'd come from a good home, wouldn't she be crying to get back there? If she had a good mother, would she be blithely cooing in a strange room, gurgling at a new rattle? Perhaps the mother who dressed her in fine clothes also neglected her. After all, she'd abandoned her in a store!

By six o'clock, I couldn't resist tuning in to the news any longer. I settled with the baby in the den, in Warren's big leather recliner — now I was glad his girlfriend hadn't wanted it. My heart pounded as I pressed the remote to turn on the set. I turned so the baby couldn't see the screen from her place in my lap. I didn't want her to see her mother.

As the picture came on, I worried. Were they on the lookout for me?

There was the first President Bush guessing the week-old war in Iraq would be over in a few days. Then, news from the Central Park jogger trial. Then, what I'd been bracing myself for: a reporter stood outside IKEA, holding a microphone: *A search is on for missing infant Natalie Featherstone abducted today . . .*

Her name was Natalie. She didn't look like a Natalie. She was four months old. Four months and six days.

They had no lead on who'd taken her! Relief ballooned in my brain.

The screen filled with the glistening, tear-streaked face of her mother. Marilyn. She was a striking woman, beautiful even in her distress. Her hair was long and blond and fell in gentle waves in front of her face as she leaned toward the camera, which made her seem so close I drew back, afraid for a moment she could actually see us. I was fearful for myself and sorry for her. Very sorry. Her baby had been taken. I had taken her baby, who was on my lap, sucking peacefully on a bottle. I was glad she didn't seem to recognize Marilyn's voice. What can a four-month-old baby know of her mother? What can she remember? A fragrance? A gesture? The feel of her hands?

"I turned away from the shopping cart for only a second," Marilyn was saying. But this was a lie! She was a liar! She'd left the baby for much longer than that. She'd abandoned a small, helpless baby in a shopping cart in the middle of a store in a bad area. What if someone had come along besides me? Someone who meant to harm her, lock her up, raise her in a basement? There are so many crazy people out there, I thought, protectively stroking the baby's arm.

The camera pulled back to reveal Marilyn's husband, pink-faced and square-jawed, in expensive-looking jacket and tie.

The distraught parents . . .

He held up a photo of himself and his wife holding the baby. The camera went in for a close-up. It was a photo not of the baby, but of their car! A red BMW took up most of the picture. The camera pulled back and I could see, in the splay of their legs against the green lawn, they'd gotten everything they'd wanted so far in life.

The infant in the picture looked nothing like the baby I held in my lap and I realized they hadn't bothered to take recent photos. The camera was on them again and she put her hand to her throat as if checking for the persistence of vocal cords there. She leaned her cheek against his shoulder and he put his arm around her in a comforting hug. They still had each other. My longing for a baby was at least the equal of theirs.

The FBI has launched a tristate search for the kidnapper . . .

Kidnapper. Until then, that word hadn't occurred to me.

Suddenly everything in me started to rise. I managed to get the baby safely to her crib in the next room before kneeling on the floor and retching into the plastic waste-basket decorated with characters from *Pinocchio.* I knelt for a long while, cushioning my knees on the rug, while everything in me, everything I'd ever consumed, it seemed, came up into the basket and now the room reeked with the smell of my vomit.

I took the basket to the bathroom and emptied it and washed it and brought it back to the baby's room. The baby was crying and I picked her up and took her to the rocker and rocked her to sleep.

13
MARILYN

I didn't want to go to sleep that night, or nights for weeks after. I didn't want to lie down in the dark knowing I'd wake to a house without Natalie. I'd pace the house, walking in figure eights, needing to go somewhere, to feel as if I were doing something. The doctor gave me meds to knock me out, but I didn't want to take them at first. I'd never taken anything stronger than aspirin. What if Natalie turned up in the night and I was unconscious and couldn't go to her right away?

After about a week, I gave in. Tom warned me I couldn't function anymore without sleep. But sleep wasn't restful. It was full of nightmares. Nightmares about Natalie in which she was screaming, reaching for me and I couldn't help her, her hands were always just out of my grasp. Or, I dreamed that I'd find her, she'd been in her swing all along, and my body would flood with gratitude and relief and I'd pick her up but she'd slip out of my grasp and fall through a hole in the floorboards and I'd be wakened by a strange sound and Tom taking me in his arms, telling me the strange sound was coming from me.

Even worse than the nights were the mornings, climbing out of a deep well of sleep, slowly encountering the light, hearing the waking song of my baby, getting ready to get out of bed and tend to her, when I'd have to remember all over again — she was gone.

14
LUCY

I returned her again and again, in my mind.
All that night, and throughout the next day,
I saw scenes in which I was handing the
baby back to her mother. I imagined walking boldly through the doors of IKEA, saying that someone had given her to me, or
that I had found her somewhere, in a
playground, crying, left alone on the grass,
in need of a diaper change. But what playground? And what had I, a childless woman,
been doing in a playground? And where had
I been when the baby was taken? I had no
alibi. I knew from TV, I needed an alibi.

I couldn't keep her, much as I wanted to,
much as I felt an inexplicable connection
between us. But how would I give her back?
I imagined returning her, under cloak of
night, to her doorstep. I knew where the
parents lived. It was all over the news. I
imagined swaddling her in soft blankets,
leaving her in a basket on their welcome

mat, ringing the doorbell and hurrying away. But how could I hurry away fast enough to not be seen by vigilant neighbors or police who I assumed were watching the house? After a sleepless night, I woke with a plan.

That morning, holding her on my lap as she took a bottle, I told her how much I loved her, how sorry I was we couldn't stay together. Baby, I said, (I called her Baby) I'll never, ever forget you. I gave her little terry-clothed arm a squeeze, and at this, she pulled her mouth away from the bottle and gazed at me, as if taking in what I was telling her.

I washed and ironed the sunsuit and bib she'd worn to IKEA, dressed her in it, and brought out a sweater my sister had knitted for the baby I was never able to have. I wanted to leave the baby with something to show that the person who'd taken her was a kind person who had cared for her well.

I drove a few towns away, to a Babies To Go. How reluctantly I unstrapped the criss-crossings for the last time, picked her up, and settled her on my shoulder. Once in the store, I followed signs for cribs, which were in the rear. I dithered for some time deciding which one would be best to leave her in, glad to be spared the attention of salespeople huddled in a far corner over boxes of takeout.

I chose an old-fashioned rocking cradle, plump with white pillows and bolstered in frilled fabric dotted with bumblebees. White ribbon weaved prettily through its wooden slats. Slowly, I lifted her from my shoulder, resting her head on the ruffled pillow, prodded the cradle into gentle motion, rocking her gently until she was asleep. I kissed my fingertip and touched it to her soft forehead, then stood and hurried toward the front of the store, tears gathering so that I could barely see my way to the pay phone by the front door. I put in a quarter and listened to several mechanized messages thanking me for calling IKEA.

I'd meant to say where the baby was, then hang up. But before a human answered, I was distracted by a cry from the back of the store. That cry changed my mind. The sound of her sadness pulled at my core. I couldn't bear for her to be abandoned again. I replaced the receiver and hurried back to rescue her from the cradle.

"Mommy's here," I crooned. It was the first time I'd ever called myself that. The word flooded me, filling crevices I didn't know I had. I held the baby tight, reveling in the pleasure of her small, warm body against me, a pleasure I'd resigned myself to never feeling again. I swayed with her back and forth, murmuring "there, there" and other small mantras that mothers do, until she quieted, head on my shoulder.

I knew what I was doing was wrong according to law. But what I was doing felt right, according to the laws of nature.

I carried her to the aisle of car seats. It took a few minutes to divert the attention of a salesclerk from his carton of Chinese food, to help me pick out the best one.

Driving home with my baby in the seat behind me, I kept checking the rearview mirror to make sure she was safe, begging the universe to give Marilyn more babies, knowing that none could replace the one in my care.

15
LUCY

I had to give her another name, of course. She'd been Natalie for four months. She'd no doubt come to recognize the sound (na-ta-lee) and associate it, according to *Dr. Spock,* with fulfillment of needs or pleasure. I didn't want to wrest that accomplishment from her. I didn't want to damage her development. And yet, I needed to call her something else. A name different but not too distant from the one she was used to. I didn't want her to feel as if her identity had been robbed. I didn't want to subject her to psychological vertigo.

After we came home from Babies To Go, I sat on the floor in her room, pulling baby-name books from the shelf. I had plenty of baby-name books. Warren and I had perused them at leisure in the heady days of what we thought was impending parenthood. None of the names we'd chosen seemed right to me now.

The baby lay beside me on the braided rug, playing with paper which she was crinkling and putting into her mouth. She liked sucking on paper. It was clean paper. Engraved Tiffany stationery, fresh from the box. I imagined the baby would have her own engraved stationery someday. What name would be on it?

Her new name couldn't begin with an *A*, *E*, or *O*. I'd avoid initials that could turn into acronyms. In grade school, I'd had a friend, Zena Thomson, whose middle name was Isabelle and for years she had been taunted with "Zit."

Bella. Chloe. Haley. Mia.

Besides an actress whose work I admired, Mia was also the name of a friend's older sister, a girl who was pretty, poised, sophisticated — all the things I hadn't been as a girl.

The name in the mouth produced a sound similar to Natalie: Mee-a.

"Mia," I tried, and the baby looked up.

Years later, after a playdate with a friend whose sitter spoke Spanish, Mia told me that her name in that language meant "mine."

"Did you name me that or was that my born name?" she wanted to know.

91

"Your born name," I said. "It's beautiful. I didn't want to change it."

"My first mommy named me that because she didn't want to give me away, right?"

"Right," I said, lifting her, pressing her against me, swallowing the lump in my throat, until she demanded her freedom and wriggled away.

The day after I named her was a Monday, and at 9 a.m., I called Sandra, the creative manager at work. I told her I was in Kansas. She knew about my quest for a child — everyone at work knew about it at that point. I said I was picking up a four-month-old baby from a high school student who'd changed her mind about raising her. Such deception is unimaginable now, when caller ID would display the area code of the landline I was calling from, but then it was possible. Sandra was a single mother herself. She told me to take as much time as I needed.

In the first days with Mia, I wouldn't let her out of my sight. I'd take her into each room with me, strap her into a high chair while I worked in the kitchen mixing formula, heating it, mashing banana, which Dr. Spock suggested should be the first fruit. I'd stand there working the fork, pressing tines into the soft white pulp, crossing and recrossing patterns until the banana was mushy enough for a baby to eat, thinking how lucky I was not to be at the ad agency, hashing and rehashing client copy instead. I even set her up in a bouncy chair in the bathroom so I could keep an eye on her while I was taking a shower. I carried a monitor around the house while she slept, listening for the reassuring sound of her breath. I'd sometimes keep watch, hovering over her crib rail, gazing at her as she fell asleep, marveling at the rise and fall of her little square back, the glisten of sweat on her dimpled arms, the daintiness of her baby snores.

You'd think a four-month-old taken from her mother would put up a fuss. But I recall her in those first days with me being less upset than she seemed to be puzzled. Perhaps I am deluding myself. Perhaps I have blocked out a wailing resistance. But I don't think so.

Picture it, my friend had said, *and it will come true.* I was filled with gratitude for my good fortune — and remorse for the way it had come to me.

I'd sometimes call my sister "from Kansas," putting questions to her, but most things having to do with taking care of a baby — how to burp them, carry them, get them to sleep — couldn't be explained over the phone. Cheryl kept offering to fly down to help and I had a devil of a time talking her out of the trip.

Every few days, I'd call in to the office, reporting progress. "She rolled over today for the first time!" I'd say, failing to mention that the bed she'd rolled over in had been mine in New Jersey. Or "Another delay," I'd lie. "The birth father needs to cosign and they can't find him."

I got a message from the art director who'd helped me place the ad saying how happy she was for me, but that deadlines were urgent and she was pairing up with another writer. I didn't care.

I lived those first weeks of motherhood in dread of the doorbell. The few times it rang, I felt every hair on my body upend. I feared that something would break in my case and that the authorities — or even the wronged mother herself — would show up at my door to take her back. The few times the bell rang, I never answered it. Instead, I'd peep through a gap in the drapes. The bell ringers wore benign-looking uniforms in post office blue or UPS brown. But what if they were disguised to gain access? What if I was a suspect being spied upon? They'd leave packages on my doorstep but I'd wait until after I put Mia down for the night before creeping out to retrieve them. The packages were baby gifts. Baby clothes from my sister, a Sony video camera from friends at work. (The agency I worked for had the Sony account.) Once a flyer fell from the door when I opened it: *Missing Infant,* it read beneath a photo of *Baby Natalie.* I crumpled the paper and threw it away, glad that the photo looked nothing like her.

I didn't answer the phone. I rarely went out, waiting for dark before backing the car out of the driveway, so no one could see that I had a car seat, to buy groceries in distant towns.

What worried me most during those weeks was that she would get sick with something. I'd have to bring her to emergency and the jig would be up. I guessed there were alerts to airports and hospitals for a baby fitting her description. Each time I changed her diaper, I did a complete body check, scouting for redness or rashes or lumps. I kept careful notes on her feeding and poop schedules, as one book advised — although later, I realized that advice had been for nursing mothers, to inform them if their babies were getting enough nourishment.

Mia usually slept through the night, but one 3 a.m. she was crying inconsolably, though her diaper was dry and she didn't have a fever. Remembering the little lump I'd felt in her gum, I guessed she was teething. In despair, not knowing how else to soothe her, I sat on the rocker with her in my lap and undid the top of my nightgown. I thought maybe milk would come, maybe I could calm her with it. Weren't there stories of wet nurses and women in bomb shelters nursing babies whose mothers had died? These thoughts were crazy, but I didn't care — I was desperate to give Mia whatever she wanted.

The sight of my breast did calm her immediately and I guessed that she'd been breastfed before, though she'd been weaned by the time she came to me — I knew by the odiferousness of that first diaper. She stared at what was being offered, with a glance at my face as if asking permission, then moved her face forward and seized my nipple between her gums. It hurt like hell, as if my nipple was being crushed between stones. I winced and pulled back and she resumed her crying, screaming louder this time, as if I had tricked her, which I suppose I had.

I wished that those first weeks could have

gone on forever, our tiny world of eating, sleeping, rocking, reading.

It was as if Mia thought she was on a great adventure. She seemed to take pleasure in exploring new sights, new surfaces, new smells, new sounds. She didn't take naps, though the books said she should. She hadn't read those books. She slept through the night, though. I was grateful for that. I'd begin each day with a feeling of excitement, as I used to feel as a child on Christmas morning. I'd never been a light sleeper, but now I was out of bed at the first sound of her "talking" to herself in her crib in the morning, my heart somersaulting, hurrying to the nursery to take in the gratifying sight and scent of her, realizing anew — I was somebody's mother!

I'd sing her little songs and talk to her as I attended her toilette. Then, I'd settle her in a jump chair, I'd go to the front door, and after checking from the window to make sure no neighbors were about, I'd duck out and grab the paper from the front porch. I'd sit at the table feeding Mia and turning the pages slowly, cautiously, scanning headlines for news of what had happened, closing the paper, grateful for yet another twenty-four hours with her.

Generally, people in advertising consider

PR to be a lesser profession, but my own estimation of the field rose considerably when I saw that after a few days of media attention the story was made to sink out of sight. IKEA was opening a new store in Los Angeles. They didn't want bad publicity.

Each day, she curled her tiny fist around my fingers, becoming more and more mine.

16
MARILYN

The night of the day that Natalie was taken, state troopers brought in dogs to find her scent. They asked me to give them a piece of her clothing. I went to her room — it felt empty as a tomb — and stood in the middle of it, trying to see through tears, to find something to give the troopers. I didn't want to part with a single thing that had been hers. Finally, I lifted the blanket from her crib. It was still a soft heap on the mattress. I hadn't folded it after her nap. It had little lambs on it. Soft, so soft. I pictured them finding her, giving it to her. She would be comforted by something from home.

Later, much later, I asked for it back, but they said they had to keep it sealed in a baggie, for dogs.

The FBI was brought in. A police detective set up shop on our coffee table. Detective Brown showed up every day at 8 a.m., started making calls on a special phone they installed. Others would come by — neighbors, friends — and he'd assign them tasks for the day: paperwork, mostly, so he could do his job of trying to find Natalie. Whenever the phone rang, my stomach contracted. The detective quieted everyone. Everything stopped, so the only sound in the house was those long rings. I'd reach for the handset, fingers shaking, wondering if I was about to talk to Natalie's kidnapper. We were expecting (dreading) a call for ransom. Tom and I had been told to sound calm and keep a caller on the line for as long as possible, so the FBI would be able to trace the call. It had been decided that I'd answer the phone instead of Tom, my voice would be less threatening. Each time the phone rang, I'd reach for the handset, and try not to sob. But a ransom call never came.

I nurtured hope, against odds, that someone would call to say our baby had been found unharmed, that they had taken Natalie by mistake, there'd been some terrible misunderstanding. But, of course, that call didn't come either.

For months, day and night, we searched for our baby. We couldn't stop looking. Friends and neighbors, some we'd never met before, joined us in the search. Every evening, car pools drove out to IKEA, volunteers fanned out through fields surrounding the store, flashlight beams playing on the grass after dark. People waded through ditches and opened trunks of abandoned cars. I was relieved that nobody found her in one. I didn't want her to be found dead.

We put up posters everywhere: telephone poles, malls, school bulletin boards. Tom's office made copies and paid bike messengers to leave them at the offices they went to. We hired teenagers to leaflet neighboring towns. We turned the living room into headquarters for a "Take Back Natalie" campaign. Our home didn't feel like a home anymore, it was a public place. Our lost child belonged not just to us, but to everyone. We were inundated not only by people who wanted to help, but by curiosity seekers coming up on our lawn, peeping through windows, leaving smears on the glass that separated them from unthinkable disaster. People tied yellow ribbons on everything that was vertical: trees, shrubs, the mailbox post. On the news they said local stores had run out of yellow ribbon stock. Then someone tied a bunch of yellow balloons to the wishing well. Those balloons bobbed for weeks. I realized whoever had put them there must be replacing them, day after day. Then one morning I saw the balloons deflated, drooped on the grass. I knew that person had given up hope.

On our living room credenza were always coffee and sandwiches. For years afterward, the smell of coffee urns made me nauseous.

AT&T offered to extend my leave, but I quit instead. I couldn't stomach the idea of going back to work. How could I return to the life I had once considered normal, of doing something all day that took me away from what was now my purpose — to find Natalie or help people who could. I couldn't imagine summoning interest in a job anymore. Because of a job, I had lost my child.

Detective Brown showed up every morning just as Tom was heading out to work. How can you function at work? I asked Tom and he told me that work was the only place he *could* function. "We still need to pay the mortgage," he said, which was true, though I knew if he'd asked the firm for paid leave, they probably would have given it to him. He was a partner by then. We began dealing with the tragedy in different ways. His way was denial. Mine was denial of everything except the loss of our daughter. We lost the language we had together. He rarely spoke. We no longer touched. Once, he brushed by me in the kitchen and said "excuse me" as if I were a stranger on a subway. I felt pushed away by those words, as if he had actually shoved me.

Months passed and one day, after being there every morning, Detective Brown didn't show up. When he hadn't come by noon, I called Tom at the office and Tom tracked him down. The detective was back at his desk in the precinct. He said he'd been assigned to move on. Move on! How could he move on, knowing our baby was still out there, somewhere, without us? I never doubted her continuing presence on this planet. Every pore of my skin was alive with the certainty that though she was gone from us, she was still part of this earth.

17
CHERYL

It was all so believable. I remember Lucy calling from Kansas to tell us the news. I knew she'd put an ad in the paper out there. So I believed her when she said she was in Wichita to pick up a baby from a girl who had gotten in trouble.

I recall her telling us how expensive private adoption was. She told us what it cost, a sum that rocked Doug and me and made us even more grateful we'd been able to have our two boys the natural way. It never occurred to me to question the adoption. Why would I? I never imagined my sister would lie about that.

I offered to fly down to help her, but she was dead set against it, even after she got the baby back to New Jersey. Part of me was glad, I have to admit — leaving my own family wouldn't have been easy. The boys were in middle school and Mom was gone by then and I didn't have anybody but

Doug to help out and he was busy, on the road a lot.

Looking back, maybe I should have suspected something. But I wrote off her refusal of my help as a simple matter of pride. Lucy is two years older than I am. You never ask an older sibling too many questions.

I'm just grateful our mother isn't still alive, to have to suffer the pain of knowing the truth about Lucy. Someone capable of such an act and such a deception. My sister is not who anyone thought her to be.

18
LUCY

I knew I had to go back to work. But I dreaded leaving Mia all day. I thought about quitting my job and going freelance. Free-lancers commanded hefty day rates and could come and go at will. But I knew I couldn't depend on freelance to sustain the life I wanted for us. I needed the certainty of a biweekly paycheck, with health benefits.

I cast about in my mind for a profession that would let me stay home with a baby. But what profession would let me stay home with a baby while at the same time paying enough to support us? It was 1990. Telecom-muting wasn't an option yet. My office was in midtown Manhattan. There were ad agencies in New Jersey I might have worked at instead, but none had the stature of Scali, McCabe, Sloves, which was one of the most creative shops on Madison Avenue, proven in part by the fact that it was no longer on Madison. I had a child to support for the next eighteen years. I couldn't afford to throw away my career.

I decided that if I was going to go back to my job, I had to move to the city. I had to be able to get to my baby from the office in a matter of minutes, had to be able to get to the hospital in case of emergency, which would be impossible if I had to depend on the vagaries of De Camp buses or PATH trains or traffic clogging the Lincoln Tunnel.

I began to scour the *New York Times* classifieds. I'd get up early with the baby and retrieve the paper from my doormat, opening the door and shutting it quickly against the gray dawn, before neighbors were out. I read it while holding Mia on my lap at the kitchen table, sometimes letting her play with the red grease pencil from the office I used to circle 2BRS, DRMN. I knew I wanted a doorman. Mia was just five months old, but already I was picturing the teenager she would become, returning home at night from a dance, lithe and long-haired, tiny-skirted and bare-legged. I didn't want her standing in a dark entrance, fumbling for keys. I wanted a brightly lit canopy and a doorman who would look out for her. A building close to a subway, which would mean a short walk home, short enough that muggers wouldn't have time to mug her. It was New York before Giuliani. There were still plenty of muggers.

I was nervous about seeing apartments with a real estate agent, baby in tow. What if one of them identified her, somehow, from the news? I was relieved not to have to sign up with an agency, after all. I learned of an apartment before it was listed. An account woman at the office took a job with a client in Düsseldorf. She put an ad in the Scali newsletter saying she was putting her co-op on the market. She gave me a good deal. And so I traded a light and airy 3 BR in Montclair for a rear 2 BR in Morningside Heights. It was a back apartment on the first floor. But it had a doorman. And a canopy entrance lit brightly at night, for safety. It was a short walk from the 110th Street stop. The apartment was dark, but I didn't mind. The dark suited me now, cloaking me in its protective veil.

One benefit I hadn't realized before taking the apartment was that it was across the street from a newly built playground in Riverside Park. I became grateful for this amenity as soon as I moved in.

The playground was a place I could take the baby, unafraid. No one knew I wasn't really a mother. No one glanced suspiciously my way. No one glanced at me, period, which was fine with me. I'd sit by the river in the fresh, wide air absorbing the baby-raising wisdom of women around me, discussing answers to questions that flummoxed me then — what was the best formula, how to find a pediatrician, which were the good preschools and how to get into them?

Mia was six months old now, she could sit in a sandbox, and I perched on its wooden perimeter watching her play, learning all I needed to know to take care of her, rarely having to say a thing.

I learned about Mommy and Me classes given in a nearby church basement, and that if you weren't there to sign up at 7 a.m. on the day classes opened, you'd be shut out. I learned which kind of stroller was easiest to fold, for a bus or cab trip. And what to do for a baby's cold (humidifier). I learned about childproofing a house (no thumbtacks!) and what shade of poop meant a baby was sick, realizing how little I'd known about life, having been protected from its messiness by spending so much clean time in offices.

Once, guiding Mia down the chute of a slide, I overheard a woman on a bench behind me confess her guilt about having an affair. "I can't help myself," she said, in a voice she didn't bother to lower. "The second I saw him, it was like I got carried away by a wave." The listeners nodded, murmuring supportive comments, which surprised me, and made me feel suddenly piqued. Because if I told them of being similarly swept away by besottedness, I doubted they'd make the same allowances for me.

19
CHERYL

Soon after Lucy got Mia, I did something I thought would be a nice surprise for her. I contacted an old school friend at our home-town paper and I got her to put in a baby announcement. When the announcement came out, I clipped it and mailed it to Lucy and got a call from her right away. I thought she was calling to thank me. But instead, she was angry! She shouted at me, accusing me of having overstepped bounds, invading her privacy. I had to pull the receiver away from my ear. I apologized, but couldn't understand her reaction, how such a small thing could provoke such vitriol in her. I chalked it up to her moving to New York City, where people like keeping their dis-tance, preferring to live as strangers, I guess.

20
LUCY

The hardest part of going back to work was hiring a sitter. How could I leave Mia? How could I abandon her as she'd been abandoned before? How could I leave her with someone who might whisk her away, beguiled by her as I had been? I had nightmares in which I'd return to a dark, empty apartment echoing with hollowness left in her wake. But I had to go back to work to support us. As the days of my maternity leave dwindled, I made myself look up nanny agencies in the phone book. I called the one with the most trustworthy name. Professional Nannies Institute. I liked the sound of it, the promise of the title, which implied that it dealt only with women for whom taking care of children was a profession. Surely they wouldn't jeopardize a career by making off with one of their charges. I called, imagining a pipeline direct from London through which Mary Poppins look-alikes would slide into this country. But though the woman who answered the phone had a reassuringly British accent, she told me that few nannies came from England anymore. The institute was a school in name only. The only course it gave was in getting a green card. The fees appalled me. I said I'd call her back and hung up.

Several mothers in the playground had found sitters by answering ads in the pages of the *Irish Echo,* a weekly paper in which classifieds were a kind of clearinghouse for babysitting jobs in New York. But the prospects I interviewed were disappointments: a girl from Dublin who came for the interview carrying a big bag of pink candied popcorn — how could Mia acquire good eating habits from her?; a young woman from Trinidad who wanted to bring her infant son to the job, so she could babysit him, too — but if there were a fire, which baby would she rescue first?; a woman from Barbados who'd been Claudette Colbert's laundress — but how much would she know about taking care of a baby?

I realized I was looking for someone who was not only capable but like-minded. I began to fathom the commitment required for a mother-sitter relationship to work. It would be akin to a marriage. Indeed, some mothers at the playground saw more of their sitter than they did of their spouse.

A sitter would be someone who would wield great influence over my daughter, someone I'd have to trust to guide her development. A sitter could make my life miserable or wonderful. This imbued the decision with enormous weight. I began to get cold feet. I toyed again with the notion of finding a job that would let me stay home with my baby. I could start a business. A couple I knew had left advertising to start a catalog company selling baby clothes. The company had become successful — I sometimes saw people reading their catalogs on the subway — but that success had taken years. I didn't have years.

Then, one afternoon while pushing Mia in her stroller to the corner market, I saw a sign on a bus stop. *Babysitter — Mush Experience.* The sign was handwritten and I wondered if the "Mush" was intentional, meant to be ironic. The penmanship was Palmer Method, tight but graceful loops, the kind of writing that hasn't been taught for decades. I knew an older woman had written the notice. I was partial to hiring an older woman. An older woman would prove more responsible, I'd heard at the playground.

I called the number and spoke with someone with an accent, who wasn't the babysitter. She said she was the babysitter's
cousin. The babysitter wasn't home now,
but she was a very good babysitter, the
cousin said. The cousin had trusted her own
son to her, but now she stayed home and
didn't need a babysitter anymore. The
babysitter had two interviews arranged for
the next day, did I want an interview with
her? Yes, I said, and we set a time. The
woman on the phone offered to come with
the babysitter. Because the babysitter's
English wasn't too good, she said. This
alarmed me. I didn't want someone taking
care of my baby who couldn't speak English.
I said I'd changed my mind about the appointment, but, apparently, there was confusion because the next day, at the appointed
hour, the doorbell rang.

It was the babysitter. She'd come alone.
She was a kind, gentle-looking Chinese
woman about my age. She had dressed for
the interview in an old-fashioned silk dress
that reminded me of dresses my mother had
worn. It would have been rude to turn her
away.

She insisted she couldn't wear shoes into
the apartment and, over my protests, slipped
them off on the doormat. She was shorter

without heels, and though I am not a big woman, I felt oversize as I led her, barefoot, down the hall to the living room, where Mia was playing in her jump seat. Mia had been wary of other sitters I'd interviewed, but she began to bounce happily when she saw this woman, as if they were already friends.

I gestured to a place on the sofa, and I settled myself opposite.

I asked her about her experience with babies. Her English wasn't as bad as it could be.

She said she'd taken care of her cousin's son. Also, she had a son herself, back in China. She reached for her purse and took out a plastic wallet and thumbed a photo out of its billfold. The boy wore a school tie and posed on a bicycle, one foot on a pedal, one on the ground.

"I raised him until twelve," she said, gazing at the picture. Its serrated edges were bent and she gently pressed them back into place. Now the boy was fourteen, she said, and lived with her husband and parents in Shanghai.

She slid the image carefully back into its sleeve and I thought of the sadness of having to leave your child in a different country on the other side of the world. I couldn't imagine it.

21
WENDY

I left my son to go to Meiguo. Beautiful country. That is the Chinese name for America. I left in 1988, when Lin was just twelve. Feng and I wanted a better life for him. We wanted a better life for our family. At this time, China is still very poor. Many people want to leave China, go to other countries to live and to work: America, Germany, Canada. America was first choice, a country so rich, it was said children drank milk there like water. In China, many things were still rationed. You needed *liangpiao* — coupons — to buy everything: meat, cooking oil, even rice. How much you could buy was according to how big your family. Except eggs. Two dozen eggs were allowed each family a month, no matter what size family you had. *Liangpiao* was like gold. When my mother died two years ago, we found *liangpiao* carefully wrapped in a handkerchief, in a box in her room, kept in case difficult times returned.

My cousin worked in New York City. He and his wife had a restaurant in Chinatown and they needed someone to care for their son. So our plan was for me to go to the U.S. first, then later, Feng can follow with Lin.

In the 1980s, it was very hard to get visa to go to U.S. You stood on long lines outside the embassy for days, your family bringing you food. The U.S. required you to have bank statement that showed equivalent of three thousand American dollars. We borrowed money from my parents. Feng's parents also offered money, but we do not accept. Because we know that they do not let two spouses go abroad at the same time, too afraid they will stay. Once you are turned down, you can't apply again for six months.

I got a visa because of Feng's love of American jazz. It was illegal then to listen to American broadcasts in China. To do it, Feng built a shortwave radio in secret. This, too, was against the law. No one could know or he would be arrested. I didn't want him to have it, but he didn't listen to me. He turned it on low, late at night, after I went to sleep. This radio got American news, too.

The night before I went for my interview,

we practiced what I should say. I almost could not get to sleep that night, rehearsing things in my head: how to hold myself, how fast to talk, when to look like I'm thinking, when to answer right away. But finally it is morning and Feng is shaking me.

"Wake up," he is saying, and tells me he heard something on the radio that can help me get a visa. He says it is my winning card, but that I must not reveal it until the interview is over. "The interview isn't over until it is over," he says.

Later, I stood at an embassy window, nervously answering question after question, trying to hold myself upright during one answer, bowing my head at another. The man looked at my paperwork and then his hands reached for a big, red stamp. I knew red meant "refused." And then I played the card Feng had given me.

I took a deep breath. "I congratulate you."

The man looked up. He looked at me for the first time. "Why do you congratulate me?"

"Because your country has a space shuttle that succeeded in reaching the moon."

This is what Feng had heard. The Americans' last moon shuttle had crashed but their next one had just succeeded in landing.

"Really?" The man turned to another man passing behind him. He spoke in English, but I knew he was asking if what I said was true.

When he turned back to me, his face had softened. The papers were between us and he pulled them back. When he pushed them toward me again, instead of a red stamp of refusal, I saw a black stamp of acceptance. I ran all the way home. Feng was waiting for me in the little park outside our housing complex. He knew by my face that his plan had succeeded. We began to cry, partly out of happiness but also because we knew this would mean I would go away, that I'd be separated from him and our son for a long time.

After my first excitement, I began to worry. I wondered if it would be worth the sacrifice to leave my family. When I confessed to friends my fears about going, they told me not to wish away my good luck. They said not to worry about Lin, my mother and Feng could raise him. But when they said these words, it felt like they were throwing stones at my sides.

The day I boarded the plane, I expected to feel excitement, but I felt only fear and great sadness. I sat by a window, waving to Feng and Lin, who stood in the airport window, waving until the plane pulled away. I tried not to cry. I wanted my son to see I was brave.

The cabin was warm and I went to the lavatory to take off the long underwear that Chinese wore then. It was only October, but I'd worn it to make room in my suitcase for the many gifts I was bringing my cousin. I stayed there a long time, crying quietly into the wool. I felt like I was separating myself from everything I knew, everything I loved.

When I first came to America, I was shocked by how dirty it was. Even the floors of the modern airport were dirty. Also, the waste! In China, bones are saved to make soup, but in the restaurant in Chinatown, we throw them away. Even though food is very expensive. A basket of eggs that cost pennies in China cost dollars in America. So I am surprised that here, rich people are thin and poor people are fat.

One thing I couldn't wait to see was Christmas. We'd heard about American Christmas in China. But Christmas wasn't a special day at the restaurant. Christmas was just like an ordinary day, only busier. Because families who don't celebrate Christmas come to eat at Chinese restaurants instead.

After two years, my cousin and his wife moved the restaurant to Queens. She stays home and we didn't need two ladies to take care of one baby. So now I must find another job. I must keep earning money to send home. I put up many signs in good neighborhoods, hoping a nice family would see this sign. This is how I met Lucy. At first, I cannot believe how much she will pay me for one hour. It is much more than I earned from my cousin's wife. And Lucy needs many hours, which is good for me. I don't have anything to do here but work.

I send money for Lin to go to a good school. I send money for his new clothes and new bike. I call home every week, but calling is so expensive that all we can afford is for everyone to say hi. I'd call at a certain time and they'd pass the phone from one to another: "Hi, this is Feng, I'm okay, are you?" "Hi, it's Mama, I'm okay, are you?" I'd go home every two years, bringing toys for Lin and English books that I'd read to him. We wrote many letters. I still have his to me. I'm sorry that Lin threw away the ones I wrote to him.

After two more years, when Lin was sixteen, Feng was also allowed to leave China. But officials wouldn't let him bring

Lin, for fear that they would not return. So Feng comes by himself to this country, leaving Lin with my mother. I have my own apartment by now. With Feng getting dollars, too, I can soon go home and help Lin through the good high school that now we can afford. But the only work Feng can find is dry-cleaning work. The smells are so bad, he says, it's for dogs to do. He is paid so little, he must walk forty blocks instead of taking the subway, or he earns no money. He can't find work like mine: high-paying and clean. So Feng goes home and our plan doesn't work. I work for Lucy until Mia is fifteen, going back to China only once a year. Then, my mother falls sick and I must go back to Shanghai to take care of her. But Lin is already grown up by now.

Every day I was with Mia, I loved that girl. But always in America, I missed my son who I love so much, enough to leave him.

22
LUCY

The next day when she came to work, I asked what her name was. She had written it on a scrap of paper, but Mia had gotten hold of it and it was unreadable.

She didn't answer at first.

"What is your name?" I enunciated, more slowly, thinking she hadn't understood.

She startled me with "What do you want it to be?"

What kind of question was that?

She said she needed an American name. She'd started English lessons at a church in Chinatown and their homework this week was to come up with an American name.

She gazed at me hopefully and I couldn't explain my American resistance to taking away her good name and giving her another.

I asked what her Chinese name was. Wan-ling, she said. That name was beautiful, I told her. She didn't need another. But she said she wanted an American name. She thought it would help her be more American.

Mia squirmed in my arms and I thought of the baby-name books.

We looked up names that started with *W*. There weren't many. Winifred was awful. Wanda was worse. Winona? I said. Winsome? Wendy? As soon as I said Wendy, she repeated it, as if tasting the word.

"Wendy." She smiled, pointing to herself, and it was the first time I saw the Chinese way of pointing — putting forefinger to nose instead of to chest.

She pulled a clean, folded handkerchief from inside her sleeve and leaned toward Mia, gently wiping drool from her mouth.

"But you call me Ayi," she said, gently lifting her from me. "Auntie," she explained to me.

Mia grinned a two-tooth grin, already smitten. As was I.

I did worry about putting someone in charge of my child who didn't have full command of the language. But while Wendy's English was lacking, she was beautifully versed in the language that mattered most to a six-month-old, the nonverbal language of taking care of a baby. She sat on the floor playing games with Mia, seeming never to tire of pushing blocks through a hole or building towers of plastic bricks. She'd sing songs in Chinese and read from board books and from colorful comic books she brought from Chinatown along with videotapes of the adventures of Monkey King, rewinding to scenes that made Mia laugh.

I was comforted by the fact that we lived in a first-floor apartment where a doorman was always just steps away. Nine-one-one services were particularly good in our neighborhood. We lived on a wide street.

I bought a beeper and devised an elaborate system by which Wendy could always communicate with me. (These were the days before cell phones.) "333" meant all was well and that the baby just wanted to hear the sound of my voice. "999" meant Wendy had a minor problem or question and I was to call as soon as it was convenient. "666" meant EMERGENCY — call home right away. Why had I made the codes so similar? Several times I saw the beeper upside down and misread the 999 as 666 and my heart jumped and I couldn't reach fast enough for that little black square vibrating as if it was a heart, it was my heart, it was my lifeline to Mia. But as long as it was quiet, I could trust all was well.

23
LUCY

No harm came to Mia when Wendy took care of her. The 666 never flashed on that screen. It was only in my care that Mia got hurt. Like the day I taught her to ride a bike. She fell on the sidewalk and there was so much blood from her knee, I scooped her up and ran with her to the doctor's office, three blocks away. She needed stitches and I held her hand and her face toward mine so she wouldn't have to look at the needle. He gave her three stitches. He advised six so there wouldn't be scarring, but I couldn't bear subjecting her to more trauma than necessary.

And before that, was a day I thought I had lost her. Wendy never lost her, but I did. That day, I discovered the magnitude of the wrong I'd done Marilyn, the brutality of the assault I had dealt her.

It happened in Bon Point — a fancy baby-goods store on Madison Avenue, gone now.

Mia was still a baby, about one and a half. It was early Saturday morning. No other shopper was in the store. I'd rushed in with her to pick out a present for some baby shower we were on our way to.

As I was talking with a woman at the counter about various offerings under the glass, Mia was playing at my feet, or so I thought. I'd given her one of the plastic playthings Wendy kept in a net bag on her stroller. At a certain point, I glanced down, and Mia wasn't there. I remember not being able to take my eyes from the place where she'd been, so certain that my eyes were playing a trick. It took a moment for my mind to take in that she must have crawled away. She wasn't anywhere I could see, but she couldn't have gone far. She couldn't walk yet. She was a late walker. "Where is my baby?" I shouted to the woman behind the counter, though she was standing just an arm's length away. Her eyes widened behind tortoiseshell readers and she promptly called out to the other saleswoman: *Shut the front door!* It was such an immediate reaction, I worried that they'd had this kind of trouble before. Why had they left the doors open? Store entrances were never left open on upper Madison then. Carnegie Hill, as the neighborhood

128

was called, was not so gentrified as it is now.

The other woman hurried up the few steps to the entrance and pulled the doors shut. But I went after her, and flung them open again, emerging onto the broad sidewalk, looking down its length, for a figure making away with my baby. Madison Avenue looked deserted, the long pavements empty as in a ghost town and — though this is impossible — in my memory of that moment, tumbleweeds come at me, propelled by a whistling wind down the empty thoroughfare.

There was a station wagon parked directly in front of the store. Its windows were tinted. I lunged forward and pressed my forehead against the pane of the front passenger window, cupping my eyes with my hands to see through the glass. There were kids in the car, but none of them Mia. A middle-aged man behind the wheel looked up from his newspaper, startled. Without a word or gesture of apology to the man — which even in the moment, I registered as being uncharacteristic of me, raised to be unfailingly cordial — I turned and hurried back to the store. The woman at the front door opened it for me and asked my daughter's name and soon the store sang out with our chorus: *Mia! Mia? Mia!*

Each call of her name was a blow to my

chest and I realized that the pain I'd caused Marilyn was physical. I made promises to the universe: if Mia was found, I'd set things right. I'd give her back. I'd figure out some way to do this without getting caught. I was highly paid to be a solver of problems. If I just put my mind to it, I'd come up with a way to solve this problem, too. If Mia was all right, if she wasn't harmed, or dead, I would do anything, anything wanted of me. All I could think of, saying it over and over again in my head, was a prayer, a mantra: please, please, please let Mia come back to me.

I continued calling out her name, imbuing the word alternately with beseechingness (*Mia?*), impatience (*Mia!*), desperation (*MIA!*).

Soon, I thought, the cops would be brought in and I pictured myself breaking under their interrogations. I'd confess my secret, not caring about consequences. Consequences wouldn't matter if Mia were gone.

And then the air resonated with the words: "Here she is!" I hurried in the direction of the saleswoman's voice. There was Mia. She was quite safe, sitting in the middle of a circular rack of hanging clothes that the saleswoman had parted. She'd been hiding.

Mia looked up at me, calm, unfazed. Her eyes had the glazed look of satisfaction she always had after she pooped — something she preferred to do in private, despite the fact that her diaper concealed the act. "Mia!" I cried, tears blurring my vision as I reached through merchandise to pull her toward me. The fumes coming from her seemed the sweetest scent I'd ever inhaled.

We didn't go to the baby shower. After changing her diaper in a dressing room — the saleswomen fell over themselves showing me into it — I took Mia home. In the cab, I sat holding her on my lap, my hands still shaking with gratitude for her.

It was fall. We drove through Central Park to the West Side, beneath yellows and reds and golds glinting against a blue sky, past Rollerbladers, bikers, strollers, and runners, all moving in the same direction, as if an exodus were taking place.

Coming out of the park, we passed a sign for the Big Apple Circus. I made a mental note to buy tickets and realized that I wasn't going to keep my promise to the universe, after all.

24
WENDY

Mia was a big, fat baby, so carrying her is not easy for me. She didn't walk until she was more than one and a half. This is very late for a baby to walk. Lin took his first step before his Zhua Zhou party, the party for babies who turn one year old. It is the day we stop calling him his milk name, which is a name to fool the gods into thinking a boy is not worthy of attention, so they won't take him back. His milk name was MuMu, which means "wood." My husband and I don't really believe this tradition, but we also don't want to risk our son's fate.

I know Mia's not walking is my fault. I knew this is true, because I was afraid of her getting hurt. I was afraid to let Mia learn to walk in the apartment because the floors didn't have carpet. Some floors were marble, some floors wood, each hard in its own way. Lucy didn't want carpet, she thought floors were beautiful and didn't want to cover them up. This is another example of American thinking.

I worried that Mia would fall down and hit her head on the hard floors. I carried her everywhere — from kitchen to bedroom to living room to watch Monkey King on television. Finally, one day, my arms feel so tired, I almost drop her. Now I know I need to teach her to walk. The only place of soft floor was a round rug in Mia's room, a rug near her crib, so that if baby falls out, she won't land on hard floor. I make Mia practice her walking there.

At first, Mia doesn't want to walk. I know why. She thinks: Why do I need to walk? Mia sits like little Buddha, everything is brought to her or she is brought to everything. I talk, talk, talk to her, over and over, telling her she needs to learn how to walk. I tell her she is a big girl now, she has to stand straight and walk like a grown-up lady. But many days, she only sits, holding up her arms, crying "Ayi! Ayi!," waiting for me to pick her up. I try to trick her, leaving the room to see if she'll do this thing by herself. But she doesn't. She crawls to me in the doorway, lifts herself to standing by holding on to my leg, crying for me to pick her up in my arms.

One day, we are in the park, playing in the

sandbox. Another Chinese lady is there with the baby she takes care of. This baby is younger than Mia, but already walking. The baby is a boy and he pushes himself up and walks across the sand to take Mia's shovel out of her hand and bring it back to the place he is playing. Mia doesn't cry, she looks only surprised. Then she, too, pushes herself up and takes a few steps by herself across the sand to take back her shovel. When I see this, I clap and shout. I am so happy. I tell the other babysitter and she claps, too, even though now her baby is crying. Our clapping and shouting make Mia walk again and again.

On this day, I did not tell Lucy that Mia first walked in the sandbox. I keep this secret because I am a babysitter who is also a mother. I know a mother wants to be there to see her baby's first steps. She doesn't want babysitter to see this before her. So when Lucy comes home, I wait for her to find us. We are sitting on the rug in Mia's room, playing a game. When Lucy comes in, I pull Mia to her feet and start clapping like it is part of our game. Suddenly Mia takes a step toward Lucy and another, before she falls down.

"She's walking!" Lucy says, throwing down her big bag and running to Mia. She picks her up and I smile and look surprised like I have never seen this before. Lucy looks at me and tears come to her eyes and I wonder if she knows that these are not Mia's first steps, but is glad for my silence.

25
LUCY

I was always holding my breath, steeling myself for retribution. When would it come? I had no idea. But I suspected that some kind of payback from fate was in store.

When Mia was three, I got her into the Florence School across town. Florence was — still is — all girls. I wanted an all-girls school for her. I'd gone to one and liked learning in the company of those of my sex. When I did school tours, I noticed boys got the attention, making noise on their mats.

I needed a birth certificate and adoption papers to enroll her, of course. Faking them was easier than I thought it would be. I'd read in the paper about a town hall that had burned down in Kansas. All the records in it had been lost. A paste-up man in the bullpen created a birth certificate for me. I told him it was a joke for a client. I chose April 26 for her birthday, a safe few weeks after her real one, which I knew, of course, from the news.

I bought a Polaroid camera because for the first few years, I was afraid to take real pictures of her. I worried that an attentive film developer might see something to arouse his suspicion. This was before digital. Film had to be developed in photo shops, long strands of film had to be uncurled from tin canisters and developed in baths, then printed, requiring attentive eyes on each frame. Until Mia was in kindergarten, I took only pictures that could develop themselves. I have two of them with me. I keep them safe inside one of her gloves in the drawer of a table, in the dark so the images won't fade. One is of Mia getting her first haircut. Here she is, aged two, shrouded in a smart, silky black robe embroidered with the name of a Madison Avenue salon, head bent under the hands of a stylist, her eyes wide, gazing warily at the scissors poised at a curly strand on her forehead. Here's another of her a couple of years later, dressed as Alice in Wonderland for Halloween. She wears a white smocked apron over a pale blue dress and patent-leather Mary Janes bought from a fancy shoe store near Florence. You couldn't button the strap of the Mary Janes with your fingers, you had to use an old-fashioned buttonhook that came with the shoes. Later I learned from Mia that Wendy hated those shoes, that the laborious process of using that buttonhook was the only thing that caused her to lose her patience. Wendy never complained to me about it, though.

I'd get Mia ready for school after I got ready for work. I'd roll down the tops of her regulation anklets as I dressed her, smoothing the lace, trying to block thoughts of what would come to be, what would happen to Mia, if the world was just. I'd shut my mind's eye against horrifying images such as Mia's lace-covered ankles being severed from her legs, occasioned by some brutal accident in which she fell under a bus that proceeded to run over her — this had happened, years before, to a girl at the school whose name was engraved on a plaque in the school library. The girl's parents had another daughter, in Mia's class. They were good people, not deserving of such a thing, far less deserving of it than I was, I knew.

I worried that something might break in the FBI case, that police would come to our building and take her away. For years I braced myself as I came home to the lobby, gauging the doorman's face for a look that told me the police had been there.

I didn't stop worrying until Mia was five, after something that happened on a class trip.

I'd volunteered to be a chaperone on her kindergarten's visit to a downtown pie factory. This was when Chelsea still had lots of factories, before the factories became glassed-in showcases for art. Many mothers of girls in the class were stay-at-home moms and I was glad for opportunities to prove to them and to Mia that although I had a job that took me many hours of the day away from her, I was as attentive to my daughter as they were to theirs.

We were a group of about twenty: fifteen five-year-olds, two teachers, and a few mothers besides me. Mia was glad I had volunteered, being young enough to still want me around. I'd been assigned responsibility for a group of three: Mia and two of her little friends. I remember how happy she was that day, which made me happy, too. Watching her cavort at the bus stop with others in their pleated gray uniforms and red-checked aprons that made them look like miniature milkmaids.

After a tour of the factory, during which the girls frequently giggled at the sight of themselves in obligatory hairnets, we emerged into the street, where there was a retail outlet for pies. The line was long, and as I stood at the end of it, holding Mia's hand, a police car drew up to the curb outside the pie-store window. My throat closed and my heart started up like a punching fist, and as the officers took their place in line behind me, I worried that it was beating so hard it would set into telltale motion the gold pin on my silk blouse.

There was no reason to assume that the appearance of the police in the store was in any way connected to me. Yet my mind raged with the possibility that this was so, that their presence meant that authorities were still in pursuit of a long-grown-cold trail of an abduction. I could almost feel their breath on the back of my neck.

I let Mia's hand slip out of my own and turned to the officers. With a bright smile, I offered to let them go ahead of us in line. The officers were young, in their mid-twenties. One was a woman and I wondered if she was a mother, with a mother's sixth sense. She smiled at me, then down at the little brood of my charges. I was glad that her gaze did not linger on Mia.

"No'm," said her partner, touching the beak of his cap. "We can wait." Was this meant ironically? By "wait," did he mean he could wait me out, to make the mistake that would connect me with the crime I'd committed, to which I'd not yet been linked?

There was no logical reason for this kind of thinking, but it sprang from a fear that grabbed my innards and squeezed, coiling around them like snakes.

I turned back to face the counter. We were far back in line, the last of our group, having been waylaid by a trip to the restroom.

I felt the officers' gaze bore into the back of my head. They were standing close behind me, close enough, it seemed, for thoughts to jump from my brain into theirs, thoughts I concentrated on keeping contained within the bones of my skull, a ridiculous exercise, I realized, even as I was doing it, but I felt compelled to focus on doing it anyway.

What if they — the woman — was reading my mind? What if she intuited the connection between Mia and me? Mia's baby face had once been on a milk carton, before the practice of picturing missing kids on milk cartons had been discontinued. That photo had borne little resemblance to how Mia looked then, even less to how she looked now, but what if the policewoman had poured from that carton, had remembered the face, was trained in tactics of police artists who age faces, elongating the

141

cheeks, adding hair, giving the nose structure, the lips, the eyes?

The sweet fragrance wafting from pies
made me suddenly sick, and without a
word, I grabbed the hands of the two girls
who weren't mine, thinking that my action
would prove to the cops behind me that one
of these was my child. I'll never forget the
look of betrayal on Mia's face as she realized
I was leaving the store with other children,
not her. She followed us out, as I knew she
would. "For air," I explained to my charges,
sitting us all on a bench outside the store,
until after the police left, passing us on the
sidewalk without a glance, their attention
focused on forkfuls of pie.

It was then I knew — I'd get away with it.

26
MARILYN

In the days after the kidnapping, I felt so shot through with guilt, sometimes I could barely pull myself out of bed.

How could I have walked away from my baby? Tom never asked me that in so many words, but I knew he wondered it. I wondered it, too. The weight of what I had done sometimes pressed on my chest, making me feel pinned in place, unable to move.

Other times, I couldn't stop moving. I was manic. My grief felt like terror. I cleaned and cleaned. I cleaned everything in that house: walls of the nursery, baths, kitchen, scrubbing until I'd used up every bottle of cleaning product we had in the cabinet. All day long, I'd scour surfaces until falling into bed chapped-handed, bone-tired. I rubbed and rubbed at the wine I'd spilled by the side of the bed, but that spot never came out. I washed Natalie's floor on my hands and knees. I ripped down her white curtains and bleached them, not wearing gloves. I meant to punish the hands that had lost her. I washed her walls, her crib sheets, her changing table, anything that was hers and I hoped would be hers again. As I was scrubbing, making things perfect for when she came back, I'd torture myself, replaying that day again and again, making it come out every way but the way that it had: *I don't take the baby shopping, I stay home and work. I don't answer the phone in the store, I never hear it, buried deep in my bag. I answer the phone, but the call is dropped and I hurry to finish shopping and take Natalie home, where I return the call, oblivious to the tragedy I am averting by doing this.*

I resented the way Tom began to avoid the situation, his attempts to seal off pain, to deny the horror that was undeniable.

Soon we began to inhabit opposite ends of a day: he claimed early mornings, I claimed the nights. Our orbits rarely intersected. But one night, finally climbing into bed, I saw that the other half of the bed was empty. I went to find him, maybe he was sick. I passed Natalie's room and saw him there, in the moonlight, on his knees on the carpet. He gripped the crib slats, his forehead resting against the bars. I couldn't hear anything, but could tell by the shaking of his back, he was sobbing. I never saw Tom cry before. I had done this: brought my husband to his knees. I went to bed and never mentioned it to him.

Days seemed to go by in slow motion and hyperspeed at the same time. Mostly, I felt like nothing connected me to the ground. I spent hours each day trying to imagine where Natalie was. I wondered why something so terrible had happened to Tom and me. But really, it was my fault. Tom never came out and said this. But I know he thought it. I thought it, too. His parents certainly did. They came that first weekend. Neither of them ever met my eyes, not once.

Every time I saw Tom, I saw Natalie's face. Her forehead. The shape of her eyes, her chin. I stopped wanting to look at him. He wasn't her. He couldn't bring her back. Nobody could.

One day, I heard the song from Natalie's swing. I was in the laundry room. I assumed Tom had started it going, for some reason. Anger surged in me as I hurried down the hall to her bedroom, but when I saw the swing, it was perfectly still. I didn't know how its music had come, but later I realized that it had been Natalie, reassuring me she was still in the world.

As Tom and I became more and more

isolated from each other, we became isolated from others, too. Neighbors had flooded into the house to help initially, but after a few months, they preferred to avoid us. Once, at the grocery store, a friend from book club turned her cart around when she saw me, hurrying off in the other direction. I didn't blame her. No one knew what to say. I'd stopped going to book club. I'd stopped going anywhere, stopped even going out of the house unless I had to. I began to resent people whose children hadn't vanished.

Who were we now that our baby was gone? Were we still even parents? Tom wanted to know. I assured him we were parents and would always be. We were parents of a little girl who is out there somewhere. But Tom stopped believing that. He stopped hoping. We separated, thinking we were cutting the problem in half and now we would have to deal with only our half of it. But separation just made things harder, for me.

27
TOM

There we were in 1990, stumbling along as new parents, learning how to take care of a baby, learning what our daughter wanted, what she liked, getting a sense of who she was, her personality. We talked about her constantly, Marilyn and I, planning her future, dreaming about what she would do, who we would help her turn out to be. Maybe she'd be a rock star. Maybe she'd be the first rock-star president.

Then, one day, without warning or explanation, that person, that part of our life, was gone. My wife went shopping with our daughter, and then, she wasn't shopping with her anymore. A baby was ours, and then, suddenly, she wasn't. There were no notes or phone calls, so we knew it wasn't for ransom.

I worked with detectives searching for her. We led search parties at night, using flashlights. Sometimes I'd go into the office on no sleep at all, stumble out of the elevator not knowing where I was.

For the first few months, my imagination went wild with all kinds of scenarios, like Russian mobsters grabbing our daughter, selling her to rich Germans.

Then one night, I thought I heard Natalie cry. I woke up knowing what I heard was impossible, but there it was, impossibly, her little cry. I got out of bed and went into her room, thinking I might see our baby back in her crib. How could this be? I was still half dreaming, but it didn't feel like a dream. I looked down at her crib, and could see in the moonlight, of course she wasn't there. The mattress was empty. And then, I knew she wasn't coming back to us. It had been months since we lost her. I was a man in mourning for a daughter who would never return. I had to face facts.

Tragedy happens to lots of people. You can decide to let it destroy you, or you can decide to move on.

I made myself stop thinking about what had become of our baby. I couldn't imagine what had happened to her, and didn't want to. What good would it do?

I wanted my wife to stop imagining, too. I thought it would be healthier for her to live in the present. I thought it would be better for us to move on, to stop living for the baby we didn't have anymore, start living for us. But I didn't have the words to say this to her, at least not words she was able to hear.

28
MARILYN

I could no longer trust myself. I couldn't rely on my own judgment. I'd made a terrible choice in stepping away from the baby. How could I trust myself not to make such mistakes in the future?

I stopped cooking and often forgot to eat. My hair started coming out in clumps in the shower — I didn't care. Sometimes, instead of cleaning, I spent the day in bed with a book. All I read were books on kidnapping, children who had disappeared — Charles Lindbergh's baby, Etan Patz, Adam Walsh. I thought stories of other kidnappings might hold some clue, might lead to the whereabouts of my own child who'd been taken.

There was a list of psychics the FBI worked with, and some days, I'd find myself calling them all, barraging them with questions, trying to tease out any information they could glean from the universe. After I hung up the phone, I'd clean something. Or I'd walk. I'd walk and walk. I'd walk for hours, to keep from being in an empty house. I lost thirty pounds. At first, I was glad. I wanted to shrink, to disappear. I'd lost all my pregnancy weight, and more.

I began to imagine ways I could kill myself. Pills would be painless. But that would mean my daughter would lose me twice. I had to stay alive for her sake.

I began seeing a therapist. I was desperate for someone to talk to, someone who'd listen, who'd know how to help put me back together again. Tom had left by this time.

The therapist did help. She explained that losing a child was like having a nerve severed. When a child dies, eventually the skin grows over the nerve, so the pain is reduced, though it never goes away. But because I didn't know where my child was, my nerve would stay raw, constantly exposed. Until she was found, I couldn't expect myself to heal. Because I'd have to keep imagining what had happened to her. All I could do was think of ways to distract myself from the pain.

Memories of Natalie would hijack my thoughts while driving to the grocery or reading a magazine in a waiting room — suddenly I'd hear her squealing happily as she splashed bathwater or see her tiny hands opening and closing as she slept — and then I couldn't breathe, my stomach twisted, contractions intensifying until I had to grit my teeth to keep from screaming.

Changing surroundings might help, said the therapist. She suggested I consider a move. At first, I resisted this suggestion, worried that Natalie would somehow come back to the house and I wouldn't be there for her. But when a former colleague called, offering me a job at Clorox in San Francisco, my friends — the few still talking to me — encouraged me to start fresh. They helped me see that staying in the house wouldn't bring Natalie back. She'd been taken at four months. It's not like she'd ever come walking back there.

I didn't think I could pack up that house. I didn't think I had the emotional muscle to do it. But packing up the house turned out to be a great salve. First, it kept my mind and hands busy, it kept me in the present moment, not the past. I couldn't let my mind wander down bleak paths when I had to concentrate, had to make decisions, had to do the work of going through all my belongings, deciding what to take, what to leave behind. It forced me to come to terms with loss. So many things I'd held on to because of who they'd belonged to once: my grandmother's wedding dress, my grandfather's stamp collection. Now I saw they were just things. The dress wasn't my grandmother; the stamps weren't my grandfather. And Natalie's things — her tiny shoes, her little coats, her crib and swing and playpen — they weren't Natalie. Giving up her things wasn't giving up on her. I could still have hope that she'd come back to me.

And yet, when my plane took off for California, I felt like I was abandoning her.

Yoga saved me. It really did. I put my toe in the water slowly at first. Clorox offered Vinyasa sessions in the employee lounge at lunchtime. It was good exercise. It made me feel strong and in control in a way I hadn't felt since it happened.

Then I saw a flyer for yoga designed to reduce anxiety and increase happiness levels in the brain. I was willing to try anything that would do that. From the first day, I was hooked. Just walking barefoot into the spare, white space made me feel hopeful, as though the serenity all around me could be put inside me, too. I also liked the teacher. Sonya was someone who I could tell had been in the practice a long time. Her manner was gentle; her eyes were wise and full of compassion. She taught me to breathe. I realized I hadn't known how to do that before.

Each yoga session, no matter what practice, ends with Savasana, which means you lie on your back on the floor, eyes closed, releasing any residual tension. Sonya would go around the room as we lay, gently pressing a finger onto our foreheads, "the third eye," and when she did that, all my anxiety floated away. One day, at the end of the class, she offered meditation. And so I was introduced to the dharma. How Sonya explained it resonated with me: that the Buddhist way is about living in the present, about letting go of what could have been, what should have been different.

Through the practice, I've come to learn that pain is inevitable in this world, but suffering is optional. No matter what happens, there are attitudes and practices that help you survive, even thrive. I learned to feel pain as it manifested in my body, to recognize the tightness in my muscles, the change in my breath when I thought about what had happened, and to use this awareness to open up opportunities for healing and growth. To be ready and open to Natalie when she came back. I knew she'd come back.

After studying Iyengar for a while, which is all about getting the poses right, Sonya moved me on to Ashtanga yoga, which is about connecting the poses to each other. I'm a Gemini. I thrive on connections.

Through someone I met at yoga, I joined a grief group. I met others who had been through wrenching experiences. I learned how many ways there are to suffer the loss of a child — one woman's teenage son had been a star soccer player, but was now paralyzed, no reason, no diagnosis. Another mom's talkative four-year-old boy disappeared, not bodily, but lost his ability to speak. A couple lost their three daughters on Christmas Eve; the tree in the living room had caught fire while they were asleep.

We had to learn that what had happened to us, to our children, had just happened. Nothing had been "done" to us, or to them. We weren't being punished. I learned to believe that I had not been singled out.

I learned to take refuge in wherever the light is, because anything else is darkness that can pull you down deep.

I learned that every time I thought of my child, I was sending her love. I learned as long as I believed I would be reconnected to Natalie, it would happen. I learned to make choices to promote that alignment.

When I'd done the work of becoming one with knowledge that creates happiness, I met Grant. He did carpentry for the church my grief group was in. I met him coming out of a session. He stood on a ladder, fixing the light above the entrance door. The ladder was blocking my way, and as he apologized, looking down at me from the top rung, saying he'd be down in a minute, all I could think about were the crinkles at the side of his eyes, how he looked like someone who loved to laugh. I was ready for happiness.

29
GRANT

When I met Marilyn, she was an executive at a big company. I didn't think she would go for a man who worked with his hands. I'd dated women like that before. They tend to have expectations no man can meet. I made a choice a long time ago, to do the kind of work you can see. When I was a kid, I turned down a scholarship offered by a boarding school back East. Some people thought I was wrong to turn down opportunity like that. But I didn't view it as opportunity. I saw it as obligation I didn't want to fulfill. My father had a contracting business and taught me everything he knew. I liked that work. I knew if I went to that boarding school, I wouldn't go into business with him. I never regretted it. My father died in his fifties. I was grateful for the time we'd had together. I'm sorry that Marilyn never got to meet him.

When I met her, I'd just bought an old

factory in San Mateo and was renovating it myself, on weekends. She started helping me strip it back to brick, replacing the windows, jacking and leveling the chestnut floors, putting in electric, sanding and varnishing. I work with only green materials. I like to sustain what's already there. Marilyn wasn't afraid to get her hands dirty. I knew right away she was different from women I'd dated before.

We married in 1995, two years after she moved west, five years after her daughter was taken. She took my name. I didn't ask her to do that, but she wanted to.

We were blessed with three children — two boys and a girl. She quit her job after the first came along. The last came when Marilyn was forty-three. That one took a bit of praying. And a lot of homeopathic meds.

Early on, we talked about whether or not to tell the kids about Natalie. We decided it would be confusing and possibly scary for them. Maybe that was a mistake. Maybe it would have been better if they had gotten used to the idea of having a sister, so her turning up wasn't a shock for them. But honestly, I didn't expect she'd turn up.

30
CHERYL

I didn't meet Mia until she was seven months old. Lucy brought her upstate for Thanksgiving. It's a five-hour drive from Manhattan to Emmettsville. Lucy took a cab! She said there were no rental cars left, she'd forgotten to make a reservation. She didn't want to take a train or bus with a baby. I'll never forget the sight of a bright yellow Checker cab chugging up our steep driveway, driven by a man in a blue turban. I wasn't sure what the protocol was — should I invite him in to stretch his legs, use the restroom? But before I could do that, Lucy had paid him and he was on his way. Lucy knew how to handle any situation. That is something I've always admired about her.

I remember how we used to play house. I'd be a mother with two dolls. Lucy would be a mother with two dolls and a nanny. Even then, Lucy knew what she wanted.

And Lucy always knew how to get what she wanted.

31
LUCY

I told Mia she was adopted, when she was three and a half. *Are You My Mother?* was her favorite book for a while. One night, I was sitting on her bed, reading it to her for the zillionth time. When we came to the end, something about the moment seemed right. I explained that while most mommies have to take the baby given to them, I was a luckier kind of mommy. I got to choose my baby myself. She took it in, nodding. Then asked me to read her the story again.

I heard her the next day telling the news to a friend we saw on the bus: "My mommy didn't have me, she *picked* me!" she crowed, repeating this happily many times during her childhood, and whenever I heard her say it, a hot coin formed in my chest, knowing it was true in a way that she couldn't imagine.

What I hated most was the lying. I know

that sounds suspect, coming from someone who lied for so long. But I hated having to commit an elaborate construction to memory, carefully placing one lie on top of another, almost convincing myself of the truth of each one, building a palace of them. Or, rather, a prison. I told so many lies I started to believe them myself. Fooling oneself turns out to be easiest of all.

Everyone lies, I reminded myself. Lies are necessary, by collective agreement. Saying what others want to hear is lying. People do it every day. They lie about having had a good time at a party, they lie about your age and theirs, lie that you haven't changed since they last saw you in high school. I heard a mother lie to her babysitter, saying she had an early-morning meeting, when she really went to the gym. Women at the playground lied to their husbands about how much it cost to upholster a sofa or renovate a kitchen. Husbands at the office lied on the phone to their wives in beach houses, saying they had to stay in the city for work, when they didn't. Lies were the very foundation of the industry I worked in, despite laws against them. The first thing I learned as a junior copywriter was how to lie legally, using phrases called weasels — misleading statements like "studies show" (what studies?) or "gives the appearance of younger skin" (because no product can legally claim to "make skin look younger").

I especially hated lying to Mia, even as I tucked her into bed, nodding along with the Berenstain Bears, who informed us never, ever to lie because "trust is one thing you can't put back together again." I stroked Mia's soft arm as I read her the story, feeling sorry that she was being raised by a liar.

As in the story, the longer I kept the lie alive, the bigger it got. I had to tell it to more and more people. Now the circle of people who thought Mia had been adopted in Kansas included not only Wendy, but mothers at school who sometimes asked about her adoption and I found myself expounding imaginatively on the intrusiveness of social services visits, the mountains of paperwork involved. I could never feel better by confessing my lie, as the Berenstain Bears were encouraged to do. Telling Mia the truth at this point would be cruel. If she learned the truth, she'd be scarred for life. Mia was happy. I couldn't stand the thought of her being wrested from the only home she knew.

I'd seen a baby returned to her birth mother. A surrogate mother had demanded her baby back when the child was two. I'll never forget the footage that played and replayed on TV: a distraught toddler screaming in the arms of a stranger who would now be her mother. I could never let that happen to Mia.

Sometimes you have to choose from wrong choices. Sometimes, the right choice is which choice feels the least wrong.

I knew that eventually I'd have to tell Mia the truth. She deserved to know her true origins. Part of me thought that if I waited long enough, if I used just the right words, perhaps she'd be able to understand. I pictured our future selves sitting by a fire — she, a middle-aged woman, married perhaps, with her own children, certainly happy, and me, gray and gentled, the age of benevolence, speaking honestly, finally, with tenderness, saying all that I have had to keep from her.

What mother doesn't keep things from her daughter?

■ ■ ■ ■

PART TWO

■ ■ ■ ■

Nothing makes us so lonely as our secrets.
— PAUL TOURNIER, *GUILT AND GRACE*

32
LUCY

Mia was always precocious. It wasn't just that she was smart. She was wise. And surprisingly self-disciplined, even when she was little. I remember taking her to see the premiere of *Toy Story.* She was not even six. We went to the opening in Radio City Music Hall. I took the afternoon off and picked her up from school myself. I didn't trust Wendy to navigate midtown. Her English still wasn't good and her knowledge of the city was limited.

We arrived early, before the crowds; I stopped at the candy counter with Mia to buy her a treat. She chose Chuckles, those brightly colored fruit jellies I'd loved as a kid. She'd never had them before. The only package size they sold was jumbo, but I said yes. She was rarely allowed candy and I wanted the day to be special for her. I was working crazy hours — we'd just gotten the Revlon account — and I went weeks without seeing my daughter in daylight. I paid for the candy and we followed an usher to our seats, which were in a special section thanks to comps from a media buyer.

I took off her coat and we settled into velvet cushions and I opened the wrapping and held out the package to her, childishly hoping she wouldn't choose black, which was my favorite, the one Cheryl could never believe I liked. But Mia startled me by reaching out, not for the candy, but to stay my hand.

"Let's wait until the movie to eat them," she said.

And so I smoothed back the cellophane, feeling abashed, marveling at the capacity for self-denial in the small being beside me, agitating with knowledge of my own lack of it, which accounted for Mia's presence not only in the chair beside me, but her very presence in my life.

33

CHERYL

I always wished I was more connected to Mia. I was her only aunt. Doug, the boys, and I were her only family besides Lucy. In Doug's family, nobody talks to each other anymore. Lucy and Mia would come upstate for holidays, to our house. I inherited the old Victorian we grew up in. Our parents bought it for a song in the early fifties because it wasn't modern, which was the style everyone wanted back then. Lucy got everything in the safety-deposit box except for the deed. There were stock certificates and our mother's jewelry, which went to Lucy because she had a daughter. But neither of them ever wore the jewelry, as far as I could tell. That always made me a little bit sad. Maybe it wasn't their style. But I would have worn it.

Christmas mornings were always fraught with Lucy here, trying to minimize the pile of presents for Mia under the tree, trying to make them balance out with the ones we'd wrapped for the boys. Mia had another Christmas at her house, the boys once told me, and I silently thanked Lucy for not delivering the extent of her bounty in front of them. But she was always generous to the boys. We were grateful for that.

I remember one Christmas when a bonus had come through for Doug, I opened my present from him and it was a Kate Spade bag. I was thrilled. Those bags went for hundreds of dollars. "I have one in red," said Mia, and I couldn't believe it. What did a nine-year-old kid need a designer bag for?

"All my friends have them," she said. And then I saw Lucy shut her down with a look.

We didn't see them for the rest of the year. We never went down to the city to visit. It's a five-hour drive, too far to go for a day, and their apartment wasn't big enough to host the four of us overnight. The only time we stayed there was when Lucy took Mia — and the nanny! — to Disney World. What fun we had living in their place for a long weekend, pretending to be New Yorkers, seeing the sights New Yorkers get to see every day. We fed their cat, who ate food so fancy it didn't come in a can. It came in a pouch you had to peel and reseal and keep in the fridge. I'm not big on cats, but

Pumpkin was cute: soft and cuddly and orange. I knew that Lucy wasn't a cat person either. She'd got the cat after seeing a mouse in their apartment.

Mia was always more into school than my boys were, maybe because she started school so early. I didn't send my boys until kindergarten. They never liked reading, but Mia always did. One Christmas when she was about eight, she asked me if I wanted to be in her book club. "Who else is in it?" I asked. The answer was no one. Her mother was too busy. Her nanny couldn't read English. So I agreed, of course, to be in her book club. I was always looking for ways to connect with her. I picked the first book, choosing one of the Ramona series, which I'd loved at her age. She wrote me a letter saying she'd read it in a day and that she'd always wanted a little sister, but now this book put her off that desire. In the letter, she gave me her choice for our next book. I'd expected it might be another book in the series, but it wasn't. It was Edith Hamilton's *Mythology*! I thought maybe she had to read it for school, was killing two birds with one stone. But it turned out she really wanted to read it. I have to admit, I never got through it. The boys were teenagers and I'd gone back to work as a nurse and I didn't have a lot of leisure for reading. That was the end of our book club, of course. Which I always felt bad about. I wished I could have been closer to her as she grew up. But Lucy always kept Mia pretty much to herself. I told Lucy that Mia was welcome to visit us during the summer. I would have taken time off from work when she came. But Lucy opted to send her to expensive sleep-away camps instead.

34
LUCY

This is what I remember: the lovely scent of her baby head and the weight of it in my lap; her first glimpse of ocean, calling it "Bubbles"; that her favorite toy was my toothbrush; that the sun made her sneeze.

A man I once worked with lost his wife, and worried he was losing his memory of her. He'd forgotten the color of her eyes, he said. I'll never forget Mia's eyes, the startling blue of a glacier.

How could I have done it? What was in me, a decent person, that made me capable of such an indecent act?

Taking time — oh, now I have nothing but time — to look back on my actions, to try and make sense of them, to arrange them and order them, to account for what my life has become — my mind catches on an incident I haven't thought of in years.

The incident happened when I was six. It was my first day of school, a Catholic school. My mother had enrolled me, though its tuition wasn't inconsequential to a secretary struggling to raise two girls on her own. She'd made it abundantly clear to us that a good education was worth any expense, a belief I hope I have passed on to Mia.

She'd ordered a uniform from a company authorized to provide them and I remember the smell of the brown paper as she untied the string on the package, the woolly scent of the dark pleated skirt she removed with both hands, as if it were holy. I admired myself in a mirror on the back of her bedroom door. The skirt fit perfectly and I thought it made me look smart. I gazed at it as she knelt beside me, unspooling a marked tape and taking my measure. As I took off the skirt, she cautioned me to be careful — she meant to return it.

"I'll make you one just like it," she promised, and helped me out of the skirt so I wouldn't step on the hem. She folded it carefully and rewrapped it in brown paper, pressing the paper where it had already been creased, then gathered Cheryl up from her nap and, giving me the rewrapped package to hold as I sat in the front seat beside her, drove us downtown to see Mrs. Mulcahy, who owned a discount fabric emporium.

Mrs. Mulcahy admired the skirt's cloth, clucking appreciatively as she pinched a pleat between thumb and forefinger, then flipped up the countertop, coming around to our side, and led us down a long musty aisle where she and my mother squinted at dark bolts of fabric until Mrs. Mulcahy called a boy to pull one of them out from the stack.

My mother did a fine job on the uniform. Several nights I drifted to sleep to the comforting hum of her sewing machine, acquired with Green Stamps that Cheryl and I pasted into pamphlets after every trip to the A&P. With what care we positioned each inside the green squares — we worried the stamps wouldn't be honored if they were even a little bit crooked.

It took her longer than it usually did to sew something — she whipped up most of our clothes in a matter of hours. The pleats were tripping her up, she said. She didn't have a pleater attachment, had to create them by pushing and prodding the material awkwardly under the needle. But when she was finished, it looked just like the original and I marveled at how clever she was to create what less clever mothers had to pay dearly for.

My pride in my mother's handiwork that

day was short-lived, however. As soon as I got to school, a girl behind me in line proclaimed my uniform to be counterfeit — she could tell by the zipper. I knew that every kid in the class would soon know it, too, and I hated my mother for her betrayal, for tricking me into not seeing a thing that was obviously perceptible to others, and for denying me what they had, what should have been mine.

My sister doesn't remember it this way. Our mother sewed her uniform, too, and her fine job as a seamstress inspired Cheryl to learn how to sew, a skill I made sure I never acquired.

So much of who you are has to do with your mother. From her, you acquire your first moral ideas, your first assessments of character. And because of this, I assure you — my mother is not to be blamed. She was honest to a fault, painfully earnest about appropriating only what was indisputably hers. She hailed from the Midwest and though raised in Chicago, maintained a farmer's sensibility all of her life: rise with the dawn, do work, take what's yours and no more, don't buy new when old will do. She was a good example to me, a good role model. The only thing she can be accused of inculcating in me was a wish to be like her — to be a good mother.

You forgive your parents if you live long enough. But I don't expect Mia will ever forgive me. I don't forgive myself.

35
CHERYL

For my fiftieth birthday a few years ago, Doug sent out index cards to a bunch of people asking them to record words of wisdom for me, since I'd reached the age where one is supposed to be wise. Mia's card was my favorite: *Don't leave home without your keys.* It was such a witty thing to say. But sad, too. She was fifteen and her nanny had gone back to China. Mia was too old, of course, for another nanny. But fifteen is still a kid, after all. Which meant for all that Lucy lavished on her, my niece didn't have some things my kids took for granted, like someone to greet them when they got home from school.

Of course, I had the kind of work where I could juggle my hours. I wasn't in a cutthroat office like she was. But Lucy always wanted a big life. From the time she was little, she talked about leaving home and going down to the city. I was the opposite. I liked it here. I liked living in a place where I knew people and people knew me, a place where it was safe to bring up a family.

Family has always been important to me. Years ago, on 9/11 when I saw the attack on the news, I was frantic, worrying about Lucy and Mia. I kept calling down to the city, calling and calling until I finally got through. I thought she'd want to come up to be with us, like so many from Emmettsville did that week, wanting, needing to reunite with family. But not Lucy. She said that she and Mia were fine. When I called a few days later, she said they were going to a candlelight service in a park. It was a slap in the face to hear she sought comfort in the company of strangers, instead of wanting to be with us, her own family.

36
LANCE

Lucy was a creative director on dog food when I met her at the ad agency in 1998. The executive creative director was a friend of mine who gave me use of an office to write in. I was just getting started, had just published *Red Dogs* and was looking to capitalize on that success, work it into a series. In exchange for the office, I agreed to be on call for copy emergencies. I found it impossible to work on my book there during the day. Too much commotion. I ended up writing there mostly at night. It's my best time to get work done anyway. No phones, no noise, the city twinkling below. It was on the thirtieth floor and had a great view.

Lucy would be coming into the office around 8:30 a.m., just about the time I was powering down, to go home. She'd get in after she dropped off her daughter at some fancy uptown school. No one showed up on the creative floor before ten. Lucy seemed

like any other New York mother to me —
neurotic but not especially crazy. We got to
be friends. More than friends. We'd talk
about writing. I'd bounce ideas off her —
after working all night, I'd be glad for
someone to talk to. Eventually, the talk led
to other things. Carrying on in the office
was new to her. She said she'd never done
it before and I believed her. She practically
had a heart attack the morning her boss
walked in on us in his office — we didn't
confine things to our own offices, that was
part of the fun. He gave us a break, just
turned around and went back out — a lot
of crazy stuff went on in those days, before
advertising became a numbers game.

I knew Lucy wanted to write about other
things besides dog food. One day, I asked if
she wanted to moonlight for me. I had ideas
for more series than I had time to write.
The Crying Stone was the first book we did
together. It hit the best-seller list and stayed
there for weeks. Of course, only my name
was on the cover — that was part of the
deal. The publisher felt the reading public
wouldn't take well to two names. Anonym-
ity was fine with Lucy at first. But after the
first couple of books, she wanted her name
on the cover, too.

I didn't want to press the publisher for it.

I figured the money was good enough compensation for her. The stories, the characters, the plots were all mine — all she did was execute them, like a seamstress in the garment district brings a clothing designer's ideas to life. But does the seamstress get her name on the garment? No.

Usually, I'd have to rework what she'd written. I should have charged her for the PhD she was getting in fiction. I taught her the rules of telling a good story. Cut the parts people skip. Don't waste time on description. A good story moves forward, all action, action, action. Each chapter a cliffhanger. That's what busy people who buy books want to read.

Baby Drive was the first book of hers I didn't have to touch. The pacing was great and the scenes all rang true in a way they didn't in drafts of other books she wrote for me.

Now I know why.

37
LUCY

A few years after I met him, Lance offered to try me out as a ghostwriter. He gave me an outline and asked for five chapters. I sweated those chapters. How hard it was to go from writing sixty-eight words, the length of a thirty-second commercial, to thousands of words, one after another. Lance's outline was seventy pages, almost a book in itself. I admired his pacing, the way he let a story unfold with a leisure that narratives in commercials couldn't afford. I worried I wouldn't be up to the job of writing something that wasn't a print ad or commercial, but he took me on.

Lance would come up with the plot twists, chapter by chapter. I never admitted to him what a hard time I had writing some of those chapters. They weren't the kind of books I read for my own pleasure: historical novels or domestic fiction. These were thrillers, full of gore and violence and gruesome sex play. Lance had done research. These were the books that millions wanted to buy.

In advertising, I'd sometimes feel guilty writing copy that promoted frivolous luxury or products that posed risks. More than once, for a pharmaceutical client, I'd had to urge a voice-over to sound cheery while announcing alarming side effects like "gambling urges" or "suicidal ideation."

But writing Lance Orloff stories often made me feel even worse. The scenes were grisly. Dismemberment. Torture. Necrophilia. Scenes had to be sensational enough to shock a reader who didn't shock easily. Writing them sometimes gave me stomach pains. But — Mia was in middle school, college wasn't far off, and it was the most lucrative freelance gig that ever came my way. I'd long ago set up a college fund for her, but I'd lost a lot to reversals in biotech stocks.

I didn't quit my day job, of course. Freelance doesn't come with benefits. I'd write the books at night and on weekends. I'd come home after dealing with office politics and client revisions and sit down to whatever Chinese meal Wendy had cooked before she left for the day, help Mia with homework if she needed it, then sit at my desk for as long as I could, tapping out pages.

"If you work for yourself, how come you have such a mean boss?" Mia asked one sunny Sunday I spent behind my computer. But she was a child. She knew nothing of finances. And I didn't want her to have to.

As soon as I got my name on a cover, I thought, I'd be able to forge a future in publishing. It was work I could do no matter how old I got. I was in my fifties. Advertising was a young person's business.

Without my name on a cover, who was I, to a publisher? Just one more copywriter with a manuscript in a drawer.

We kept it quiet, but Lance and I had a thing for a while. He wasn't my type. But the way his brain worked — the way he could not only dash off campaign ideas for clients, but mastermind the plots of novel after novel, come up with narrative twists, the way he could take my pages and, with a few cuts or edits, heighten what I was trying to do — I found that very sexy. He was a few years younger than I. It made coming into work in the morning exciting.

I never brought him home to meet Mia. She remained my only significant other. I didn't want to risk consequences of letting anyone come between us. I'd seen those movies. They never turned out well. And, I didn't dare let myself become involved with someone I'd fall in love with, with whom I'd be tempted to share my secret.

I never told my secret to anyone. Anyone.

After our first two books together, Lance moved out of the agency in midtown. Orloff Enterprises acquired its own office: a spacious, all-white loft down in SoHo.

The way it worked was, Lance would bounce ideas for books off me before doing up outlines. He'd throw out book summaries, elevator pitches, on the phone or at lunch, to gauge my response. Siamese-Twin Serial Killers! Roving Gang of Girl Cannibals! I was never as good as he was at concocting stories; my ideas were never gruesome enough for his taste. But I could weigh in on which of his ideas would most appeal to our audience, which, according to publishing data, encompassed a surprisingly wide range of readers from high school dropouts to college professors.

Baby Drive came as a complete surprise to me. We'd never talked about a kidnapping story. Lance's outlines were long and I used printers at the office to print them out. I recall standing in the copier room, watching pages for *Baby Drive* roll out of the machine. I saw the words "baby" and "kidnapping" and my first reaction was to look behind me, to make sure that no one else was in the room.

I read the synopsis: *sociopathic woman kidnaps a baby to replace the one she has lost.*

Was Lance onto me somehow? Had I blurted out something in my sleep? We weren't together anymore. Things had cooled once he moved downtown, which I thought was a result of our diminished proximity, but maybe they'd cooled for other reasons. Did he know something? He had a phalanx of obliging detectives on small retainers, who sometimes helped him research details of his plotlines. Perhaps he'd talked about me, and one of them had made the connection.

My face grew hot as pages piled up in the printer tray. The words seemed to leap from the machine in accusation: *baby lust, mother envy, infertility dreams.* I gathered pages as soon as they'd cooled and took them to read in my office, closing the door behind me.

The baby in the story was a girl, but in other ways, the story he'd written was different from mine. She had been taken from a hospital, not a store. The woman was single and childless, like me. She got away with it until the daughter was a teenager and found out and murdered her in her sleep. I had a terrible, fleeting vision of Mia, coming at me in bed, with an ice pick.

I canceled a meeting and grabbed a cab headed downtown. I needed to see Lance's face when I questioned him. Confronting him in person was the only way I'd be able to detect any trace of his suspicion of me.

He thought I'd shown up because I liked the outline.

"It's good, isn't it?" he said, self-congratulatory. "I thought of the story last week, watching *Law & Order.* We haven't done kidnapping before and I don't know why — it tested off the charts in our last data probe."

Lance had figured out how to make book writing as well oiled a machine as the ad business was, employing algorithms and focus groups to help him determine the themes of his novels.

I tried to talk him out of it. Kidnapping was too common, I protested. It was a cliché, the subject of too many movies and books already.

"You're right," Lance conceded, and momentarily giving me hope. But what he meant was, we needed to add plot twists. Unexpected character traits. And lots of what our readers expected: gore.

The only change I convinced him to make

was to change the sex of the kidnapped baby.

"Yes, a boy," Lance agreed, rubbing his hands together. "Incest opportunity."

I knew I'd have to get the story out of me quick, or succumb to failure of courage. I wrote *Baby Drive* all at once, in a rush, taking a vacation from work, spending weeks in a cheap hotel in New Jersey.

I told Mia I had a shoot in L.A. By this time, she was in college; it was her junior-year summer. She was home, working on a senator's reelection campaign and taking a prep course for the LSAT. I couldn't write that story in our apartment, with her there. I didn't want my writing it — or who I knew I had to become while I was writing it — to taint the sanctuary of our home, to denormalize the wholesome environment I'd worked to create. I was afraid that the story I'd have to generate would poison the air, that Mia would sense the disturbance, divine the truth.

It was a hellish few weeks. I spent them at a Red Roof Inn, just across the river, in my rattiest bathrobe, constricted as a prisoner, moving only a few steps each day, from bed to desk to door for takeout — but the writing poured out of me. I tap, tap, tapped myself back to that day, to the desire, the thrill, the heart-pounding fear, and every so often, I'd kneel by the toilet, shaking, my body revolting at what I had to recall.

I took some consolation in knowing that Mia had had a happy childhood. She hadn't been abused as my protagonist's son was, raised by a woman who didn't let him out of her sight, subjecting him to a host of emotional traumas and a variety of sexual deviances. But I couldn't help seeing myself as a reader would — someone who had stolen a baby, taken her from another mother. I had treated Mia kindly, provided for her generously, but there had been brutality in my wresting her from the life she'd been meant to live. That was how a reader would see it. No amount of explaining, no rationalization could spare me from that dispassionate conclusion.

I wrote in a fever. The writing came more easily than it had with any of the other books I'd written for Lance. At my little desk lit by a lamp bolted to it, words moved through me, spilling into the ocean of words on the screen, filling up page after page almost without my having to think.

But again and again, I had to retreat to the bathroom, hugging the porcelain. Each time, I rested for a while afterward, holding on to the bowl, as if I was afraid of being uprooted, as if the room were caught up in some sort of a twister, as if I had to hang on for dear life.

After twenty-seven days, I came to the end of the book. As soon as I pressed send, I took off my ratty robe, fell across the bed, pulled my knees to my chest, and, in an almost fetal position, cried myself into a twelve-hour sleep.

I awoke feeling lighter, as if something in me had been exorcised. I walked barefoot across the thin carpet to take my first shower in days, feeling as if I was lifting into the air.

38
LUCY

Usually, Lance started a new book with me almost as soon as I'd handed in a manuscript. But that didn't happen after *Baby Drive.* He put off our briefing, told me on the phone he hadn't had any new ideas. I suggested I meet him in SoHo to talk; we'd come up with something. He agreed. But when I went down there, almost as soon as I showed up, he made me a drink, though it was still before noon, and gestured me into one of the white director's chairs, which I didn't like sitting in, they made my feet dangle.

He told me he wouldn't be needing me anymore. He said this quickly, without inflection, as if he were telling me a twist in a plot. He said my dismissal had nothing to do with me, or with him. The publisher wanted to move away from the series.

"You're a good writer," he said. "You'll be able to work on your own."

I tried to contain the upheaval inside me, to keep from spilling my Bloody Mary on his white chair.

"Because I've got a present for you," he said, and I guessed he was talking about a severance. No severance was in our contract, but I thought our personal relationship might induce him to give me one.

He brought out an envelope from behind his back and presented it to me with a flourish.

It was a large padded envelope from the publisher, the kind they sent early galleys in.

I drained half the drink, set the glass on the table, and opened the envelope. It wasn't a bonus. It was the galleys for *Baby Drive.* How was this a present? Was he suggesting I didn't have to read the 285 pages for typos, other errors, that he'd take over that job himself, sparing me, was that his idea of a parting gift?

"Look at the cover," he said.

I looked. There was my name — Lucy Wakefield — on a book about kidnapping. Undeniably, indisputably, unmistakably, there it was, just below Lance's. Though the type size was smaller, the letters looked bold and colossal, the font jumping off the page. My face went hot, as if I'd been smacked.

"I knew you'd be happy," Lance said. "You can make a lot more being out on your own."

My first thought was to ask him to change it, even though a set of galleys would have been hard to change. But I couldn't bring myself to do that. My name on a book would help me make a name for myself. I needed that, now that he was letting me go. I reassured myself that the book contained nothing that could technically link the story to mine. But, as he refilled my drink, and our glasses clinked, unease coiled in the pit of my stomach and lodged there.

39
LANCE

Lucy wrote *Baby Drive* in far less time than it usually took her to get a book out. That boded well for her going out on her own. I knew I was going to have to drop her. That series had reached the end of its run and the publisher was after me for a new one. I'd already started working on a new series, but with somebody else. Another copywriter who, like most, wanted out of the business. She was younger, her stuff had more punch. We'd already begun seeing each other. Lucy and I had run our course. But I owed it to Lucy not to leave her in the lurch. I gave her what she wanted, her name on the cover. I did everything I could to set her up right. I gave her part billing on the invite to the pub party in Dumbo so she could make connections. I invited her to come with me on tour, to a few of the better stops: Seattle, Portland, Frisco, though she had to do that at her own expense — the publisher wasn't going to foot her bill. At first she said no, but I talked her into it. If she wanted to be an author brand, she had to start getting her face out there.

40
LUCY

Marilyn lived outside San Mateo, which — I'd checked MapQuest — was thirty-three miles away from San Francisco, a good distance. Still, I was nervous as my plane touched down at SFO. What if I saw her? I knew what she looked like, or what she had looked like. What if she happened to be in the airport when I got off the plane? If she passed me, she wouldn't recognize me, of course. She wouldn't know who I was. And yet I fretted about the possibility of running into her, at the airport, or elsewhere, watch her detect some stink of guilt I exuded.

I knew where she lived. I'd been keeping track of her for years, always needing to know that she'd come to no harm. Following the news, I tracked her relocation from New Jersey to California, her divorce from a clean-shaven husband and marriage to a bearded one. Several times, before caller ID, I worked up the courage to call their house, pretending to be a market researcher. I was always nervous, worried she'd hear the urgency I tried to conceal. She never did, though. In this way, I discovered she'd had other children. One, two, three. I was glad.

As I entered the airport, I saw Hari Krishnas, moving swiftly, their orange robes lifting from their bodies like sails, and for a second, I thought I saw her face under a veil. The woman in flowing orange wasn't Marilyn, of course. But she resembled the Marilyn I'd seen on television twenty-one years before. Marilyn's face would be older now, I realized with relief as the woman floated past me, leaving a scent of cinnamon in her wake.

There was almost no danger of my running into Marilyn, I reassured myself as I maneuvered my roller bag into the trunk of a cab. And what if I did see her? There was nothing she'd see that would link me to her, or to something that had happened on the other side of the country, over two decades ago. How deliberate I'd been while writing the book to craft scenes and settings that wouldn't betray me.

But when the cab left the bridge and turned onto Market Street, crowded with lunch-hour pedestrians, I pulled back from the window, suddenly certain of seeing Marilyn in the crowd on the sidewalk. For a terrifying moment, I thought I saw her crossing in front of us as we were stopped at a light. Her proximity — or my sense of her proximity — made my insides liquefy.

41
MARILYN

Ever since it happened, I'd been reading books on kidnapping or watching movies about it. It didn't matter to me whether or not the stories were true. I hated myself for being so obsessive about wanting to absorb every detail about how it was done, how someone got away with it, or didn't. Sometimes I'd have to put down the book or walk out of the movie because I couldn't breathe. I didn't want to think about any of those things happening to Natalie. Tom couldn't understand why I'd torture myself, and really, I couldn't explain it. But something was driving me, and later, Sonya explained it was my mother's instinct, keeping myself open for coded messages, intimations that would lead me to Natalie.

So when I read *Baby Drive* I was open to knowing it was telling me something. It wasn't the story of my baby. The baby was a boy. But he was stolen at four months, just like Natalie was. And there was something in the way the story was told, the intensity of it . . . something in the way that the aftermath of having a baby was described, that spoke to me. As I read page after page, my skin prickled and something cold came up my spine. There wasn't anything in the story that described my baby. And yet I felt somehow, this story was connected to me.

I read the book at night in the bathtub, turning page after page, all the while sensing Natalie's presence. I finished reading it in less than an evening. It was a gruesome tale, full of base horrors preying on the lower regions of the mind. But something made me feel that it was drawing me nearer to my daughter. I had to knock terrible visions of her out of my mind. I wouldn't let myself descend into madness again. I told myself wherever she was, she was all right. The book was fiction, a made-up story, a thriller. None of the story's facts were real.

That night, I had a powerfully vivid dream about Natalie, the first dream I'd had about her in a while. In my dream, it was night. She was all grown up, in a nightgown, standing in a high window, without a pane. "Want me to teach you?" she asked, then jumped out the window and lifted into the stars, and suddenly I was with her, flying behind her, wind in my hair. There was a full moon. Over the years, I'd often talked to the moon, knowing wherever Natalie was, it was the same moon she was looking at. Even as I was dreaming, I knew that the dream was a dream, but that this part of it was real: that Natalie was reaching out to me, telling me she was alive and fine and that soon we would be together again.

The next day, I saw an ad in the *Chronicle* for a reading by the writer of the book, Lance Orloff. It was at the big Barnes & Noble, in San Francisco, where I'd meant to go anyway. I wanted to check out the "If You Lived" kids' series for Chloe. Another homeschooling mom, like myself, had told me about this series that makes history fun instead of something to dread. Our local bookstores didn't stock them. Grant was home between jobs and could stay with Chloe. I drove up to the city, not knowing (and yet knowing) that my daughter was on her way back to me.

42
LUCY

Coming into the store, I saw posters announcing an appearance by Lance Orloff. My name wasn't mentioned. He looked tan and jaunty in his photos, but he'd stayed back in our last stop, Seattle, because he'd been too ill to fly. He told me he had a flu, but I guessed it was a hangover. An old college buddy had come to the reading and they'd gone out afterward. He hadn't let the publicist know he wouldn't come to the reading. If he'd told her, the reading would have been canceled. My life would have continued just as it was.

I was nervous about doing the reading without Lance. At Elliott Bay (Seattle) and Powell's (Portland), we'd worked out a duet: he'd talk about how he came up with the story, he'd read for ten minutes, then I'd read for five.

This Barnes & Noble was huge. I took the escalator upstairs, to the corner of the store set up for the reading, and as I rose, looking down on the people and merchandise on the first floor, I began to feel more and more confident, as if I was rising into a headiness of what it means to be a real writer, not a copywriter anymore. I imagined the books I might write, without Lance. He'd already scheduled me a meeting with his agent.

The reading area was near the café and the smell of coffee was strong, and I was so nervous, the smell made me nauseous. About forty people were gathered on folding chairs, or milling about, looking at books or magazines. A woman was adjusting the mic at the lectern and I went up to her and introduced myself. When I told her that Lance wasn't going to make it, her eyes bulged behind her tie-dye-colored glass frames. But she simply sighed and asked for my name and lowered the mic to my height. She apologized to the audience, explaining Lance's absence, saying that his cowriter would be reading instead. I heard what seemed a collective groan, and when a man got up, gave a little snort, then gathered his man-purse and huffed away, others followed and then others, so that when I tested the mic, there were only about ten people left.

Still, I was excited to be reading solo to

an audience, even a small one, words I had written, words that told a story instead of extolling the virtues of a product for sale.

I thanked people for coming — and for staying — then, with little preliminary, I began to read, looking up now and then from the page, using tricks I had learned in executive trainings: speak slowly, more slowly than sounds natural to you; breathe between sentences; look up and look at everyone in the room.

Then, I saw something that made my throat close. In the back row was a woman who looked like Marilyn. She had the same facial structure. I stepped away from the mic, afraid my heart was beating so hard the sound might be picked up and amplified.

But perhaps it wasn't Marilyn. I'd thought I'd seen her many times that day. What were the chances she'd actually be here?

I stepped back to the mic and continued to read, trying to keep my voice from shaking.

Each time I looked up, my eyes settled on her. Her face, its angularity; the way she touched her hand to her throat, evoked, indisputably, the woman televised into my living room in New Jersey years ago.

I began to read very fast, not looking up,

205

just wanting to get to the end. I skipped a whole paragraph, which no one seemed to notice.

I kept my eye on the cell phone I'd placed on the lectern. Its screen was a timer, ticking off the minutes. It said 7:47. When it got to 10:00, I knew I could stop. But I couldn't wait. At 8:48, I looked up abruptly. "And to find out what happens next, you'll have to buy the book," I said brightly, as if I'd cut the reading short for the purpose of sales.

43

MARILYN

I was surprised Lance Orloff wasn't at the reading. A writer no one had heard of was at the podium instead. She was too short for the microphone. A store employee had to adjust it. "Hello?" she said, as if it were a question. Her voice wobbled. I saw she was nervous. She explained that Lance couldn't come and apologized that she'd be reading instead. I decided to stay, although most of the people I was sitting with left. She waited until the commotion was over before she began to read, rarely looking up from the page, stumbling over the words. I guessed that she was embarrassed that the audience had dwindled down to just a few people.

Her voice trembled as she read: *I told myself: I was only taking the baby outside for a moment, to get him out of the cold of the air-conditioning.*

And suddenly I was flooded with memories from that terrible day. I remembered how cold it was in the store, what a relief it was from the August heat. I remembered the bolt that shot through my stomach when I saw that my baby wasn't where I had left her.

I decided I'd stay and say something to her when the reading was over. I'd tell her that the book resonated with me, that I'd been the victim of a real-life kidnapping, see what her reaction would be to that.

The line to see her was slow, even though just a couple of people were in it. She didn't just sign a book, she made small talk. Still, I waited my turn. I wanted to get close. I felt I had to get next to her, that the nearness of her presence would tell me — something.

But waiting in line, I began to lose heart. What was I thinking? What would I say? Ask her if she knew where my kidnapped baby was? That sounded ridiculous. Here was a woman who was a professional writer, a woman in a smart haircut, wearing an expensive suit. Lucy Wakefield couldn't possibly have anything to do with my baby's kidnapping. And yet, I sensed there was a connection.

It occurred to me that I should have brought my copy of the book, to get it signed. I took one from a stack by the podium, I put on my reading glasses, and opened it to the right page. The man in front of me stepped away and her eyes fell on me. Immediately her face changed. It wasn't just her expression that shifted. It was her breath. I heard a sharp intake. Her cheeks darkened. She looked scared as a trapped animal.

My legs went wobbly. "I liked your book." I handed the book to her, but she didn't take it. I couldn't decide what to say next. I was too focused on watching what was going on in her face. Her neck was flushed. She looked at me, but her eyes cut away again. And then, the podium started to buzz. It was her phone going off. The screen lit up with a face that looked remarkably familiar, someone who looked like a younger me! I felt certain — impossible as it was — that this girl was my baby, all grown up, even though the name on the screen wasn't hers. It was *Mia.* The author knew where my daughter was! Could she have had something to do with taking her? I felt this in a rush, as if she was in that very moment yanking my baby out of my arms.

Then Lucy Wakefield picked up the phone and turned it so I couldn't see the screen anymore and I wondered if — as had happened so many times before — my imagination had played a trick.

44
LUCY

Several people lined up to have their books signed. I tried to prolong conversation with each, seeing that Marilyn — I was convinced it was her — was behind them, thinking she might grow impatient and be on her way.

Why was she here? Could she simply be another of Lance's fans? He had millions of fans. He'd even started doing ads on TV.

I took my time with each person ahead of her in line. One by one, I flattered them, asked questions, dragged out answers to questions asked of me, I signed not just my name, but long, flowery messages in the book I balanced on the lectern between us, rolling my pen across more than one page.

But all the while, Marilyn remained steadfast behind them. And then, suddenly, there she was. She said her name. Marilyn. I was face-to-face with the woman who'd given birth to my daughter. She said something else, but I couldn't understand what it was.

My brain didn't work. I was just watching her lips, watching her face, which was so like the face of my daughter. Fear shot through me but I worked to keep my expression blank. I glanced from side to side, half expecting to see the approach of people in uniform.

I stood frozen in place, my pen motionless in the air. We looked at each other, across the lectern, like opponents gazing from opposite sides of a boxing ring, sizing each other up. Did she know who I was? The bond between us felt palpable.

I saw how much she'd aged since the night I'd seen her on television. Her skin had dulled, her features softened. Her hair was gray. I saw the pain in her face. I was responsible for it. I had taken her baby, had inflicted on her the worst thing a mother can imagine.

But what could I do now? I couldn't undo it. I couldn't return her baby to her, make the intervening years of loss go away. Her daughter was my daughter. My daughter was grown. My child had been taken, too, in a sense. She'd left home for college. She'd turned twenty-one on her last birthday. Nothing could bring back the baby she had been, to either of us; that baby was lost to both of us now.

Marilyn handed a book to me, but I didn't take it, just stood dumb and stiff. I couldn't recall what to do with my hands.

And then my phone, still lying on the lectern, went off. It was on silent, but it started to vibrate and Mia's face filled the screen, along with her name in bright, identifying letters. The vibrations were moving the screen across the wooden surface, toward Marilyn. She looked down at it. Her features rearranged. Her face flushed and her eyes grew large, magnified by tortoise-shell half-moon readers she wore on a beaded chain. It took forever for my hand to close over the phone, removing my daughter from her line of sight.

"Hi, honey," I said into the phone, trying to sound calm. I turned away, plugging my ear as if against the din of the store, but the store was now eerily quiet.

"It's over," said my daughter.

My heart leapt to my throat.

"What?" I said.

"IT'S OVER!" Mia repeated. "MY LSAT!"

Only then did I remember the exam she was taking that day, the one she'd been studying for, for months, and as she told me about it, I kept the phone to my ear, frowning to intimate that the call was some

sort of emergency, shrugged apology, gathered up my bag, and took two steps at a
time down the escalator and out the front
doors, losing myself in the crowds on the
sidewalk, hurrying back to the hotel.

45
MARILYN

When the author had left, I looked down at the book and saw the dedication for the first time. It was dedicated to Mia, the name that had appeared on her cell phone.

That night, I waited until the kids were in bed, and Grant, too. When it was dark and silent except for their snoring, I tiptoed into the family room and fired up the computer. My heart was rocking in my rib cage, thumping so loudly, I was afraid it would wake up the entire house. I went into Facebook and looked up "Mia Wakefield."

There were several Mia Wakefields. The book jacket said the author lived in Manhattan and I added that to narrow the search.

Three had blank female silhouettes next to their names. The fourth featured the face of a little girl. I clicked the photo to enlarge it, and as the spinning ball did its work of making the image big enough to see, the immensity of the situation took hold of me, making it hard to breathe. I sat perfectly still as the ball spun around, until finally it stopped and turned into the face of my daughter. I drew back from the screen as if something had pushed me hard in the chest. It was an old Polaroid picture, blurry, but I knew it was her. She looked to be about three. She was beautiful. I saw both Tom and myself in her face. I was glad she looked vigorous and healthy. I clicked on the two other photos in her public album. In one, she was about eighteen, bundled in ski clothes, her skin luminescent against the snow. I searched her face, trying to take her in, literally trying to breathe her back into me. I enlarged her on-screen again and again, trying to see her every pore, trying to examine her for signs of damage, until her image broke into tiny unrecognizable boxes. I resized the boxes until it became her again. The last photo was of her at a party. I was glad she had friends.

I longed to reach out to her, but wondered how she'd feel about hearing from me out of the blue. Did she even know I existed?

I wanted to "friend" her, but at that time Facebook required categories and how would I categorize myself in the request? I wasn't her *classmate* or *colleague* or *acquaintance* or *coworker*. Needless to say,

215

there wasn't an option for *mother.*

I decided to send the request with a message. But what would I say? There are no ready words for a situation like this. I didn't want to scare her or sound like some crazy stalker. I knew I couldn't write what I really wanted to say: *Whoever raised you weren't your parents, they were your kidnappers!* I sat there, drafting and deleting message after message.

Darling Daughter, I am your mother who's been searching for you for years. Too emotional. It might scare her.

I am so happy I found you here. I have never stopped looking. Too stalkerish.

I went to bed. Then woke up with a start, having finally been given the right words, in my sleep. I eased out of bed, careful not to wake Grant, and tiptoed out of the room, to the computer.

I think I'm your mother, I typed. *This is not a joke.* It was honest. Direct. Unthreatening, I hoped.

I stared at the message a long time before sending it. One thing I've learned, and something I've taught my kids, is not to do anything on a computer before you take a deep, cleansing breath. You can't take back anything you sent into the Internet, which is as futile as trying to put a broken egg back in its shell.

I inhaled deeply, as Pranayama breathing practice has taught me. But still I didn't send the message. Instead I got up and made myself some valerian-root tea and returned with the mug warming my hands.

I sipped while staring at the words I'd typed on the screen, wondering about the reaction it would provoke in my daughter. Surely the message would be confusing to her. Would she be curious? Dismissive? I was praying by this time that it was not wishful thinking, that it wasn't another lead that proved to go nowhere.

And what impact would my reaching out to her have on my family, our family, hers and mine? People she hadn't met, who hadn't met her, yet who were bound to her by blood, by bone. I worried about Connor, just turned sixteen. Could he accept an older sister into his life? And what about Thatch, two years younger and having a hard time adjusting to high school? Would this discovery make him feel even more unmoored? And how would Chloe, just ten, react to not being the only girl in the family anymore? What about Grant? How would he feel about bringing another child — not his child — into our fold?

But all of these questions were moot, I realized. There was no way I'd resist reaching out to my daughter, no way I could put off the urgent need to see her. To hold her again in my arms.

I waited until the tea was down to its dregs. I set down the mug. I took a deep, clarifying breath, in and out, deep, from my diaphragm, reached out a damp, shaking hand to the keyboard, and pressed return.

46
LUCY

Nothing happened, not right away. But what if Marilyn showed up again? What if she was following me, had alerted the authorities to make an arrest? I braced myself at the airport, flying home the next day, sweating when security lingered over my driver's license, expecting, at any moment, to be whisked into a holding pen. But all proceeded as if nothing had changed.

After I was back in New York for a few weeks, and still nothing happened, I convinced myself that my fears were unfounded, that my imagination had run rampant, that Marilyn just happened to be another Lance Orloff fan and that things would go on as they always had.

And then, I came home and found the apartment ransacked.

47
MIA

Getting that message really made me freak. It was late at night; I was trying to finish a paper. Now I could hardly read. The words jumped on the screen. I'd heard about kids Facebook-searching their birth mothers, but I'd never heard of a mother looking for a kid this way. I'd thought about my birth mother, of course, and wondered about her, but never so much that I wanted to find her. I didn't want to be rejected twice. Also, I figured that looking for my birth mother would be hurtful to my mom. I always thought I'd be the one to look for my birth mom someday when I was ready. I wasn't sure if I wanted to connect with someone who thought it was okay to take that right away from me. Even if she turned out to be my actual birth mother. I didn't friend her. But I didn't delete her friend request either.

Then came Thanksgiving at Aunt Cheryl's and then came exams and then I was home for winter break and working on a paper again, and just to distract myself, I pulled up pending friend messages. There was Marilyn's. For the first time, I clicked into her albums. They were mostly of her kids. Something about those kids looked eerily familiar. Without knowing why, I started to cry. Probably part of me must have guessed I was looking at pictures of people I was genetically related to for the first time.

That night, I asked Lucy about my adoption. I didn't want to ask her directly about Marilyn. If she was my birth mother, something told me to keep it from Lucy. Lucy was my mother. I didn't want her to think that I wanted another one.

We were in the kitchen, doing dishes. She was bringing up a pot from the dishwater, handing it to me to dry.

Ayi had gone back to China by this time, so we didn't have Chinese for dinner anymore. I'd made the spaghetti and Lucy was supposed to clean up, that was the deal: whoever cooked didn't have to clean up. But sometimes I stuck around to help because really, I felt kind of sorry for her. She worked hard. She didn't have any friends. She didn't have time for anybody but me. I used to ask why she didn't try to meet someone. She said she worked too many hours to have a relationship. Her only friends were work buddies and they had families of their own to be with on weekends or nights when they weren't at the office working with her. I couldn't imagine how it would feel not to have friends to hang out with. But Lucy seemed fine about it. She liked working, she said. I guess, after her marriage didn't work out, her work was what she wanted to be married to.

I'd burned the sauce a little, and some of it was still stuck on the bottom of the pot. I handed it back to her.

"What was the name of the adoption agency?" I asked, trying to sound casual.

She took back the pot and examined my face.

"I didn't adopt you through an agency, don't you remember?"

"No," I lied, though of course I remembered. She hadn't told me the story in years. I wanted to hear the details again. I didn't want to tell her about the lady who friended me. She didn't get social media. She was all about privacy.

"A girl in Kansas answered my ad in the paper. She was fifteen, too young to be raising a baby. She tried it for four months and didn't want to give you up, but she knew you needed a better home than the one she could provide."

She'd never before mentioned that my birth mother was so young. That would make her thirty-six. In the Facebook photos, Marilyn looked older than that. So I guessed she wasn't my birth mom, after all.

Now Lucy was scrubbing the bottom of the pot with a copper cleaner, something she hardly ever bothered to do. I saw that the conversation was upsetting her, which made sense. She was my mom. She didn't want to talk about me having another mother.

"Did you meet her?"

"Who?"

"My birth mother!"

"Yes, I met her just the once. I can't believe you don't remember this story. We met in a lawyer's conference room, so the mother could interview me and see if I was the right mother for you. Lots of other people wanted you."

"Yeah, I was amazing right from the start." I wanted her to go on with the story instead of switching subjects like she usually did when we talked about things she didn't want to discuss. "So why'd she pick you?"

"At first, I really worried she wouldn't. I was the only single mother she was considering, but she was okay with that. She'd been raised by a single mother and was a single mother herself. I told her that not having a husband would mean I'd have much more time to devote to a baby. I so wanted a baby, Mia. You can't imagine how much."

"What about my dad?" I'd always imagined my teenage birth parents, beautiful and in love, like Romeo and Juliet. I'd never asked directly about them. It was like some sort of unspoken agreement between us.

"He was a boy in another school who didn't even know he got a girl pregnant. He was very handsome, the girl said. And smart." She wiped her hands on the back of the mom jeans she always changed into as soon as she came home from work.

"What was the girl's name?" Marilyn's last name was Mornay. Maybe she was my birth mother's mother.

"Kimberly something. She died a few years later, the lawyer told me. In a car accident."

"What?!" This was new information. She'd never told me my birth mother was dead. In fact, through the years, I'd always thought of my birth mother on my birthday and wondered if she thought of me every April 26, too.

"I hadn't wanted to tell you when you

were younger. I thought it would make you too sad. But now you're old enough to know."

The phone rang and she searched for a handset like we always had to do when the phone rang. The ringing phone didn't interest me. None of my friends ever called on a landline.

I stood, leaning against the wet counter, holding the dirty, wet towel, waiting for the earthquake inside me to be over so I could put one foot after the other and walk out of the room.

Something about the story didn't feel right.

That night, I confirmed Marilyn's friend request.

48
MARILYN

Mia didn't accept me on Facebook at first. But one day, I saw she'd become my friend. The first thing I looked for on her page was her birth date. The day was wrong, but the month and year were correct. Someone could have changed it, for obvious reasons.

After that, I began to post a lot more. Shots of the kids, our house, Grant, my ceramics. I became very aware of what I was posting because I knew I was introducing my daughter to her real family. But I didn't message her. I knew I should wait for her to feel ready to make that first move.

I spent hours absorbing her virtual presence — picking up details of her life from her funny photos, her wry posts, her musings, her frettings about tests, her love for animals. It was like I was trying to soak up my daughter, as if I could pour her from the screen. I knew she was still in college from her profile. I got her cell number from a comment she left for someone. My hands shook as I wrote down the numbers. These were the numbers that would let me hear my daughter's voice. But I knew not to call her. Not yet.

I clicked voraciously, searching each photo for likenesses, scrutinizing every feature. There were Tom's dimples, my blue eyes and disobedient hair. A picture of her at the beach revealed my complexion, always in need of sunscreen. It felt strange to stare at photos of my own daughter, feeling how deeply we are connected, yet realize that I didn't know her at all. In one photo, the set of her chin (Tom's chin) made her look like a strong person. I was glad. She'd need to be strong.

A photo of her as a little girl sent a bolt through my heart. There she was, about five, a little straw-blond girl in a white night-gown, at night, running on a sidewalk, hold-ing a lit sparkler. Who had taken the picture? Who had been watching her with a lighted firework in her hand?

In another photo, she looked to be about seven. I recognized my sweet, lost child. I was glad to see she was smiling, happy. She was holding someone's hand, the hand of someone who wasn't in the frame, the hand of someone who wasn't me and I got a strong burning in the center of my chest as I stared at her face, imagining all the milestones I'd missed, the birthdays, the firsts, the time she said "Mother," and I mourned the loss of our years together, grateful that the Oneness was finally guiding her home. Of course, I'd been given the gift of other children, other childhoods to witness. But none could make up for the one I had lost.

For years, I had lived with constant worry about my daughter's well-being. Now here she was, grown, entirely different from my memory of her as a baby. I was glad beyond words, but it also hurt. With each piece of information, I was slapped in the face with the realization that I had not been part of her life for over two decades.

I clicked on another photo. She had a boyfriend! They were kissing and a sparkling sea was behind them. Were they still together? They must be, I thought, or she would have taken down the picture. Was he good to her? From what I could see of him, he looked like a nice boy, intelligent. But was he kind? Loving? Another photo was a close-up. He was pushing a strand of hair from her face. How serious were they? According to her profile, she was still at Middlebury, she hadn't graduated from college yet. My heart filled with desire to hold her, to impart to her wisdom and love and maternal cautions.

Once I had seen all the photos, I cycled through them again and again, savoring them slowly, reclaiming my daughter bit by bit, but not reaching out to scare her away, until the joyous day when I received an answering message from her.

Who are you, really?

I didn't want to scare her. I didn't want to give her a reason to unfriend me. I didn't want to sound crazy, telling her she'd been kidnapped. But that is what I had to say.

49
Mɪᴀ

The first night I friended Marilyn, I looked at her page. She did kind of look like me. Her eyes were the same. I could see that one of her front teeth was crooked, which is the reason I had braces for years.

She lived far away, in California. Her *About* said she was from New Jersey, there was no mention of Kansas. She seemed like a nice lady, but I didn't know that many mothers on Facebook to compare her page to. Lucy wasn't on Facebook. She was old school. She got pressured at work to set up a page and asked me to help her the few times she updated it. "Why do I need this again?" she'd ask, and I'd shrug. Honestly, I didn't want a mother on Facebook. I didn't need to share stuff with her that I do with my friends. My boyfriend's mom was on Facebook. That was bad enough.

Marilyn's profile said she did ceramics in the basement and homeschooled her kids.

Her kids were who I was most interested in. I zoomed into pics to see faces better, and something pricked the backs of my arms. There were people around a birthday cake and one of the boys looked almost exactly like me. It was weird to see my face on a boy. I began to wonder if Marilyn's message was right. Could this be the woman who had given me up as a baby? But she couldn't have been fifteen when she did it — so, also, that part of the story didn't make sense.

Then, one day, I messaged her and almost instantly, a reply message came back. The message was so long it took up almost the entire screen. She said her baby was kidnapped in 1990 and she was convinced that I was the baby kidnapped from her. She sent me links to newspaper reports about it. But I didn't look like the kidnapped baby in the pictures.

She told me my real name was Natalie. I tried to imagine being a baby named Natalie. I couldn't.

The only evidence she was going on was that my mom had written a book about kidnapping. I replied that my mother wrote books about murder and bank robbery, too, I said, but that doesn't mean she's a murderer or a robber.

I began to think she was crazy, which was

kind of a relief. I liked my life. I didn't want it to change. And having a birth mother would definitely change it.

50
DETECTIVE BROWN

It was days before my retirement party when the call came in. I didn't know who Mrs. Mornay was at first. Then she said she used to be Mrs. Featherstone, and of course, I remembered. Her case haunted me for decades. She said she'd kept my card in her wallet all these years. She said she'd found her daughter on Facebook and asked if I could help.

I told her not to get her hopes up. Chances were, this girl on Facebook wasn't her missing daughter. It's rare that victims of non-family abductions show up after this many years. If a child isn't found in the first twenty-four hours, the chance of recovery goes into low percentages. If the child is still missing after four months, the chance of recovery is down to almost nothing.

So when she wanted me to push for a DNA test, I was reluctant. But I decided not to hand in my papers just yet.

51
Mia

A detective called me on my cell. He said he was calling on behalf of a Marilyn Mornay who had contacted him because she had a daughter who'd been abducted in 1990 and thought I might be her. Now she was sending the cops after me? That made me freak.

At first, I refused to take the test. The detective told me the chances were slim that I was the baby. He just wanted to rule me out. He said I could take my time about deciding whether or not to take it, I didn't need to give him an answer right away. But I told him he shouldn't wait around for a yes.

What made me decide to take the test was getting into a fight with Lucy.

She wanted to go to a beach for New Year's, but I wanted to go out with my friends and my boyfriend. It was nice of her to offer a trip to Puerto Rico and all, but

New Year's was important to me! It would be the last one I had while I was in college. Who knows if I'd even be able to celebrate next year. I was applying to law schools, and if I got into a good one, I wouldn't have any time to party. Also, this would be the last New Year's with my friends before we all graduated and started real lives. We had a thing for New Year's. My best friend and I always wore gold outfits. I loved my mom but I really didn't want to spend New Year's with her.

When Lucy gets mad, she looks like an alien — her eyes get small, her forehead crinkles, she pushes her tongue into her cheek and makes it bulge out, which is how she looked when I told her to go to Puerto Rico without me.

Around eleven that night, I was on my way out. I'd just gotten home for winter break, I was going out to meet friends at a club. Lucy was in ratty pajamas and fluffy slippers and her hair was a mess. She was yelling at me for what I was wearing! She was saying my skirt was an invite to trouble on the subway, and as I watched her mouth move, I thought, This woman has no idea what she's talking about. This woman who raised me is actually crazy.

The next day, I was still mad at Lucy and went into Marilyn's albums again. There were new pictures of kids opening presents under a tree. I got a jolt of recognition seeing that boy again, and now there was a girl who looked like me, too. Part of being adopted means you always want to "belong." I used to watch families walking down sidewalks and think how like a club they were. These people looked like they were in the same club as me.

I called the detective back. He told me where to get tested. It would be free and I didn't even need to make an appointment. But it was weeks before I could make myself go there.

February 1, 2012. The day that changed my life forever. I was sitting at my favorite place to work when I'm home — Starbucks on the corner. J-Term had just ended — Middlebury gives you January to take classes on campus or intern or volunteer somewhere. I'd spent it interning for a law firm downtown, something my prelaw adviser had arranged. I was working on the write-up, when suddenly the results of the

DNA test came in. I'd forgotten I'd signed up to receive results by e-mail. The subject line was *Personal and Confidential.* I stared at it for a while. It was snowing out and I was sitting right by the door and cold gusts blew in on me each time it opened, but suddenly I was sweating. I kept staring at the *Get Results* icon, unable to click. My heart was pounding, even though I knew — or thought I knew — that the results would be negative. I closed my eyes and pressed. When I opened my eyes, I saw the word in big green letters: *POSITIVE.* Next to that word was "99.9%." But the number I focused on was a number that wasn't there. The number I saw in my mind was .1%. That was the chance that the test results were wrong. I wanted them to be wrong. I wanted the whole thing to be a mistake. It was important to think up an explanation for the existence of two things that couldn't coexist:

1. The results were correct *and at the same time*
2. My mother wasn't a liar and a kidnapper

■ ■ ■ ■

But I couldn't think up an explanation right away. I gathered up my papers and went out into the cold. The flakes were sharp and cut into my eyes. I was glad for that, so that when the doorman opened the door for me, he didn't realize that I was crying. It was around six, too early for Lucy to be home.

All kinds of stories were going through my head, stories that would explain the unexplainable. If the *Positive* turned out to be true, how could I have come to Lucy without her having stolen me? That my mother had stolen me was, frankly, unimaginable. She was a good person. Stealing was something she was totally against.

If I *was* the baby stolen from the Facebook lady, I decided that Lucy wasn't the one who had stolen me. She probably hadn't even known the baby she was adopting had been kidnapped. I'd seen a *CSI* episode about this. I knew I'd been adopted through a lawyer in Kansas. Was the lawyer still around? I could do a search. The lawyer's name was probably on my birth certificate.

I went to Lucy's bedroom, to the walk-in closet where all our important papers are kept in a fireproof box, hidden in the back, under her hanging clothes. It was a beige metal box. I hadn't opened the box in years, not since I was nine and playing Harriet the Spy with my friends. I flipped open the top and there were the same file folders I remembered, neatly arranged and labeled: *Leases, Social Security, Insurance, Birth Certificate.* I eased out the last file. It contained two pieces of paper, folded in thirds. The paper I unfolded first was pink, decorated with old-fashioned drawings of babies. *Lucy Kane Wakefield born October 10, 1954 in Emmettsville, New York.* Slowly, hands trembling, I unfolded the other. Of course I'd seen my birth certificate before. I'd needed it for camps, trips, college applications. But I'd never examined it closely.

Certification of Birth. I felt glad seeing the word. That's what I was looking for: *Certification.*

April 26, 1990
Nortonville, Kansas
Name: Mia Woodrich
Mother's Maiden Name: Kimberly Woodrich

I tried to imagine the fifteen-year-old Kimberly. I pictured a pregnant, blond cheerleader. I was sad she was dead.

Father's Name: Unknown

No lawyer's name was listed. It was signed

by the town registrar and sealed with elaborate stamps. I let out a huge breath I didn't know I was holding. The Facebook lady was wrong. The DNA test was wrong, too. I really was who I thought I was. I had certification to prove it.

I sat back, filling up with relief, realizing how ridiculous it had been to be taken in by somebody on Facebook who is probably crazy, though who could blame her for going crazy. Such an awful thing had happened to her.

Then I saw something glint on the far wall of the closet. I wouldn't have seen it, except for where I was sitting. I crawled toward it, on hands and knees, the hems of Lucy's perfume-scented clothes brushing my face, reminding me of being little again.

It was a key. The key was held to the wall with a piece of tape so old, it had melted to glue. I peeled the key off the wall. The key was old-fashioned, a brass metal ring with a long, toothy spine. The key hadn't been there when I was a kid, or I would have seen it. The prying beams from our flashlights were thorough.

What did it open? A door? A box? I felt around in the dark, but all that was there on the carpet was dusty shoes and boots she didn't wear anymore.

I crawled back out from under her clothes and stood up, looking around the closet. There was a built-in dresser, but the drawers didn't lock. Maybe it was the key to her jewelry box? I stepped out of the closet, to the box she kept on top of a bureau. The box wasn't locked; the lid lifted easily, and there was my grandmother's jewelry. My mom had let me wear it for Halloween once, when I was Cruella. I looked under her bed, under her night table, behind doors of a cabinet for something that required a key. I went back to the closet and looked around. Then, I noticed locks on the luggage stored on the top shelf, three suitcases, stacked on top of each other, an old hardbox luggage set my mom had gotten before she went to college. When I was little, she'd promised the luggage to me when I went to college, but of course no one wanted that kind of luggage anymore.

I got a stepladder from the kitchen and maneuvered it into the closet. I mounted its steps and pulled the first suitcase down from the dusty shelf. It was the smallest one. The suitcases graduated in size, like matryoshka dolls. I set the suitcase on the floor and pushed at brass tabs on either side of brown stripes. The tabs clicked as soon as I touched them and the suitcase sprang open. It was empty. The pink silk lining was faded and dusty. The dust made me sneeze. I got back on the ladder and pulled down the next suitcase. Its tabs opened right away under my thumbs. It, too, was empty. The last suitcase was bigger than the others, and much heavier, harder to work down from the shelf. When I got it to the floor, I positioned my hands over the brass tabs and pulled my thumbs in opposite directions. Nothing happened. I tried again. Nothing. I pushed the key into a brass opening by the leather handle and turned it, springing the tabs with a click so loud it made me jump. As I raised the lid, the smell of old paper, old clothes, gave me a sick feeling.

By the time the lid lifted, I already knew.

I peeled back tissue and neatly folded inside was an old baby outfit. The pink striped sunsuit Marilyn had described. Folded beneath, were newspapers, brown and stiff with age. BABY KIDNAPPED said a headline. INFANT ABDUCTED FROM SHOPPING CART said another. The dateline of each was the date Marilyn had told me, *August 10, 1990, August 10, 1990, August 10, 1990.*

The closet walls seemed to close in and I felt as if I were about to be crushed. The floor shifted. It was like I was suddenly on that adventure-park ride where you're strapped to the wall feeling the floor fall out from under you. I got out of that closet as fast as I could, out of that room, down the hallway, hurrying past everything in the house that now looked radically different. The house was suddenly a museum for the way things were. Framed photos of me on the walls weren't of me, they captured the childhood of someone I didn't know anymore. Notes stuck on the refrigerator, papier-mâché sculptures I'd made in school on a table — these were now artifacts from another time and place to which I could never, ever return.

When I got to my room, I took my big duffel bag out from under my bed and stuffed it with clothes and things I'd need for a while. I didn't know where I was going. All I knew was, I had to get out. I felt as if bugs were crawling all over me.

I bent down to say good-bye to the cat. I was sorry for Pumpkin. Lucy might forget to feed him. I went to the kitchen and refilled his bowl and as I squeezed food from the pouch, I worried about what would happen to him.

Once out in the hallway, I couldn't get my key in the door. The metal glittered maliciously as I aimed and failed again and again at the keyhole. I'd locked this door thousands of times since I wore my first house key on a ribbon around my neck. Now the door seemed to be saying *You don't live here anymore.*

52
LUCY

In some respects, a co-op with a doorman is like a small town: eyes are everywhere, which gives residents the illusion that you and your belongings are always guarded and safe. It's not always an illusion. We lived in our apartment for twenty-one years, ever since Mia was six months old, and we'd never been robbed.

So that night when I got home and found the door unlocked, walked in, and saw the hall mirror askew, the basket of mail up-turned on the bench, the brass bowl of change spilled on the foyer rug, I knew what was inevitable had finally come to pass — we'd had a break-in — and yet it came as a shock to me.

My first worry was for Mia. Was she okay? One of her blue gloves without fingertips lay on the rug.

My instinct was to turn back and enlist the doorman. But I didn't want him to call the police. As quietly as I could, I dropped my bag, slipped off my boots, and walked noiselessly on the balls of my feet toward her bedroom.

Our apartment was full of hallways and the one I was in felt darker and longer as I made my way down it to Mia's room. The apartment was silent. The only sounds were coming from the lobby: the buzz of a house phone, the yap of a dog.

My hand shook as I felt for the switch on the wall and flicked on the light. Mia is a neatnik, her room is always orderly, things boxed or hung or separated into marked bins, but now it was a mess, closet doors awry, clothes still on hangers but fallen to the floor, drawers protruding from the chest, jeans and shirts and sweats spilling over the sides. I was relieved that her keys were gone from the finger hook by the door. Mia is safe. She hadn't been home. How upset she'll be, I thought, when she sees the mess a robber has made of her room.

I went back down the hall to the living room and kitchen — not too much damage. Still, I felt violated. Mia's old school artwork pieces had been smashed to the floor. Why did they have to be vindictive?

I continued to my bedroom, still walking carefully, but by this time, I wasn't scared. I felt certain that no one else was in the apartment. There was a perceptible lack of charge in the air.

I flicked on the light in my bedroom and the first thing I looked to see was still there — my old silk jewelry box, which contained nothing intrinsically valuable, but was of great value to me: costume pieces from my mother and grandmother, which I hoped to pass on to Mia someday. The box was open, and I was relieved to see that the jewelry was still in it. But the door to my closet was ajar. The light was on. I approached warily. I thought again of alerting the doorman — but I didn't want him to report the robbery yet.

I proceeded into the closet. My mouth went dry. There, on the floor, was the sunsuit I hadn't looked at in years, the outfit Mia had been wearing the first time I saw her. It looked so tiny. I got down on my knees and lifted it from the carpet. It was hard to believe that Mia could ever have been small enough to wear it. The faded seersucker was stiff. It smelled of talcum. Beneath the sunsuit, her little starched white bib, yellowed. The thought of a stranger's hands on them brought tears to my eyes.

Below that, newspaper clippings, browned

and brittle.

My first thought was that the intruders weren't robbers, they were police with a warrant. But wouldn't they have taken this evidence away?

The suitcase hadn't been jimmied. It had been opened with the key. The key was still in the lock. Someone had found it. Then I saw that the documents file had been opened. I thought of the plumber's assistant who'd worked in our apartment recently. He'd spoken no English and his eyes had darted furtively into rooms he passed on the way to the kitchen. Perhaps he'd come back, looking for money or papers with which to forge identity. But I didn't keep cash lying around. And the papers were still there.

Why had I kept them, those things that could incriminate me? Why hadn't I buried them long ago in a bag of garbage and tossed them away? Because these were the only remnants I had of the day Mia came to me. I couldn't part with them. For years, I'd secreted them away in a safety-deposit box at a bank. Then thousands of records and heirlooms disappeared on September 11, in the pulverized vaults of the Trade Center banks. I was glad my things weren't among them, but realized that no safety-deposit box was perfectly safe. I stopped paying the monthly fee and brought the things home, finding a place to conceal them until the day I'd tell Mia. I meant to tell Mia someday.

I lifted one of the newspaper pages and part of it crumbled onto the carpet. This was the piece that ran in the *Post,* the one I'd meant to show Mia first: BABY SNATCHED AS MAMA YAKS. Only the *Post* had told the truth, that Marilyn's baby had been taken because she'd walked away from her.

Carefully, tenderly, I put the things back in the suitcase, the suitcase back in its place. How disappointed the thief must have been by its contents.

I put the ladder away and arranged the papers back in their files and dropped the key in the file box, too. I'd tell the police that nothing had been taken from the bedroom, which was true.

I realized I was shivering, though I was still wearing my coat. I reached into its pocket and brought out my phone. I needed to call Mia, to warn her that we'd been robbed so she wouldn't get a shock when she walked through the door.

I put in her number, but the call went to voice mail. Like many kids, Mia often doesn't answer the phone. You have to text first.

Call me b4 u come home. I didn't want to say we'd been robbed in a text.

When she didn't reply, I followed with okay?

Maybe she was in the subway, out of cell range. She said she'd be working on her paper. Maybe she was still at Starbucks. I'd run around the corner to check.

Francisco knew something was wrong as soon as he saw my face.

"You miss her, right?"

"What?"

"Mia went back to school, right? Half hour ago, I put her and her big bag in a cab."

And only then did I realize what must have happened. Something turned to ice under my breastbone.

"Where was the cab going?"

But he didn't know.

53
Mia

Francisco helped me put my duffel into the trunk of a cab. Francisco was my favorite doorman. I'd known him since I was six months old. We used to take a picture of me and him every year by the fountain, which Ayi helped me put in an album. I'd take it to the lobby and show him sometimes. Once, he borrowed it to show his family. He'd welcomed guests for my birthday parties when I was a kid, and for parties on the roof that my mom didn't know about when I was in high school. Now I wasn't even giving him a real good-bye.

When I thanked him for helping me with my bag, he saw I was crying.

He gave me a thumbs-up, like he always does. "Soon you graduate and come back to New York." I realized he thought I was going back to Vermont. Tears stung as I watched him turn his back to the cab and become a silhouette under the lit canopy.

Being inside the warm cab was like being inside a cocoon. Soft and dark, its warmth a refuge from the cold.

"Where to?" asked the cabbie.

Really, I didn't want to go anywhere. I just wanted to drive around for a while, to think.

"Sixty-Sixth and York." I told him an address that would take me all the way across town, as far to the east as I was now on the west. Getting there would give me time I needed to figure out where I was going, what I was going to do.

I didn't often spend money on cabs, and when I did, I was usually conscious of clicks of the meter, leaning forward to keep watch on the fare, worrying about how high the numbers are going. But this time, I sat back and just looked out the window. I didn't care how much the ride ended up costing. I would use the gold credit card she'd given me for emergencies. And then I'd throw it in the East River.

I thought I had a mom who didn't lie. She'd been honest about things other mothers lied about. She told me the truth about Santa as soon as I really wanted to know, warning me not to tell other kids. She told me the facts of life in fourth grade so I didn't freak out in Growth & Development, like a lot of my friends whose moms didn't have the guts to tell them things yet. It's like she took every picture I had of my childhood and spray painted over it.

The cab was hurtling across the park. This always happens. When you want to get someplace fast in New York, the cab crawls, but when you want to give yourself time to get warm, or talk something out, or figure out where you want to go next, there's no traffic and you get a driver like I had, trying to get you there in record time.

"Can you please just slow down?" I asked, making a show of buckling my seat belt, as if fear of an accident was the reason I wanted the driver to do the opposite of what he thought his job was, what everybody in New York thinks their job is — to get somewhere fast.

We were crossing Central Park. The trees kept coming. The branches were snow-covered and stretched up to the moon. It was like that Disney film I saw as a kid where the trees in the forest turn into sad women begging. I was one of them now, wishing for something that the moon couldn't give me, what no one could: make what had happened, un-happen. The cab stopped at a light and my stomach pitched forward. Then, right away, the cab started up, speeding through the park, and I watched the useless, beautiful moon appear and disappear behind branches until we got to the other side, to Fifth Avenue, where the buildings began again and the moon disappeared behind them for good.

How could she have done something so wrong? It wasn't just that my mother was gone. My image of her as a good person had been taken away. What else had she lied about?

We stopped for a light right in front of my school. My old school. The Florence School is where I'd come every day for years, a big, limestone mansion, a long-ago gift to a Victorian bride from her father. We were stopped in front of its circular driveway, where horses used to drop off ladies in carriages, where Ayi used to wait for me at three o'clock with all the other sitters and mothers. Had Ayi known? Something rose in my stomach. I decided she hadn't known. She must have believed, as I did, that I'd been adopted. Ayi had told me many stories about my birth mother, stories that comforted me, even though, after a certain age, I knew she was making the stories up. She'd describe the last moments before my birth mother had to give me away, how tightly she hugged me for the last time, her long kiss on my forehead before leaving me, which Ayi said she had to make herself do in order for me to grow up in a life she wanted for me. She told the stories as if they were true, with a sincerity she couldn't have managed if she'd known I was stolen.

The bricks of the building were so white they glowed in the dark. Sometimes, when I was little and having a bad day, I'd put my hand up to one of the bricks and touching it would make me feel instantly better. I imagined jumping out of the cab right then, to run to the building and flatten my palm against it. But I didn't, of course.

The cab turned down the side street, passing the school. Suddenly the cabbie spoke. "Don't worry, he'll call." His eyes were kind in the rearview mirror and I realized I was crying. I felt in my pockets for a tissue, but didn't have one. I wiped my face with the angora scarf my mom had given to me for Christmas. My mom. My mom wasn't my mom. Was her name even Lucy?

Where could I go? I'd have to decide soon. I couldn't let the driver dump me and my duffel bag outside in the snow, at some random address.

Ordinarily, when I had a problem this big, I'd call my mom.

"What's with you girls talking to your moms every day," my boyfriend's mother had asked me. "When I was your age, I never called my mom." I knew plenty of girls who didn't talk to their moms every day. Now I'd be one of them.

I wished I could talk to Todd but he was still on J-Term in Guatemala, building water systems where they didn't even have plumbing, let alone phone or Internet. Ashley, my best friend, a fellow Florence survivor (the word now felt loaded — going fifteen years to the same school was nothing compared to what else I'd survived, it turned out), was already back at New Haven and I considered telling the driver to keep driving east, onto the highway that would take me to Connecticut and I'd pay him double, not caring how much it took out of the gold card. But I thought of Ashley's face when I'd tell her the news. She'd be shocked and sorry and would want to know all about it and telling her would be complicated and nothing she could say would change anything, and then I thought of Ms. Laniere.

Ms. Laniere was the coolest teacher at Florence. She was an English teacher and almost not like an adult because she treated you like an adult even when you were a kid in high school. I'd gone to her house a bunch of times. She'd helped with my essay to get into Midd. We were close for a while.

With most parents, the parental relationship is based on petty economics. Like, how many beers did you have? Did you have a cigarette? But Ms. Laniere took the long view. She trusted you knew the deal. She trusted you wouldn't wind up alcoholic after drinking one beer. She even let girls live with her sometimes, like when their parents were getting a divorce. "Call me anytime," she'd said. She'd probably thought I'd forgotten about her. I decided to text.

My thumbs went into motion: Hey from Mia.

Mia! appeared. Is that you?

My thumbs kept going.

The cab was slowing as we got to York. Suddenly I leaned forward, which tightened the seat belt around me.

"Sorry!" I said. "I changed my mind. Park Slope!"

He turned around to see if I was serious, I guess, then started up the car again. He didn't care. It would be a good fare.

As I was checking Ms. Laniere's exact address on my phone, it rang. The word *Mom* flashed on-screen. Tears burned as I pressed ignore. I made a mental note to change the name in my contacts. I didn't have a mom anymore.

54
CHRISTINE LANIERE

When Mia turned up on my doorstep, I was afraid she was hurt. She was sobbing, but wouldn't say what was the matter. She just wanted to sit with me, and once I saw she wasn't bleeding or in physical pain, I let her. I made a fire to warm her and we sat talking about nothing, really. I asked if she wanted to talk about it. She said no. I assumed her turmoil had to do with a boy. I talked about other things to distract her — my classes this year, hers, her internship. That seemed to calm her. Once it got late, I told her she should stay, and gave her sheets for the sofa.

She stayed a few days, and several times I was tempted to call her mother. I didn't, though. I respect kids' privacy. That's why they come to me. And Mia wasn't a kid anymore. She was twenty-one years old, an adult.

Mia has always had a good head on her

shoulders. I had her for two years in English, she was one of my best students. She was a real enthusiast for texts she liked, such as Faulkner. In fact, one Halloween she and a few girls came to school dressed as characters from *As I Lay Dying.*

She wrote a beautiful essay about how learning Chinese makes you see the world differently. The essay was nuanced and original and helped her gain early acceptance to college. I still have it:

I may be blue-eyed, but the fact is, my brain is actually half Chinese. I was raised by a Chinese nanny I called "Ayi" and grew up being a Chinese child during the day and an American one at night. I learned Chinese and English simultaneously and could dream in both. I believed monkeys ate peaches, not bananas. I wasn't allowed to sleep with my belly button showing, because this let cold air in. When I was sick, I ate *xi fan,* which is rice in water, and listened to my Ayi sing me Chinese lullabies. All my Barbies had Chinese names.

I can't believe her mother — or, Ms. Wakefield — did what she did. We had no idea at Florence, of course. She was a single mother and one of the few who worked outside the home, as the saying goes, but she'd help out when she could. I remember she made us a beautiful banner for our art show, which we still use, year after year. She didn't seem like the kind of person who would kidnap anybody. But I've worked with private school parents for decades. Nothing they do surprises me anymore.

55
LUCY

I walked back to the apartment from the lobby and finally took off my coat but didn't hang it up, just left it in a heap on the front bench. I didn't bother to pick up the pieces of mail or change scattered on the floor. They didn't matter. The only thing worth picking up was the glove. I bent down to retrieve it and squeezed it with both hands, caressing the soft wool, as if I was holding the hand of my daughter.

I walked the length of the hall, past the kitchen to the dining room, which looked out to the street. I opened the shutters and watched the parade of people lit by street-lamps. Scarves and hat strings flew out from silhouettes moving headlong into falling snow. Standing at the window, with her glove to my face, I half expected to see Mia walking home, having changed her mind. I leaned toward the window and my breath fogged the glass. I rubbed a hole in the fog with the glove. But I didn't see her.

How often I'd anticipated this moment. Before Mia knew. After she did. Sometimes, sitting across the table from her, eating a dinner that Ayi had cooked, she'd be telling me about her day at Florence, chopsticks going, happy, and I'd imagine the knowledge I was keeping from her, somehow leaching into her bones. I'd never see her trusting expression again.

The night before, she'd stayed home and we'd watched an old Woody Allen film on television. *Manhattan* had come out when I was still new to New York. I told her how much the movie had meant to me, I was so happy to be in Manhattan. Growing up in Emmettsville, I'd always wanted to live there.

"Now a canonical film like that would be called *Bushwick,*" Mia had said, reaching blue manicured nails into a Pyrex bowl of popcorn we were having for dinner, our eating habits having deteriorated since Wendy left.

I wouldn't have movie nights with her anymore. My life as a mother — which was the life that most mattered to me — was over.

I had to sit down. I slid into a chair at the marble table, and pushed my palms against the stone trying to steady myself. I tried to think, but it felt as if fireworks were going off in my head.

How long had she known? An hour? Two? Where had I been when she discovered the truth? I'd been oblivious to the significance of the moment, stepping blithely out of a conference room or into an elevator, going down, down, down, not knowing the doors were opening on a life entirely different.

What had led her to open that suitcase? It had something to do with Marilyn, I was sure. Marilyn had somehow made the connection to me, had tracked down my daughter. I felt an urgent need to explain things to Mia, to help her see my side of the story.

Come home, I texted. I can explain.

But how would I explain?

Even if I could think of a way to explain to Mia, how could I explain to the police?

The police. Fear started in my belly, crawled up my spine. I'd done the research a long time ago. Even if Marilyn didn't press charges, the feds would come after me. I had crossed state lines. Kidnapping was a felony, first degree. There was no statute of limitations. I'd get twenty years to life. Life! I could already hear the clink of the door to my cell, where I'd be on display, night and day, a bug in a jar. The cold steel bars. The constant confinement. Unrelenting fluorescent. It would never get dark. How would I survive? How does anyone?

I had to get rid of the evidence. I got up from the table and went into the kitchen and pulled a plastic trash bag from a box under the sink.

I went back to my closet and took down the suitcase again from the shelf.

I put in the key and snapped open the lid and took out the contents, one by one, and making myself look the other way so I could go through with it, pushed the sunsuit and bib and papers into the plastic bag. Dust clouded the air. I twist-tied the bag shut. Fighting tears, I walked out the front door and out to the lobby and up the stairs to the compactor chute and opened the narrow door. I pulled back the metal handle and set the bag into the rounded receptacle. I had a fleeting thought of grabbing the bag back, returning it to the apartment, finding another place to hide it, a spot so well hidden that no one would ever discover it — but I made myself push the handle, flinging the bag to the basement, where I knew from watching a long-ago *Sesame Street* episode with Mia it would be crushed the next morning, smashed flat along with hundreds of other bags, making unrecognizable what

I'd kept all those years, buried relics of the day I became a mother.

There was a conference I'd been invited to, in Shanghai. A global convention of paper manufacturers. I'd received countless such invites to conferences over the years. I never went to any of them. Nobody I knew in creative departments did. We only traveled for shoots or awards shows. We had too many deadlines to care about trade shows, no matter how interesting or exotic the location. But there was only one deadline I cared about now. How much time I had until they'd come to arrest me. How long would it be before the police figured out who I was? Had Marilyn already tipped them off? But what evidence did she have? That I'd written a book about kidnapping? By that line of logic, most thriller authors would be writing from behind bars.

I did a search for the e-mail invitation to Tissue World Asia 2012.

I knew that wherever Mia went, it wasn't to the police. She'd be mad, she'd be upset, but she'd never betray me. I knew her that well. She was my daughter. My heart went out to her. Was she okay? Of course she wasn't.

265

I downloaded the conference registration form.

I can explain, I texted. Please let me explain.

But I got no reply. The phone in my hand lay silent as a dead fish.

56
MARILYN

The phone rang while I was working on my pottery in the basement. I was in the middle of glazing a vase, which I've left unfinished. I keep it to remind myself of the joy of that day. It's always on a table with silk flowers in it.

It took me a moment to dry off my hands and pull the phone out of the pocket of my apron, but when I pressed the button to answer, no one was there. The call was from a 917 number, which I knew was Mia's. I'd given her my number in a Facebook message and told her to call anytime. I knew enough to leave the calling up to her. She'd need to feel strong enough to do it, but I knew she'd get there eventually. Mia was born in the Year of the Horse, she's good at leaping over obstacles.

I was tempted to redial the number to reestablish connection, but resisted the urge. If my daughter was having a failure of courage, I wanted to give her the chance to recover. I sat down on a stool in front of the kiln, just sat there, staring at the phone on my lap, willing it to light up again. When the kiln isn't on, it stays cool in the basement, but sweat trickled from the backs of my knees. I sat there focusing my energy on it, willing the ringtone to sound again, a ringtone I realized was eerily appropriate, a song Chloe had loaded, and now I was waiting to hear "The Girl Who Fell from a Star." I watched the second hand of a big industrial clock on the wall go around once, then twice. Again. I could hardly breathe from the pressure I felt in my stomach. Just when I thought I couldn't resist the urge to press redial, I heard the music I was waiting to hear.

"Hi, this is Mia." It was a full-grown woman's voice, not the little girl's voice I'd heard in my head all those years. My heart flooded. I held back tears.

"Hi, baby," I managed, as if I'd just spoken to her, which I had — every day for more than two decades. And then we were crying, three thousand miles apart but finally together again.

57
LUCY

I stayed up all night, filling out PDF forms for the conference. Instructions were mainly in Chinese but there was some English. The whole time I was figuring out how to fill in the blanks, I was thinking it was crazy to take off like this. Bolting out of the country. What was I doing? But what choice did I have? I needed to get away, to achieve distance so I could think straight, figure out my options and how to deal with them.

Mostly, of course, I worried about Mia.

For the first time in her life, I had no idea where she was.

Well, that isn't true. She was twenty-one years old, a senior in college. There were plenty of times I didn't know where she was. But I always knew she was safe because we had a code word. I made it up when she was fifteen and going to her first sweet sixteen party. The party was across town, on the East Side. She looked so vulnerable:

her smile shiny with braces, teetering out the door on platform heels she didn't know how to walk in yet. Even without them, she was taller than me. And beautiful. So beautiful. I half regretted the looks she'd inherited, half wished she'd looked as ordinary as I did when I was her age. It was terrifying having to send such a gorgeous creature out into New York, having to trust her well-being to the care of a teenager.

"You can call me anytime if you ever feel unsafe or uncomfortable," I told her. "Just say a code word, so your friends don't have to know, and I'll come pick you up anytime, no questions asked. *Katcheratchma.*" I made it up on the spot. I have no idea where it came from. It just popped into my head, and for some reason, both of us remembered it. Mia did use it a few times over the years — once I went to get her way out in Brooklyn when she was supposed to be at a party on the Upper East Side —

But now there was no communication.

I assumed she was staying with a friend that night. Or had gotten a ride back to school, though it was still a week before the start of spring classes. I suddenly wished college was like it was in the old days when you could call a pay phone in the dorm and someone would answer and you could check up on someone else who lived there. Mia didn't have a landline, of course. Her only landline number was mine.

She didn't answer my text until the next morning, just before I got into the subway downtown.

Explain what? Kidnapping me?

I heard a train coming into the station, but I stayed where I was on the platform steps, concentrating on controlling my shaking thumbs so they'd hit the right keys.

Call! I can explain.

NO. u CAN'T!!!!

Where are you?

Then — nothing.

I continued my walk downstairs and reached the platform just as the train was pulling out of the station. I wasn't going to work. I'd called in sick. I was going to the Chinese embassy on Forty-Second Street. I needed a visa.

If I'd signed up earlier, the conference organizers would have arranged one for me, but I was too late for that. The conference was only a few days away.

There was a scanner at the entrance of the Chinese embassy and I half expected to be stopped when I unwrapped myself from my disguising coat, hat, and scarf. But I was waved through, without incident.

Did the authorities have my name on a list? I waited in line, worrying that the bureaucrat behind the glass, sipping from a jelly jar of mud-colored tea might suspect something. My hand shook as I slipped my papers into a little well in the counter between us. I sweated as he examined my regulation photo (full color, front-facing, hatless, no exceptions), then looked up, searching my face. I was afraid he'd call for security. But he accepted my papers without question, a gesture of so little importance to him that he did it with one hand, while with the other he refilled his jar from a thermos.

The next day (I'd paid extra for rush) I spent a trembling half hour in the pickup line. When I got to the window, a stern-looking man pushed a manila envelope to me. He didn't say whether or not it contained a visa. When I asked, he shook his fingers dismissively. I retreated to a dark corner where I pried open the envelope. I slid out my passport and out fluttered a receipt for the visa. But I didn't trust that. I flipped pages in my passport until I saw it. There it was, my ticket to freedom, a stamp taking up an entire page. It was decorative and colorful as a piece of art. I stared for some time at the line drawing: a long, orange winding road atop a pink Great Wall, leading toward a brilliant red, star-spangled sun. I imagined myself balanced on that wall, following in the ancient foot treads of fugitives before me — until my reverie was interrupted by an officious woman in uniform urging me to exit if I was done with my business.

After that, I said my good-byes at the office. I couldn't believe no one was suspicious about my going all the way to Shanghai for a conference on toilet paper. Or that T&A was willing to spring for the cost, which they let me put on the company card. But everyone was busy, so busy, and I was in middle management, and had convinced them, I guess, that my demonstrated interest in the tissue category might help grow a paper-towel client we already had.

A shoot in Vancouver was coming up which I'd miss. I put one of the writers who worked for me on it, someone good enough to take over for me, if my absence grew prolonged.

I put off the meeting Lance had set up with his agent.

I bought a ticket to PVG with an open return. The conference would last a week. I didn't have plans for what I would do after that, but by then I hoped I would have figured out something. I pictured the hotel in Shanghai as an exotic retreat where I'd spend long days in a room, considering my options. In fact, I had a hard time with room choice, which I'd needed in order to qualify for the visa. I'd e-mailed to ask for a nonsmoking room and the answer came back: *Sure, if you smoke, no one care of it.* I figured I could change rooms once I got there. I didn't plan to go to the conference, of course. I didn't want to risk someone recognizing me, if the story broke.

In the days before I could get on that flight, I fretted about being apprehended. Every time I left the apartment, I steeled myself against a tap on the shoulder, a touch on the arm. When I came home, I'd search the eyes of the doorman for any change in expression or tone of voice, which would alert me to the fact that someone had been there, seeking information about me.

The apartment echoed with the absence of Mia. She'd been gone before, to camp, to college. But this absence was different, making the dark rooms darker, a tomb from which I longed to escape. Part of me wanted to run, to find Mia. Poor Mia. I knew she was hurting. But I couldn't run to her. I had to make myself run in the other direction, far away.

I fled New York on Valentine's Day. Mia and I had a Valentine's ritual. We always exchanged some sort of heart on that day. When she was little, I'd scramble candy hearts into her eggs. I'd hide a note decorated with hearts in her backpack. After she left home, I always mailed her a card with a gift check enclosed, written in pink pen.

So it's ironic that now that day will always signify for me the dissolution of our togetherness.

58
MARILYN

I wanted to fly out to see her right away. I wanted to take my daughter in my arms, I wanted to reconnect to her physically; she'd been part of me, I wanted, I *needed* to be with her, to help her begin the process of healing. And the harmonious outcome was, there was room on a flight to Newark the very next day and the flight was direct and available at a discount.

Of course, I reached out to Tom as soon as I heard from Natalie. It wasn't easy to track him down. I haven't had a phone number for him for quite some time. He moved to Costa Rica about fifteen years ago. But I had his e-mail and hoped he still had the same address. I sent him a message with the subject head shouting in caps: *OUR DAUGHTER FOUND!!!!*

He called hours later, while I was making dinner. He said he was happy that Natalie had been discovered. But he couldn't fly out right away to meet her. He thought she should bond with her mother first anyway. I couldn't understand that. I thought we should go see our daughter together. But Tom is a limited person. He is just doing the best he can.

We had a family meeting after dinner that night. Grant and I gathered the three kids in the living room, where our family focuses on important issues. It's a place soft and giving: white fluffy carpets, overstuffed sofa, walls painted a calming shade of green. This is where we came to discuss whether or not I should go back to work and the boys' decision to stop homeschooling and go to public high school.

As they settled into their places — each of us has a spot where we're most comfortable: Grant likes the cushy chair, I like the sofa, Connor and Thatch like the beanbags, Chloe lies on the flokati, her feet on the hearth — I told them I had an important announcement. We were welcoming someone new into our family. I felt a wholeness in saying the words in that room. It's where we welcomed each of them into this world, their passage gentled by water in the tank we rented each time, the midwife, and Grant floating beside me, murmuring affirmations.

"Are we getting a dog?" Thatch asked.

"A baby?" From Chloe.

When I heard "a baby" my eyes watered a little and I nodded.

Connor, sixteen, gazed at me in horror.

"No way," he said.

"Well, not an actual baby. She's all grown up now. You know that special angel whose birthday we celebrate?"

All I'd told the kids about Natalie was that our family had a guardian angel we celebrated on April 4 every year.

"That angel was my first baby. I haven't seen her since she was four months old." My throat closed and I couldn't say any more.

The kids looked at each other. I was glad that Grant was there to step in.

"How come you never told us before?" Connor asked.

"We didn't want to worry you kids, to make you think this could happen to you," said Grant.

The kids looked at each other, then at me.

"You're not the oldest!" Thatch said to Connor, grinning. It wasn't the generous response I had hoped for. Thatch is a middle child, he has issues to work through.

In a steady voice, Grant told them the story of what happened. He knew every detail. It's a story I'd told him many times before. I watched the kids' faces for how they were taking it. Thatch's hair, as usual fell in front of his face and he sank his chin in his hands, so I couldn't see his expression. He's the one I usually worry about. But, now, I worried about all three. I didn't want any of them to feel the bad energy that had capsized me for so many years.

When Grant was finished, I took a deep breath and told them I was going to New York in the morning. I was going to meet their sister. Their sister. I was excited by the thought of having her with us, having all my family together for the first time. But I worried, too. I had never left the kids for even one night before. I ached to think of how many nights I wasn't there for Natalie.

"Do you love her better than us?" Chloe said.

"Of course not!" I said, briefly considering taking her with me. But I'd need all my energy for Natalie now. "Daddy can take good care of you. Just for a few days."

"I'll take you to work tomorrow," he promised, which is something Chloe loved to do. He sometimes took her along on a job, explaining what each heavy tool was for, teaching her to level a pipe or plane a board.

"Is the angel going to move in with us?" Thatch wanted to know. This is something I wondered myself. I didn't know whether or not my daughter would want to come home with me. I needed to leave that choice up to her.

"She'll want to come home to her real family," Grant said. I hoped he was right.

I looked around the room, with new eyes, imagining it through the eyes of a girl who'd been raised in New York. I loved this house. But what would Natalie think of it? I pictured myself explaining to her the power of the hanging crystals, the mirrors positioned for water energy. Or would she already know about them?

She was my daughter, I'd given birth to her, but I had no idea of the kind of person she was.

"We can make a big welcome sign!" Chloe said, and how grateful I was for her generous resilience, and for the calm sea of Grant beneath our children, there to steady their rocking boats.

59
MIA

The next morning, at Ms. Laniere's, I stood in front of her mirror brushing my teeth. My face looked different. I was a different person. But who was that person? I didn't know. I put on a black sweater, but took it off and put on a blue one, then a green. I was surprised at how nervous I was. What would my real mother be like? Would she like me? Would I like her? What if I wasn't what she expected?

Ms. Laniere told me how to get to Newark from Brooklyn: two trains and a bus from midtown. I had to leave early. Marilyn had taken a red-eye flight.

I waited for her at the airport, feeling more alone than I had ever felt in my life. I was at baggage, watching one red bag go around and around on the carousel, going into the tunnel, coming out again.

My phone kept going off. I knew who it was. No one else would be calling this early.

I'd changed "Mom" to "Do Not Answer." I wouldn't pick up.

Her texts were getting more and more pathetic:

Please!

I love you.

I'm your mother.

I need to explain.

I couldn't turn off the phone until I met up with Marilyn. If there was a problem, she'd call my cell.

I finally texted Lucy:

I'm at EWR, about to meet my mother.

That shut her up.

Suddenly there was Marilyn coming off the escalator. I knew it was her. She was tall, like me. There was something familiar about her shoulders, her walk. I felt like I was falling down a hole with no bottom.

She saw me and started walking faster. Her clothes were bright and flowing, not right for winter, and they flowed behind her as she hurried toward me. I couldn't move. I felt numb, frozen in place.

"Baby." She smiled. I knew her voice. She dropped her bags and opened her arms and pulled me into them. For the first time I was hugging a person who was half of me. She ran her hands over my hair and my back. Then she pulled up glasses on a bead chain and put them on and stared at me through them. Her eyes were the same blue as mine. She touched my cheek.

"Look how gorgeous you are," she said. "You are beautiful."

She was beautiful, too. I was crying and so was she. She hugged me again and we stood like that. I could feel her back shaking. There was something about the way she smelled that seemed familiar. But maybe that was my imagination. We didn't let go of each other for a long time. I waited, letting her be the first to pull away. As we did, my hair got caught on one of her dangly dream-catcher earrings and we laughed, trying to extricate without hurting each other.

"It's like you're a dream and I'm trying to wake up," she said, and it was good she wasn't wearing makeup. She kept wiping her eyes with a tissue she kept in her sleeve.

"I'm not a dream." Her hair was like mine. It looked like fog around her head.

"You are the dream I had for twenty-one years." And then, she started to cry again. The tissue was useless.

My phone buzzed. Another text:
Please call me. Please.

I swiped the phone off and slid it into my back pocket.

We walked to the carousel, not saying

much. There was too much to say. She reached for my hand as we stood waiting for her bag to come out. As we stood, she took my hand in both of hers and stroked it with her thumbs. To the people around us, we must have looked like just another mother and daughter glad to see each other again. But they'd be surprised — and, I guessed, so would she — to know how awkward I felt about her grip on my hand. It was a gesture that made it look as if we had known each other forever, when really, we were as much strangers to each other as we were to everyone standing around us, all of us peering into a dark hole, hoping to recognize the next thing that came out.

"There it is," she said, and reached for a blue suitcase. Its size surprised me. It was giant, even though she was only staying for a few days, just till spring term started at Middlebury and I went back to my classes, back to my life on campus, as if nothing was changed. I thought I could do that. I really did.

60
MARILYN

I rented a car — I was stunned to discover that although my daughter was twenty-one years old, she didn't know how to drive. In my experience, kids got their licenses as soon as they could. I grew up in New Jersey and got my permit when I was sixteen. Connor got his on his fifteenth birthday. Thatch is counting the days until he can do the same. But I guess it's different for kids who grew up taking taxis or subways everywhere they needed to go.

When I asked how she got around in Vermont, she said there were plenty of kids with cars there. There were shuttle buses between campus and town. She told me that *not* driving has greatly enriched her life, has made her open to alternative ways to get places. "And you meet great people!" she said cheerfully, making me worry about her falling prey to strangers who take girls for rides. She had expensive educations, I knew.

Why hadn't she been taught something so basic?

The hardest thing to do was calling her by her kidnapped name. I have to show respect for who she was now. But who was she? How painful to be deprived of knowing my own daughter. So many questions popped into my head as we drove. I wanted to know everything about what had happened to her in the days she'd been separated from me, what had she seen, what had she done, what sounds, what touch, what colors had been imprinted on her. But I was conscious of how upset she must feel — her whole world upended — and found myself simply making small talk, to put her at ease. We had the rest of our lives to be together. There'd be time for real talk.

I'd made reservations at an Embassy Suites in Cranford, New Jersey. It hadn't been there when I'd lived in this area years ago — Grant had looked it up for me on the Internet. But before we went to the hotel, I wanted to show Mia the house where she was born. Well, the house she came to after she was born in a hospital. I thought seeing the house would help her connect with her essence, her self that had been subjugated for years.

I didn't tell her where we were going, I

didn't want to stir up any preconceived notions in her. I wanted the reconnection to be organic.

I'm bad at directions. My kids — my other kids — often navigate from the backseat, and I was surprised I didn't need the GPS to tell me where I was going, though it had been nearly two decades since I'd been to Cranford. The car seemed to know just where to turn, up this road, down that, almost without me steering the wheel, until we pulled up in front of the house that Tom and I had bought with such hopes, the house that was the embodiment of so many memories I'd tried to forget. The house was still there. They'd painted the white porch gray. They'd changed the front window and added a basketball court near the driveway. But other than that, it looked the same. I eased the car by the curb in front of it and put the car into park.

When I left this house, I'd been a different person. I was glad not to be that person anymore. I wished I could commune with my self who had lived there, the woman going through dark, panic-filled days, reassure her that things would turn out in the end.

My daughter sat next to me on the front seat. She didn't say anything. We both just sat staring up at the house on the little snow-dappled rise. I felt the Oneness flooding me, and when she closed her eyes, I guessed that she must be feeling the force of it, too.

So I was startled when she turned to me and asked where we were.

61
Mia

It was important to Marilyn that I saw my first house. She wanted me to feel a connection. She thought something in me would recognize the house. But I didn't recognize it. There wasn't anything special about it, to me, it looked just like any other house in the suburbs like houses upstate where my aunt lives.

When she told me it was the house where I'd lived as a baby, I was interested. I wanted to get out of the car and go see it. Marilyn didn't want me to, she was afraid it was bad karma. But I had to feel what it would have been like to live there. When I got out, Marilyn did, too. She stood at the curb as I walked up the driveway. I wanted to get as close as I could to the house. I wanted to touch the place I was meant to grow up in.

I walked off the asphalt and onto the lawn. I breathed in the air I would have breathed growing up here. I stood by a shrub that was shrouded in burlap. I put my hand on the stucco. There was a white wishing well in the side yard with a pail on a rope. I felt how my whole life would have been changed if this were my house. I would be a different person. I would be someone who didn't live in the city, who would have gone to a normal school, like on *Dawson's Creek*. I'd be a kid from the suburbs, a cheerleader, maybe, someone who only came into the city for field trips or museums or shopping, a kid who a city kid kind of looks down on, and I immediately hated myself for feeling that way, for being glad that I wasn't raised here because that would mean — I was glad I'd been abducted.

I looked back at Marilyn, checking out the mailbox, staring at the name that was on it now. And I hated Lucy for thinking that it was okay to take an eraser and rub out the people we were meant to be.

62
MARILYN

I didn't want to get out of the car. I didn't want to expose either of us to the bad energy that I thought might still be lingering there. But when Mia insisted on going, I got out and followed. I didn't want her going into that force field alone.

Years ago, just after it happened, there'd been yellow ribbons tied around the dogwoods and maples, which were much bigger now, and tied around the post of the mailbox. The mailbox was different, but the cedar post was still there. I found myself drawn to the cedar, to see if there were any vestiges of those ribbons on it, any traces of what I'd gone through twenty-one years ago. There weren't, and I took comfort in that. All that survived of our search for our baby . . . was our baby. She was here. The pain had subsided. For that, I was grateful.

It gave us both a start when the front door of the house opened. A woman stood behind the storm door with a baby. She poked her head out and asked if we needed help. I fibbed, saying we were looking for Longston Road and she pointed directions. I apologized for bothering her and we got back in the car.

I noticed that Mia looked very pale.

"Are you all right?" I asked. She said she felt faint.

I always travel with my bag of medicinal herbs and was glad to have the cayenne with me. I found it in my purse and reached across and held the red packet under her nose. "Breathe," I said. And she did. In a moment, the color returned to her cheeks.

"Have you fainted before?" I asked her, and she said that she had.

"But only once," she said, brighter now. "When I was in a store, having my ears pierced. It's not like it's a habit or anything."

"Twice," I said quietly.

She handed the packet back to me.

"You fainted in the birth canal." And I told her the story. She'd been born floppy and gray, and terrifyingly silent, and they'd whisked her off to a corner of the room. I couldn't bear to ask what was happening. I just lay there, looking at Tom. His eyes were damp. He was looking at me and squeezing my hand. Finally, we heard a tiny cry and I recognized that sound; as known to me as the beat of my own heart.

The next day, a neonatal specialist gave us the news that she was perfect. Then the doctor surprised us by thanking us. "I rarely get to deliver good news," she said, which told us just how lucky we were.

"I didn't know that," my daughter said quietly. There was so much she didn't know. I wanted to hug her again, I wanted to wrap my arms around her elbows that had once been enfolded inside me. But I was driving.

63
MIA

We shared a hotel room, which felt weird at first. We each had our own bed, but mornings it creeped me out to wake up and see her staring at me from across the nightstand.

Marilyn is warm and sweet and caring. She is very emotional. I've been with her three days, and she's already hugged me about a million times.

She is a very sensitive person. She sometimes knows my feelings before I do. "How are you feeling?" she asks every morning, and really, she wants to know. Not like Lucy, who never liked her real feelings to shine through. She was always kidding. When I was little, she'd do things like, when drying me off from a bath, say, "Oh no! There are purple blotches all over your back!" Then, when I was about to cry, she'd say she was joking.

We've been living on Chinese food for

three days. Marilyn is vegan but vegan choices in Cranford are lame. We go to Moon Palace breakfast, lunch, and dinner. They are always happy to see us. Marilyn is impressed I can speak Chinese with the woman who owns it, but really what we are saying is only baby talk in Chinese. I can't really speak it. My year of Mandarin at Midd taught me how much I don't know. I wanted to go on a year abroad in China, but Lucy talked me out of it. Now I know why. I'd never have been able to get a passport with fake documents.

Eating Chinese makes me sad because it reminds me of Ayi. Every afternoon I'd come home from school and hear her in the kitchen chopping things while I did my homework on the other side of the wall. The comforting sound of vegetables hitting the wok, the lovely aromas. I'd go into the kitchen for a snack and she'd give me a piece of whatever she was chopping: celery, peppers, mushrooms. She wouldn't let me eat junk.

The dishes we eat here aren't anything like Ayi's. The vegetables are too fried and the dumplings too watery. It's hard to eat Chinese food made for Americans once you've tasted it made for Chinese. But I don't complain. We're not here for the food.

Maybe I'll make Marilyn and her family a few of Ayi's dishes when I go out to meet them in San Mateo on spring break. Ayi gave me some recipes before she left, which I've never tried. That is, if I don't go to Costa Rica instead. That's where my father is. Father. It feels weird saying that word. I never had a father before. It's not like I ever wanted one. I didn't. I figured a father would take up a lot of my mom's attention, and I'd be left alone. Having a dad around would change everything. Even little things, like, we couldn't walk around in our bras anymore. I never felt like I was missing something not having a dad. But I have to say that now that I have one I'm pretty curious to meet him.

Marilyn e-mailed him as soon as she found me. He was so freaked by the kidnapping, he moved out of the country. He's anxious to meet me, Marilyn says, but she wants us — her and me — to have a chance to heal our relationship first. The mother-daughter relationship is primary energy needed to sustain emotional healing, she says.

Marilyn's hominess is kind of exotic to me. She is all that anyone could want in a mother, but I can't call her that, yet. She hasn't asked me to. She must understand that I am not ready. She's asked a lot about how I grew up and once I called Lucy "my mom" and Marilyn's eyes filled with tears. But "mom" is what I've called Lucy for twenty-one years. It's a habit.

What I don't want Marilyn to know is, I wake up at night, crying for my mom who doesn't exist anymore.

I asked housekeeping for an extra pillow and put it over my head so Marilyn won't hear.

64
LUCY

At JFK Airport, I navigated the gauntlet: check-ins, passport check, security screenings. At every point, I tried to keep from betraying panic. I braced myself for some airport employee in uniform to turn me away, say they were sorry, could I just step aside, into a room where police would handcuff me, I wasn't allowed to leave the country.

I made it to gate seating, but my worries didn't let up. News blared from TVs and I fretted that any moment, news of the kidnapping might be announced, flashing my picture across the screen. Another passenger in the boarding area might recognize me and reach out to one of the uniformed agents who were all over the airport. Was someone from Homeland Security authorized to arrest me?

A young woman in business attire slouched in a seat across from me, under one of the televisions. She kept craning her neck to stare at the screen. She'd glance at it, then turn around to me, as if the news had already been reported. Maybe it had been. Maybe it had been tweeted or Facebooked. I wouldn't know. I don't do social media. The ad agency had been after me for years to use it, and Mia had helped me set up accounts. But I never got around to actually using them.

When the woman across from me wasn't checking the television, she was scrolling the screen of her phone. She kept looking up at me. I began to sweat. I wanted to move, but I had too much to carry. I looked down, pretended to engross myself in my book so that my face was partially hidden from her. Then, a shadow fell over the page. I looked up. It was her. My mouth went dry. But she looked nervous, too. She held out her open palm to me, which seemed an odd gesture. It was as if she were inviting me to dance.

"Do you have a sewing kit?" she asked, and I saw what lay in her palm: a stray button.

I barked out a laugh, which must have unsettled her.

"Sure," I said, flipping open a flap of a bag, digging inside it for a small plastic box which I realized people probably didn't pack anymore, and no doubt this was the reason she'd approached me. No one else around us looked old enough to be carrying a sewing kit.

I exhaled almost audibly as my boarding pass was scanned, and I joined the parade down the ramp to the plane.

Right up until the moment before I had to turn off my phone, I sent Mia texts. I decorated them with <3's making emoticon hearts. But she didn't answer.

■ ■ ■ ■

PART THREE

■ ■ ■ ■

Nature infuses young Thomisid spiderlings with an innate yen to fly far from their birthplace, to form distant colonies. This preserves the species. Otherwise, they are eaten by the adults.

— NEWSLETTER OF THE AMERICAN ARACHNOLOGY SOCIETY

65

LUCY

JFK–PVG was the longest flight I'd ever taken — fifteen hours. I'd gotten my doctor to prescribe sleeping pills, but I didn't take one. I wanted to be alert when I got off the plane, in case authorities were waiting for me at the end of the runway. But I deplaned with no trouble, like everyone else.

Shanghai Airport was more modern than I had been led to believe. I wasn't prepared for an airport with gleaming floors, smartly dressed people on moving sidewalks, digital clocks, and billboards that flashed, twirled, replaced themselves every few moments showing smiling faces of A-list American film stars I could never afford to hire for testimonials in the States. I glided past Nicolas Cage hawking Montblanc watches, Brad Pitt shilling for Cadillac.

What had I expected? *The Good Earth,* where people wore conical hats and spit on the floor? I realized that most of the stories

Wendy had told me had happened before she left the country.

I retrieved my luggage and made it through customs, which was a surprisingly breezy process. A machine invited me to rate my experience: greatly satisfied, basically satisfied, not satisfied. I pressed greatly satisfied, because I was. How relieved I was to hear the *thwap, thwap, thwap* as the official time-stamped my passport in one, two, three places. Coming out of glass doors, I was stunned by the size of the waiting crowd, and relieved to spot a man holding a sign: *Mr. Lucy.* If my driver had been expecting a man, he showed no surprise. I followed him and my luggage onto one after another of the moving staircases.

I felt desperate to call Mia. Perhaps she'd relented about talking to me. There was a twelve-hour difference between us now. A digital clock declared 22:05 and I calculated that meant it was only 10 a.m., her time. She'd be back in classes at Middlebury.

The driver showed me where to change money and how to buy a SIM card at a kiosk so I could make an international call. I'd checked with Verizon before I left on how to make my iPhone work in China. The SIM card gave me another phone number. Mia must have been curious about the number that showed up on her screen, because she answered, then hung up as soon as she heard it was me.

I punched the same thirteen numbers again, just needing to hear her voice on the recording: *Hey, it's Mia. Leave a message. Hey, it's Mia. Hey, it's Mia.*

I still call her, now and then, just to hear those words, the sweetness of her timbre, pretending she is actually talking to me.

I know she thinks of me each time I set off her phone.

What appears on her screen? What does she see?

66
MIA

When I got back to Middlebury, the campus looked different. Smaller. The white clapboard buildings looked like little prisons. I didn't tell my friends what happened. Not even my boyfriend. We'd been together six months, which felt like a long time, but now Todd wasn't my boyfriend anymore. I'd texted that I had something to tell him. He texted back that he had something to tell me. He picked me up at the airport, and on the ride in from Burlington, he confessed he had slept with one of the team leaders down in Guatemala. He blamed it on Asperger's, which he uses as an excuse for everything, even though his case is so mild it's just borderline. He has a burger tattooed on his ass. "Get it?" he'd asked me, pointing to it the first time we were together. "Ass. Burger." The team leader he'd slept with had Facebooked a picture of the tattoo, which I knew was the reason he was telling me — he was afraid I had seen it. He said that sleeping with her didn't matter to him. He hoped it didn't matter to me. But his betrayal felt unspeakably cruel on top of the other betrayal I was trying to deal with, which I didn't even bother telling him about now.

When Todd dropped me off, I crawled into bed and didn't get out of it for two days. My whole world was falling apart. I couldn't even brush my teeth without crying. My friends knew something was wrong, but they thought it had only to do with my breaking up with Todd. I didn't tell them what else had happened. Partly I was afraid of anyone knowing my secret. Someone would Facebook or text about it and then my story would hit the news. I wanted to process it by myself, in private. I knew that Marilyn wanted that, too.

In those first few days after my life was turned upside down, I often caught myself blanking out, staring at my computer screen, not knowing how much time had gone by. I started having bad dreams. Terrible dreams that would wake me in the dark, leaving me dry-mouthed and panting.

I went to the clinic for sleeping pills. They helped me sleep, but I must have had a bad reaction to them. One night, I woke up in a student lounge, candy wrappers everywhere. I'd eaten an art student's Valentine Candyland display!

I knew I had to get out of there.

67
Lucy

When I got to the hotel, I learned they'd given away my room.

"Conference already start. You should come early," chided the desk clerk, pushing away the paper showing I had a confirmed reservation. The grand, glitzy hotel housing the conference was huge, but he insisted they didn't have room for one more. How could so many people want to attend a toilet-paper conference in China? I thought. "Not only China conference," he said, as if mind-reading, "Tissue *World* conference." He typed something on the computer which set a printer going behind him and handed the page that came out of it to the driver, who led me back out into the cold, cold air. I'd worn my cloth coat instead of my down. I thought Shanghai would be warmer, even in February. The overflow hotel was about a half mile away, although distance was hard to tell not only because it was dark, but because streets were so crowded with traffic, both cars and bicycles, and people veering off sidewalks, many of them shoppers carrying bags inscribed with recognizable names, to my surprise: Chanel, Nike, Tiffany's, Häagen-Dazs. It was eleven at night, but shops were still open, entrances brightly lit.

The overflow hotel was like the glitzy, modern hotel's old maiden aunt: fading, run-down, reeking with the smell of ancient cigarettes. Reluctantly, I followed the driver down the long lobby hallway to a desk at the back where a man bundled in a padded cotton coat sat smoking in front of a "No Smoking" sign. The corridor was cold.

"Is heat a problem here?" I asked, causing the man to consult in Chinese for a good five minutes with the driver, who turned to me and assured me there was a heater in my room. I asked to see the room and the man shouted something in Chinese. A young woman appeared and escorted me into a small elevator and soon I was standing in a surprisingly nicely appointed double. It wasn't fancy, but it was clean, with all the amenities you'd expect of a low-level chain hotel in the States: queen bed, hair dryer, coffeepot, huge flat-screen television. The woman picked up what I thought was the TV remote and pointed it far above the screen. I felt grateful for the rush of hot air coming from the electric heater I saw was installed near the ceiling.

It was almost midnight. Where else could I go? I hadn't slept in what felt like days. Plus, I saw the advantages of staying somewhere off the beaten track. I followed the woman downstairs and accepted the card that would unlock the front door, elevator, and my room. My driver unloaded the luggage and bid me good-bye, and I (having consulted a glossy page torn from a guidebook) tipped him from the new colorful wad in my wallet, with a bill so pink that it looked like play money.

I sat on the bed and tried to turn on the television, to see if there was American news. There was a card in English explaining how to turn on the set, but apparently the instructions left out a couple of steps. The green power light was on, but the screen stayed black. I rang the front desk and soon the woman knocked on my door, then patiently pushed a series of buttons labeled in Chinese characters until the set came on. I insisted she do it again, so I would remember — I'm not good with technology — and she complied, laughing behind her hand, apparently thinking it

311

funny that an American didn't know how to turn on a TV. Most stations were in Chinese; two were in English, but neither showed news. One was a talk show with Canadian and American expats extolling the beauty and congeniality of their new-found homes in China. The other was a Chinese-dubbed rerun of *Sex and the City.* I fell into bed without unpacking, without even undressing, listening to Samantha trade barbs with a soon-to-be mother at a baby shower wearing a hat made of gift wrappings, wondering what a Chinese audience would be making of this.

It wasn't until the next morning I realized the room didn't have windows.

"Sorry, last room," the desk clerk informed cheerfully.

The hotel had Wi-Fi, but the connection was excruciatingly slow. The connection was faster on a desktop set up in the lobby hallway. But all the templates were in Chinese. I couldn't access my e-mail or Google. Any Western news outlet I thought of wouldn't load. I hadn't been this much off the Internet since before it existed.

I didn't go to the conference, of course. I feared there'd be Western press and I didn't want any of them around to recognize me if my story broke in the States. I stayed in my windowless, dimly lit room for days, until I couldn't sit there alone any longer. But I found I couldn't go anywhere by myself. All the street signs were in Chinese, which somehow I hadn't expected.

68
LUCY

The hotel receptionist gave me brochures advertising the services of several guides, all of whom had studied English tourism at university. (An example of Chinese practicality — this is now a university curriculum choice.)

I picked Ada, not only because her photo looked friendliest, but because I liked the copy in her brochure best. Ada promised to show visitors *not only the glory but also the off-beaten paths in our city.* I'm a writer for hire — I *was* a writer for hire. I know how hard it is to come up with copy. I couldn't imagine having to do it using a language that is not your own. I liked the fact that Ada was willing to go out of her way to show someone sights beyond the ones that tourists could see on a bus tour.

Ada. Even in Shanghai, Chinese think up English names for themselves, partly out of kindness for speakers who find their names unpronounceable, partly because it's fashionable. But their ears aren't attuned to Western name fashions. So, though my guide is in her twenties, she has a name that makes her sound a hundred years old, a creaky moniker plucked from some Victorian novel. Dickens, Thackeray, the Brontës — they're all here, sold in "foreign bookstores," printed in Mandarin on pages as sheer as toilet paper, with paperback covers featuring lurid drawings of couples in suggestive poses, bearing no relation to narrative content.

Ada thinks I am here on business, though she must notice that the only business I appear to do is to write in this journal. She is always "applying" to get a job in America by trying to impress me with her good work habits and dedication to improving her English. She shows up at least ten minutes early and goes out of her way to be helpful. Yesterday, she bargained the fruit seller half off a bag of litchi nuts, though I was willing to pay the few fen he was asking.

I knew the conference had ended when the man at the front desk informed me that so did the conference rate for the hotel. The rate would be going up astronomically. Ada helped situate me in another hotel, owned by a friend of her uncle. She got them to charge me the Chinese rate, not the foreigner rate, which she says is ten times higher, a common practice here which is apparently legal.

The hotel has an oxymoronic name: New Old House. It's what's called a "service apartment," halfway between a hostel and a hotel. All the rooms have kitchenettes which consist of a hot plate and half-size refrigerator. No one here speaks English which is probably another reason why I'm getting a better rate.

This afternoon, I go to the Foreign Language Bookstore, bracing to see my face, my name. They sell a few periodicals in English: *People, Newsweek,* and the *Herald Tribune.* In the ten days I'd been going there, nothing of my story has turned up. Perhaps Mia's reuniting with Marilyn won't make the news. Marilyn got what she wanted. She has her daughter. How would it serve her interest, or Mia's, to publicize this? Perhaps Mia has told her what a good mother I was and Marilyn — and Mia — mean to forgive me. Maybe the whole thing will go away, and I will go back to the States and we can share Mia between us, like joint custody.

In the meantime, I wait.

69
LUCY

I feel sorry for Ada, so eager to seek fortune in the Motherland I've left, ignorant of the futility of her desire, at least with me as the conduit. She is a model corporate candidate, though — smart and eager and wishing to please. I mean to recommend her to former colleagues in the States, if I start up correspondence with any again.

Ada is only a few years older than Mia, and just as energetic. Though I wonder about Mia's energy now. How is she feeling? Sad? Angry? Perhaps she has answered one of my e-mails I sent her before leaving the States. I wouldn't know. I still can't access my e-mail here. She doesn't pick up my calls.

Ada meets me every day in the lobby. Yesterday, she showed me where I can swim. I haven't exercised in weeks, not since my life began to unravel. I am fifty-seven years old. I'm afraid if I let things start to slide, they'll just keep slipping and I'll look like the old ladies women used to be at my age. I'm used to biking around Central Park, 6.2 miles every day, weather permitting. I used to do it before work. I had — I still have — the co-op apartment on Riverside Drive, which we moved into when Mia was just a baby. She's graduating from college in three months. I can't believe that I won't be there to see it.

This morning I swam in the pool Ada showed me, near the hotel, a beautiful Olympic-size rectangle of clean, chlorinated water. It was only seven o'clock but bright light streamed from skylights dappling the water, which was still and inviting, as no one was in it.

I stood at the edge of the pool, contemplating big red Chinese characters on a wall, trying to puzzle them out, to determine whether or not diving was permitted, when a shout pierced the air. I turned to see a small, stern woman in uniform, hurrying toward me, pink flip-flops flapping, too big for her feet. She was waving something above her head — a bathing cap. She made me return to my locker for money to buy it, not an insignificant sum, given the fact that the latex was so thin and insubstantial it felt like pulling a condom over my head.

I had the pool to myself for a while. Being in the water worked like a tonic. I used to swim a lot before I moved to New York. The water made me feel calmer than I've felt since I got here. I did long, lazy backstrokes until I reached a wall, then breaststroked back to the other. I punctuated each lap with a turning flip by which you can tell any lap swimmer who's been on a team, even if that team was as rinky-dink as mine was, a neighborhood swim club I swam for as a kid. I don't turn flips very well anymore, and sometimes, when I come out of one, I find myself facing the wall by mistake. This happened, and when I brought my head out of the water and turned myself the right way around, I saw a Chinese man approaching the pool, glossy-skinned, having just showered, his hair contained in regulation condom.

I was annoyed to realize I'd have to share the pool. Ridiculous, I know. It is a public pool! But what really annoyed me is what came after that: he didn't do laps, but swam around the pool's perimeter, as if to claim the entire space for himself. What selfishness! I thought, resuming my laps, fuming whenever he interrupted them. Later that day, Ada told me that's how Chinese swim and I realized how insensitive I had been to prevailing custom, and that he must have been fuming underwater, too, as perturbed by my actions as I was by his.

70
MIA

Marilyn picked me up at the airport in San Francisco. It was a long drive to San Mateo and we mostly small-talked. I was too tired to get into anything heavy. When she turned the car into her driveway, I saw they'd decorated the house. There were yellow streamers and yellow balloons and a sign across the front door that said *Welcome Home!*

I saw it was a surprise for Marilyn, too. She stopped the car in the driveway, put her hand over her mouth, and cried.

I felt happy and sad at the same time. Happy to be wanted, but sad that it wasn't really my home, that no place would feel like home anymore.

When I walked into the house, I burst into tears. When you grow up in a family that isn't your birth family, sometimes you feel you're not actually real. Because you don't see yourself reflected in anyone else around you. Now, suddenly, I was among people who looked like they'd been made from the same clay. A little girl's hair, a boy's nose, the shape of his eyebrows were like silent confirmation of the way I am made. And then the immensity of the situation over-whelmed me and I leaned against a wall, trying to contain my emotion, until finally I was able to turn my sobs into laughs, and everyone, relieved, laughed along with me. Marilyn put an arm around my shoulder and told Connor to take my luggage up-stairs.

She'd made up a bed for me in Chloe's room. Chloe led me to it. Being in her room brought back the comforts of being a ten-year-old girl — a turtle in a tank, a doll-house, colorful throw pillows, floral quilts, stuffed animals sitting sentry on shelves. I said I hoped I'd be a good roommate. I'd never been one before, I told her. She said she hadn't either; she only had brothers. But this made her blush and correct herself. "I mean I USED to have only brothers. We thought you were dead!" And now she flushed even deeper, sensing another error, and I reached over to hug her, telling her not to worry, everything was going to be okay, wishing I could believe it, hating Lucy for upending not only my life, but the lives of the good-hearted people I came from.

71
MARILYN

I should have warned the kids and Grant
not to decorate the house. It never occurred
to me they would do it. And, of course, they
didn't know the meaning that yellow balloons would have for me.

A reporter was in the yard when we got
out of the car. We hadn't expected that.
Detective Brown had agreed to hold off the
media until Mia was settled. But someone
in the police force had put something on
Twitter. A reporter had seen it, put two and
two together, and tracked us down.

A picture of me and Mia ran the next day
in the *San Francisco Chronicle*. After that,
we were deluged with media. We couldn't
keep reporters off the lawn. Grant tried to
block the drive from the road with sawhorses, but they just moved the sawhorses. I
didn't dare let Connor and Thatch go to
school. I worried about them being hounded
to the point of physical danger, then being

quoted on something they knew nothing about.

Detective Brown advised us to do a press conference with police. They promised to keep it low-key. Mia didn't even have to be there. He then advised us to hire a lawyer to be a go-between with the media.

72
CHERYL

The awful way I found out was on news radio, driving home from work.

A baby kidnapped in New Jersey twenty-one years ago has been reunited with her birth mother in California. Born Natalie Featherstone in Cranford, New Jersey . . .

I had just made the turn onto Lafayette Street when I heard words I'll never forget:

. . . the girl was raised in Manhattan as Mia Wakefield.

My whole body began to shake.

But eight million people live down in New York City, surely one of them had the same name as my niece.

Ms. Wakefield, a senior at Middlebury College . . .

I had to pull off the road. I didn't cut the engine, I gripped the steering wheel to steady myself as impossible words kept pouring out of the dashboard:

. . . raised by her abductor, a New York

advertising executive . . .

I could barely control my trembling hands as I rifled through my purse for my cell phone and punched in my sister's number at work. She'd still be there. It was only 5 p.m. I got her voice mail and left a message, then tried her at home. The machine didn't pick up. I listened to the series of rings, imagined the echoes in the long, narrow hallways, the small, uncluttered rooms so much smaller than the rooms of the house we grew up in.

I thought there must be some mistake, something Lucy herself could clear up, if I could just talk to her. But I couldn't get her on the phone. I switched to calling Mia's number. But I couldn't get her either.

I put the car in gear. It was February. The roads were icy. My hands trembling on the wheel, my heart in my throat, I pulled back into traffic, rejoining the stream of cars, imagining all of them blaring my sister's name. I pulled up my coat collar, hoping that when I stopped at the light, no one I knew would be in the car next to me.

73
Mia

I hated having what happened to me in the news. I had to shut down my Facebook because so many friends were tagging me with news stories and putting them on Tumblr and Instagram and I didn't want to know about any of it. It felt like my friends weren't my friends anymore. The person who they had become friends with no longer existed.

It turns out that getting off Facebook is annoyingly hard to do. It keeps wanting you to deactivate it instead, warning you that deleting your account is irreversible, asking if you're sure again and again. One of the captchas I had to type twice was "over." By the last time I pressed enter, it felt like I was launching myself into outer space, a million miles away from the person I was.

74
MARILYN

The lawyer said we had to pick a magazine to give an exclusive to. If we didn't do that, the story would run without us and reporters would tell it any way they want. We decided to go with *People.* It was the most money — we couldn't believe how much. Enough to help Mia with law school, if she still wanted that. Enough to help with college for the kids.

The photographer brought a stylist who insisted on making up Mia and me, saying we'd look like washed-out ghosts if she didn't. She brought a huge bag of cosmetics with her, but I insisted she use the toxin-free ones I already had. They posed Mia and me together in the living room, under the hanging crystals, then in the kitchen in front of the wall of affirmations. She asked if she could take a portrait of the whole family, but I didn't want my other children's pictures in the press. So she posed the six of us on the rebounder, the trampoline in the backyard, our backs to the camera, mid-jump, none of us recognizable. *Now Marilyn won't let her children out of her sight,* says a caption. A lie. The boys go out of my sight, to school. We didn't get to see the pictures or captions before they went in the magazine. They put Mia and me on the cover. The photo was so retouched, we looked almost like sisters. The article called me a healer, which I'm not, and I've never claimed to be.

After that, we were glad to work with an IKEA public relations person who reached out to us. He offered us his expertise for free. We realized what his motivation was, that IKEA was just as eager to keep out of the news as we were. But, still, we were grateful. To help us avoid any more press, he suggested we sneak away for a few days. We went to Mount Shasta.

In the mountains, the six of us began to learn how to be a family.

75
MIA

The first day I was there, Marilyn kept asking if I was glad to be home, and I kept saying I was. But it didn't feel like home. Everything was different from the place I grew up in. The light was different. The smell was different. The furniture was different. There was wall-to-wall carpeting instead of bare floors. There was color everywhere, and decorations that Lucy would think of as clutter: candles and little flowerpots and embroidered pillows and crystals and little mirrors dangling from ceilings, making rainbows on walls. There were framed family photos on shelves and walls and side tables — baptisms, weddings, graduations. Seeing them made me feel sad at having been excluded.

It felt good to escape to the mountains. Trees, stars, mountains, moon — those things look the same wherever you are. So I did feel at home during those days we camped out, even though I hadn't been camping before. I'd been to camp, but that wasn't camping. At sleepaway camp, I slept on a bunk bed in a cabin with a bathroom inside it and trails paved with cedar chips so you'd never get lost and a camp chef to make any omelet you wanted.

This was real camping, in actual tents. I was impressed that Grant and the boys knew how to put up the tents, without even having to look at instructions. They put up a tent for them, and one for us girls. We slept in sleeping bags on special mats so the wet from the ground wouldn't seep through. We zipped up the tent at night, against mosquitoes and bears. The thought of bears didn't seem to bother them, but it terrified me and I made sure not to drink anything at night so I wouldn't have to get up to go to the bathroom. There was no bathroom, of course. You went in the woods, and I didn't want to risk it because I couldn't imagine being able to do what Grant told me to do if a bear charged: make myself stand there, waving my arms to look bigger. I knew I'd just run, which is the worst thing to do.

Grant's shoulder hurt from putting the tents up, and Marilyn rubbed peppermint oil on it, making the air smell like Christmas. I watched her, thinking this is what a normal family looks like. For the first time, I was part of one.

I loved waking to birdsong and the crackle of fire and to a mother toasting slices of bread on a stick, pouring tea from a tin pot heated over the flames, and it's like we are living in *Little House on the Prairie,* a book I was obsessed with when I was a kid.

Even here in the woods they say grace. We hold hands around the fire, bowing our heads, saying thanks for the food. They take turns saying the prayer and I bow my head to respect that.

"How come you don't ever say it," Thatch wanted to know, and I told him I didn't know any prayers. I grew up in a house where we didn't say them. "But you can be a good person without praying," I said as I was spooning apple quinoa from the pot into my bowl, and when I looked up, everyone had stopped eating. They were staring at me and I realized they were thinking my mom wasn't the greatest example of that.

"What do you believe in?" Chloe wanted to know.

"Herself," said Thatch under his breath, and I realized I'd have to be careful with him.

"Believing in yourself is a good thing,"

Marilyn said. "I'm glad Mia was taught that."

She looked over at me and our eyes met. I was grateful to her for coming to my rescue. But I kept eating, just wanting the subject to change.

I'm sorry for the kids. Their life is turned upside down, too. Connor wants to know why I want to keep my kidnapped name and I tell him it's hard to change a name you've had for twenty-one years. To me, Natalie is like a twin who died at birth, someone I never met.

Chloe asked if I miss my other mom, and before I can answer, Marilyn says, "She is not her other mom! She's her abductor!"

Which makes me feel, for some reason, dirty. It's like Lucy was some big ugly car splashing by in the rain, leaving us all splattered with mud.

I got up and went to the edge of the woods and breathed deep for a while, like Marilyn has taught me to do.

I've never tasted air this clean before. I feel like I'm bathing in its purity, that it is cleansing away the ugliness of what's happened. But once a bad thing happens to you, it keeps happening in your mind, over and over.

76
LUCY

In this country, numbers are considered auspicious. Eight is the most auspicious of all, Ada says, informing me of my double good fortune in my draw of room number: 88. She was surprised that hotel management hadn't given the room to a Chinese, who might have paid more for it. She says phone companies impose surcharges for numbers containing that numeral. Four, she says, is the opposite, a number to avoid because the word for four is the same as for death: *si*.

I sit with my pot of chrysanthemum tea at a corner table in my favorite place for breakfast, the Glad Cock Restaurant, and brace myself for my fourteenth day in this country, a day containing the unlucky number.

And then I walk to the Foreign Language Bookstore. At first, I think that nothing has changed. Steve Jobs and Henry Kissinger biographies are still in the window. But even before I make my way to the magazine section, I see what I've come for. The blood rushes out of me. There is Mia's face on the cover of *People* magazine. The headline in screaming tall type reads: KIDNAPPED SURVIVOR BEGINS LIFE WITH LONG-LOST MOM! My daughter, a survivor! As if I had done her physical harm. My eyes burn as I approach the rack. There is my daughter, pictured with Marilyn. The physical resemblance between them is striking: the same blue eyes, the same fair coloring, the cheekbones and shoulder span of a runway model. I can almost feel Mia's eyes raking over me. Is she glad to be with the beautiful mother, the good mother, the mother she should have had all along, instead of with me, the mother with the kind of looks no one notices?

I look right and left before I reach for the magazine, not wanting to be seen with it, as if it is porn. When it's in my hands, I rub my thumb over Mia's glossy cheek, and feel a jolt as if I am touching her actual skin. I don't dare open to the article in the store. What if my photo is in it? Shoppers are everywhere. Bookstores in America may be going out of business, but they seem to be thriving here. What if someone looking over my shoulder makes the connection? I take all three copies from the stand, then glance through a *Newsweek*. The story hasn't hit that magazine yet. I take a *Herald Tribune* from the newspaper rack and fold it around the glossy issues of *People* to conceal them, and slink up the aisle to check out, and make the transaction with cash, not wanting to risk a credit card that might alert the cashier to my name featured on the pages of the magazine I am buying. Perhaps the cashier has already read it. Perhaps she has sounded out my name, practicing English, so that my name is on the tip of her tongue.

I hurry out of the store and back to my hotel. It isn't until I am safely behind the closed door of my room that I dare open the magazine. I barely see through tears to read of Mia's joy in getting to know her "real mother." "Abductor" they call me. "Baby Snatcher." Nothing about how well I raised Mia, nothing about expensive schools and private tutors and bedtime stories and a full-time nanny and trips to beaches and Disney World. Nothing about how well she was loved.

Marilyn looks hippie-ish in her flyaway hair and loose garb, her arm around Mia, gazing proprietarily at the poised young woman I carefully raised, as if she had fashioned her whole in the basement, like one of her homemade ceramics. *The resemblance is unmistakable,* says the caption. But that kind of resemblance is only skin-deep.

The photo they used for me is an executive portrait used by the agency for pitches, in which I look stiff, my smile insincere. *Suspected to be hiding somewhere in China . . .*

Then I read something that makes my heart thump. . . . *where she'll be safe from the law as long as she stays because China and the U.S. don't observe extradition.*

I have a vague sense of what extradition is, but now I'm desperate to know its exact definition. I go to the computer in the lobby. I can't get Google, but I can get *Merriam-Webster* online.

Ex-tra-di-tion — the surrender of an alleged criminal.

So, if I stay in China, I can't be arrested? I type in "extradition of US criminals in China" (criminals! Typing the word brings tears to my eyes).

There is a blog post titled *The best countries for U.S. citizens to go to become invisible.* To my surprise, China is at the top of this list. According to the article (which was written by a lawyer), as long as I stayed in

China (not Hong Kong), I'd elude the reach of the U.S. law. Unwittingly, I'd managed to escape to a place where I can hide in plain sight.

But I hadn't left home thinking that I was leaving forever. I'd thought coming to China was only an interlude during which I'd gain needed distance to gather my wits and figure out how best to face down my future.

But could I stay? Could I do it? Did I have the mettle to abandon my career, my future, my family — any chance of reuniting with Mia?

And who would I be, stripped of everything that made my life recognizable where I knew no one but Wendy — but how could I explain my troubles to her?

What would I do, in a country where I didn't have friends, couldn't get work, couldn't speak a word of the inscrutable language? I was fifty-seven years old. According to research I'd read for an insurance pitch, chances were good, I'd live thirty-six more years. I didn't want to spend them all over here. But what was my alternative? Go home and rot for the rest of my life in a jail?

If convicted, she faces a maximum sentence of life in prison and a minimum sentence of twenty years.

I returned to my room and turned on the TV and spent the rest of the day staring at Qing Dynasty soap operas, alone on a narrow bed, in a fetal position, in a dark room that is numbered for luck.

77
MIA

I wish we could have stayed in the mountains forever. But we had to come back and talk to lawyers, each of whom had a thousand questions.

They gave us a pile of letters from people we don't know. Some addressed to me, some to Marilyn. Total strangers saying they're sorry for us. Most of them share their own sad stories. As if they knew us. Some send money enclosed in the envelope, which Marilyn puts in a special account that we'll give away to charity or something. We don't want that money. The letters are heartbreaking. Awful things happened to some of those kids. The lawyers won't let us answer them, which makes us feel guilty.

I'm taking an anger management workshop with Marilyn. My homework is to write in a notebook and throw rocks into the ocean, getting rid of the feelings I have for the woman who stole me. Today, I drove out to Devil's Slide with Marilyn and we stood on a cliff and let rocks fly from our fingers, saying Lucy's name, letting the hate out, driving it out of us so it doesn't seep in and poison our bones.

It's been over a month and Lucy still calls sometimes, but I never pick up. What the fuck does she want me to say? That it doesn't matter she stole me? That she was still my mother, no matter what heinous, horrible crime she committed? I don't want to speak to her, ever again.

In psych, we studied signs of a sociopath and Lucy has them all: charm, cunning, pathological lying.

What arrogance to think she was entitled to me. How dare she treat me like hers for the taking, a toy to dress up to send to expensive schools and camps so she could show off what a good mother she was. I thought she was a good mother. She was a good thief!

Now that I see Marilyn in action, I understand what a good mother is: selfless and caring and always there for her kids, who she builds her whole life around, keeping them happy and safe. I was never Lucy's priority; her work was. Ayi was always there doing drudgery while Lucy was getting ahead at her glamorous job. Ayi is the one who actually took care of me, made my favorite dishes, listened to me, held my hair back when I threw up, sat on my bed telling me stories to distract me from picking scabs off my chicken pox so I wouldn't get scarred. Lucy cared more about her computer than me!

On the drive home, I open the window to let in the smell of salt water and stretch out my arm and let my hair fly in the wind.

78
MARILYN

I thought I'd come to the place of forgiveness.

I've worked hard to heal the hole in my heart. I learned to live with my walking away from my child, which would turn out to mean walking away from her for twenty-one years.

I thought all the work I did with Sonya and others freed me from corrosive anger, resentment.

But every time I look at my daughter, I am overcome by new sorrow, realizing all that was taken from me. Today I saw a scar on her knee. Just a tiny scar, nothing disfiguring. Mia said she'd fallen, learning how to ride a bike. When she said this, my eyes went hot with tears. I should have been there, to steady her. If I had been there, I wouldn't have let her fall. I should have been by her side to see her first steps, her first word, her first day of school. I burn thinking of the woman who stole her from me. A woman with the mind-set that would allow her to steal an innocent child.

Detective Brown tells me they're on the case. An international arrest warrant has been issued for her. I ask why they can't just go get her in China, but he says they're not allowed to do that. They've frozen her passport. They've alerted Interpol. She can't stay in China forever, he tells me. The second she enters U.S. airspace, they'll arrest her. I don't want to hate people. There's already enough negative force in the world. But taking a child is taking a life. Someone who does that isn't deserving of grace or mercy.

79
CHERYL

When I turned the corner that day, after hearing the news, I saw TV trucks on our road. So I knew it was true, that Lucy was who they were talking about.

As soon as my tires crunched onto our driveway, truck doors opened and reporters spilled out. They rushed my van, which terrified me. Hands and cameras were everywhere suddenly and I was glad it was winter and my windows were up. I gunned the engine up the hill. I used the remote to open the garage, and how relieved I was when it went down behind me. Doug was already home. He'd had to pass through the same gauntlet. We called the boys. Both of them live in towns nearby. They were still at their jobs — Sam sells insurance and Jake teaches at a high school. They hadn't heard the news and no one had come to bother them yet.

Doug and I thought if we stayed inside,

behind closed doors and blinds, the reporters would get discouraged and go away. But they didn't. They stayed and stayed. Finally, that night, we opened our front door, and gave in to a few questions, thinking that would get rid of them. But the next day, we realized our mistake. The newspapers twisted our words in the statement, making it sound like I knew all along.

Lucy didn't call us until she was already in China.

"Is it true?" I asked her, and she said that it was. "How could you?" I shouted, and she said it was "complicated." That is so like her. Making what's straightforward appear to be complicated. Taking black and white and pretending it's gray.

What Lucy didn't think about is how doing what she did doesn't just affect her and Mia. It affects all of us. The paper isn't the *Emmettsville Echo* anymore. It merged with the county journal that now goes to every town in the district. We don't have a friend at the paper anymore, so Lucy's story was headline news.

Doug is on the school board and said no one mentioned a thing at the meeting, but also, no one wanted to sit next to him. Now Jake says his fiancée's parents are worried about her marrying into a family with criminal genes; he says the wedding is still on, but I wonder. I know the influence mothers have on their daughters. My own mother worried that Doug came from the wrong parish. We go late to church now so we don't have to talk to anyone.

I've spent my life trying to do the right thing: to be there for family, to be a good citizen. I never wanted a big life like Lucy did. I never wanted to stick out. And now she's made me famous all over town: a kidnapper's sister.

I know people assume I covered for her. Old friends from school knew I used to do that. Her teenage antics were harmless by today's standards, but I kept them secret from our mother, my stomach always clenched worrying she'd get hurt or do irreversible harm. But I didn't tell on her because we were sisters and sisters stuck together. That's how we were then.

Maybe I should have suspected something. But I only saw Lucy for holidays. Thanksgiving, Christmas. Those were busy days, my getting the house, the meals ready. There wasn't time for long, sisterly chats when I might have sensed something was wrong, or she might have divulged her secret to me.

I am grateful she didn't tell me her secret.

If I'd known, I would have been sick with having to keep it inside. I wouldn't have told, but I wouldn't have been able to live with it either. It's one thing to protect a relative who's done, say, a murder. Your telling won't bring the dead person back. But here, she had someone else's baby. The baby's poor parents waking up day after day, never knowing what happened to her. How could I have remained a silent party to that?

Of course, the one who's hurt most in all this is Mia. Poor Mia. I've tried to call her, but she doesn't answer her phone. Sam says she's taken down her Facebook page. Who can blame that poor girl.

I wrote her a real letter, addressing it to where her family lives in San Mateo. (Her family!) I told her how sorry I was to find out what happened. I wanted to let her know that we haven't abandoned her. We're still her aunt Cheryl and uncle Doug. Our door is always open to her.

80
MIA

We spent this weekend, just Marilyn and me, on a Forgiveness Retreat. It's a place where you go to get rid of your anger so it doesn't eat into you and cause cancer.

I hope that the person I hate most of all in the world stays in China forever. I cannot believe Marilyn can forgive her for what she did, but Marilyn says she's had decades of experience learning how to do it. She doesn't expect me to learn in one weekend.

The retreat was weird but actually helpful. It took place deep in beautiful woods. There were about twenty of us. I wasn't the youngest. There were a few teenagers, girls and boys, and I wondered what terrible thing had happened to them.

The first thing we did was pick out our drums. There were lots to choose from: big ones, little ones, leather-topped, plastic. The retreat leader, Meribelle, made Marilyn and me sit across from each other, twenty-one feet apart, the number of years we were separated. With wooden sticks, we hit the drums hard, pounding out messages to Lucy, all the things she deserved to hear. We didn't speak words, but the drums said it for us, as we hit at the skin of them, over and over.

Liar! Thief! You. Never. Were. My. Fucking. Mother. You were my captor! You ruined my life!

After that, we sat in a circle and Meribelle passed around pen and paper and told us to write down blessings for our object person. Lucy is my object person. I couldn't write anything. I walked into the woods and threw up instead. It was like I was emptying myself of the bad secret of those years, getting Lucy out of my life. Marilyn got up and came to me and held my hair back. She gave me a little packet of tissues. The tissues smelled like roses.

When we came back to the circle, Meribelle said all experiences must be treated as valuable. She asked me to say a good thing that had come from my bad experience. I couldn't think of one. Obviously, the retreat wasn't working for me.

But Marilyn hugged me and said she had one to offer. She told the group that if I hadn't been taken, I wouldn't be who I was and she loved me just the way I am. That made me cry. I guessed that's how a true mother feels. Lucy was never satisfied with the way I was, she was always trying to improve me. Dancing lessons, riding lessons, tutors, piano. I was never good enough for her, she was always concentrating on my outward manifestations. Lucy was all about outward manifestations.

81
MARILYN

A reunification specialist helped me see that just as I once accompanied Mia through the natural process of birth, now my job is to midwife her spirit, assisting at the birth of the new person she is becoming. I spent twenty-one years trying to find my daughter. Now I need to help my daughter find herself.

Mia's anger is fresh, like a fresh wound. The sooner it is attended to, the sooner it will heal. I don't want her to have to deal with anger years old, like mine. We are practicing Unmasking Yoga together — a healer comes to the house and helps us process our anger, helps us turn the heat into light.

We keep anger journals — all of us, the whole family. I want to include the other children in this process. I worry that my intense work with Mia might make them feel neglected. But if one of your children is on fire, you run to that child to put out the flames.

82
THATCH

Our family was fine until she came along.
Now we're all so pissed off, we have to keep
journals about it. I don't think Mom knows
who I am anymore, even though she still
sometimes brushes my back to help me
process things better, saying, "I love you, I
love you." Last night she was sitting on my
bed, doing the brushing thing and I looked
up and saw Mia in the doorway, eating out
of a bag of Goldfish, which Mom never allowed in the house until she showed up.
She's like an exchange student, allowed to
do anything. I knew Mom would get up
right away and go to her, and she did. Mia
doesn't ever come into our room. She told
Chloe it smells.

83
LUCY

I woke up last night, knowing something was wrong. The sheets were damp. One minute, I was burning; the next, shaking with chills. I assumed it was food poisoning, that perhaps I'd gotten it from a mango I'd bought on the street, which I stupidly hadn't washed before peeling. My head started to pound and I couldn't stop coughing. I've been coughing a lot since I came here. The pollution, I thought. But these coughs were worse. I popped some Advils I had brought from home, but they didn't help. I was suddenly thirsty. I longed for seltzer. Why is there no seltzer in China?

By dawn, I was convinced I'd acquired something awful. SARS? Bird flu? I imagined dying alone in that little room. The last thing I'd see would be a pink chair covered with white antimacassars and a door hanger warning guests not to smoke or do other disgusting behaviors in bed.

When it was finally morning, Ada rang me from the lobby and I told the desk to send her away. The room was now freezing. It was March, one of the coldest on record. The way the wall heater worked, it started ticking down the hour as soon as you put in the coins. I'd run out of the right coins. I drifted all day in and out of sleep and the next morning I lay beneath all of the clothes that I'd brought, and the hotel's thin towels, piled on top of me for warmth, but still, I was shivering. I didn't send Ada away again. I asked her to come up. The look on her face told me I was as bad off as I felt. Ada was scared, and I realized that underneath her sophisticated looks, she was just a kid. She couldn't help me. I gave her Wendy's number and asked her to call. I hadn't wanted to impose upon Wendy. What would I say? But fear made me do it. I needed her help. I needed a doctor.

Within the hour, Wendy and her husband were at my bedside, no questions asked. I wept with relief to see her familiar face, to feel the coolness of her hand on my face. The hospital they took me to was clean and efficient. I was nervous about trusting doctors I didn't understand, but I was reassured by Wendy's obvious faith in the kind, open-faced people wearing pristine white coats and jaunty white sailor's caps. Wendy stayed with me while the doctor examined me, staring at my tongue, which he coaxed farther than it's ever been from my mouth, probing my neck, pressing the cold eye of a stethoscope against my sweaty back. I was surprised to be comforted by the familiarity of that.

I couldn't understand a word he said and it took a long time for Wendy, flipping pages in her portable red vinyl-bound dictionary to find the right words to translate his diagnosis to me. It's the same little book she used to carry around when Mia was little. Now she needs reading glasses to make out its type.

She said something I couldn't understand and I looked to see where on the page she was pointing.

Pneumonia. My great-aunt had died of it. But that was in Scotland, before antibiotics.

Still, I was scared.

84
LUCY

How could I have managed without Wendy. She took me home with her after I left the hospital, telling me that her husband and son insisted I recuperate there. Their kindness is especially generous since their home isn't big, just four narrow rooms in a quaint old home on a cobblestone alley. Like my sister, Wendy lives in the same house she grew up in. Her parents are gone. Her mother passed away two years ago in the room I'm in now, which is Wendy's son's room. Lin professes not to mind sleeping on the sofa. He is thirty-six and waiting for a housing assignment, which he must receive before he can move out of his parents' house. The assignments go first to "marrieds." He says he will probably be waiting a long time.

Wendy is healing me with soups and teas and a soft rice dish she used to make when Mia was sick, *xi fan.* Mia used to beg for this, even when she was well, and now I know why. It is a rich, delicious concoction, like rice pudding.

I have no idea what medicine I am taking. Three times a day, I swallow a spoonful of sweet sticky dark medicine poured from a bottle labeled with what looks like grapes. Wendy says they are loquats. I also take pills. They are pink and shiny and enormous as horse pills. Whatever they are, they seem to be working. There was no charge for medicine, or for the treatment. I'm not sure whether this is because Wendy arranged it, or because socialized medicine is free to everyone, even foreigners. Wendy says being a doctor in China is a service job, like being a teacher.

I am writing this at Lin's computer, wearing — at Wendy's insistence — white gloves, so I don't pass on my germs, though the doctor says my contagion is over.

Lin's computer gets Internet. He's rigged it with something called VPN, which is a way to jump over the Great Firewall of China. I don't have e-mail anymore. The company must have suspended my account. I should have listened to the kids in the office who warned me to keep a personal account. I used to have AOL but closed the account after I unknowingly sent porn to everyone on my address list.

I'm surprised how much I miss the office. I used to look forward to escaping from it, not only vacations with Mia, but little getaways I'd give myself to preserve my sanity. Sometimes I'd leave for lunch early and take in a movie. If an end-of-day meeting was canceled, I'd surprise Wendy and take Mia to the park, and how privileged I felt to be with her then, getting to see my daughter as I rarely did, bathed in the caramel light of a late afternoon.

But now I'd give anything for office camaraderie, mindless chatter about weather or even awkward elevator silence. Of course, my desire for that is nothing compared to my longing for the company of Mia. The pain of missing her never goes away, like a bruise I keep touching to see if it still hurts.

85
LUCY

In Wendy's home, I try to make myself as unobtrusive as possible.

We have a routine. I wake at six, with their alarms, which have a funny, foreign sound. You wouldn't think beeps can sound foreign, but they can: *breep, breep, breep.* Sometimes the beeps are superfluous. One of the neighbors keeps a rooster, and many mornings, his riling crow long precedes the alarm. The house is ancient, but the walls are thin. I stay in bed, still woozy from illness, trying not to cough, listening to the sounds of the family getting ready for work. I revel in not having to get up to join them. I am unemployable here, my career is gone, and while that carries terrors and regrets, I do enjoy the prospect of not having to get up in the morning.

There is only one bathroom. I hear the rush of water in the pipes, the hawks of toothpaste into the sink. Then the screech of the teakettle, the twang of utensils, the drone of a TV announcer singing the news. Chinese speech is tonal and sounds like song. I'm glad that Chinese news is mostly about China. I smell *baozi* steaming, little pillows of dough that hold delectable meats rolled inside them, like secrets.

They're all gone by seven. Wendy to her job at a cosmetics counter, Feng to his inspector duties, Lin to his bank — and when I hear the front door close, I drift back to sleep if I can, then wake to reheat the water in the kettle for tea. It is a big iron kettle, weighty and old, its wooden handle indented with impressions made over time by the thumbs of Wendy's mother and grandmother.

Though I've told her not to, Wendy leaves me my favorite breakfast, tea eggs: brown eggs boiled in five-spice powder, then marinated in shells that are cracked so the whites turn speckled, like brown stained glass. Wendy says the eggs are good for my chi.

Her job is a good one, she says. She gets a commission on the makeup she sells. A friend of her family found it for her after she came back from the States. The irony is, she came to the States to make money, but says that while she was gone the Sleeping Dragon woke up and now people who stayed in Shanghai got richer than people who left to seek fortune elsewhere. I wonder if she regrets leaving Lin for all those years, and if he minds having been raised without her. But of course, I don't have the language — nor the audacity — to ask this.

Wendy comes home at three, her net bag full of groceries she has transported by bicycle. She changes out of her work uniform: dark pants and white jacket with her name in red stitching over the pocket. The characters of her name look like little dogs fighting. Then she goes downstairs for exercise. She swing-dances! Apparently, this is replacing tai chi as the favorite exercise here. She meets others her age — mostly women — in the courtyard. I sometimes watch from a window. They gather around a portable CD player bellowing out old American campfire tunes like "Moon River" and dance as people do in black-and-white movies. After an hour, she comes upstairs and I sit in the kitchen with her as she starts chopping vegetables. She won't let me help. She's still afraid of my germs.

Chop, chop, chop. I am transfixed by the way she jumps a fat cleaver over onions and carrots and ginger and beans, transforming them in an instant from one piece to many.

I haven't yet told her why I am in China. I can't bring myself to confess it to her. What will I do if she turns me out?

86
MIA

I'm three weeks older than I thought I was. Lucy not only changed my birthday, she changed my birth sign.

All my life, I read horoscopes, thinking I was a Taurus, the bull: plodding, slow, not wanting to move. I used to picture myself as Ferdinand, from the little kid's book, sitting under the tree, just smelling the flowers.

But I never wanted to just sit around smelling flowers. Whenever that book was read to me, I thought how unlike Ferdinand I was. If I were him, I wouldn't have wanted to sit in the field, I would have chosen the more exciting life in the bullring.

Now it makes sense. I'm Aries instead. It's a fire sign, meaning you've got a lot of energy.

For my birthday, Marilyn took me to have my chart read. I didn't want to, at first, but I could see it was really important to her and it was the first birthday she ever got to celebrate with me, so I felt like I owed her. It was a nice ride. The astrologer's house was high in the hills near San Francisco, a redwood cabin she built, way back in the woods. To get to her front door from the driveway, we had to cross a footbridge over a little stream and I was glad I'd worn Vans because the heels of Marilyn's sandals kept getting stuck. The door was an arch made of old wood, the windows were stained glass, and as soon as it opened, you could see cats jumping around on carpeted play shelves. It made me miss Pumpkin. A girl in our building is taking care of him. We text about him.

In Sonya's house, the cat smell was strong. There were about five cats there and I saw the place as Lucy would see it: the home of a crazy cat-lady psychic. Lucy would have disdain for what we were doing. But why do I care what she thinks, anymore? Why do I care about the thoughts of someone who isn't my mother, who isn't anything to me.

The first thing Sonya did, she looked at my hands.

"See how the lifeline diverges here?" she said, pressing a bloodred nail into my palm. "That denotes trauma in the first year of life."

Of course, she already knew what happened to me as a baby. But still, it was interesting to hear how planets play a part in what happens to you.

Like this year, Pluto crosses my sun. It's the planet of profound change, making you conscious of what is happening around you.

"Your wisdom will come in the penumbra," she said. I didn't know what she meant.

"It's the area between complete darkness and complete light," she explained. "The shadow that happens when two bodies pass."

I asked who I was going to marry. But she said she couldn't predict things like that.

87
MARILYN

Sonya helped me a lot when I first came to California. She helped me trust my instinct that my daughter was still a living light in this world. She taught me to honor my sacred energy. I went to her after I met Grant, to see if he and I were a good match. I wanted to be sure I wasn't making a mistake. Sonya assured me that Grant was a good, loving man who could support my journey. Our charts were compatible.

I often went to Sonya's around Natalie's — Mia's — birthday. All those empty birthdays I ached to hold my firstborn. I'd never gotten to celebrate even one birthday with her. The day she turned one, she'd been gone for eight months.

Last April, Sonya said she felt the nearness of a strong healing. What does that mean? I wanted to know. That my daughter would be found? Or that she wouldn't be found and that I would make peace with it?

Making peace with it would have been impossible, I thought.

Sonya said she couldn't apprehend the specifics, could only say that some kind of change felt imminent to her. A few months later, I was in the bookstore, listening to the voice of the woman who had taken her from me.

Spiritual intelligence brought my daughter back to me. I want her to know the power of that kind of intelligence.

88
MIA

After doing my chart, Sonya led us out the back door to a garden with looking-glass balls in the grass and crystals tinkling in the trees. At the edge of a pond was a little stone fire pit where low flames were burning.

Sonya handed me a piece of paper, tissue-thin with gold at the edges. "This is a receptacle for all your fears and worries," she said, "for all the things you're afraid of, all the things that terrify you. Crumple it up as hard as you can and throw it into the fire."

I looked at Marilyn. She stood next to Sonya. They were both looking at me with earnest eyes and I felt some sort of wall of resistance crumbling inside me. Why not believe, as they do, in the force of good in the world? Belief in something is the first step to making it happen — that's one of the posters I wake up to every morning. It's above Chloe's bed in the little room she's sharing with me. My snarky New Yorker side tells me it's corny, but a lot of things I believed in turned out not to be true. Maybe I need another system.

I took the piece of paper and rolled it into a ball and crushed the ball with my divergent lifelines.

"Make a wish as you throw," Marilyn said, and I had to stop for a moment to think what my wish was. What I've wished a lot since February was that my life could rewind, that I could go back to normal, that everything could be as it used to be, that I wouldn't know what I know, that I could wake up and be just a kid again, happy. I closed my eyes and wished the sun would bore into my brain and burn away my memory of Lucy.

89
MARILYN

After Mia made a wish — of course I
wondered what it was, I hoped it had nothing to do with Lucy — we took her for a
walk to the top of the hill, where it's windy
and the winds come strong enough to blow
away all negativities and you feel new
energy, new life coming in.

Sonya and I joined hands, making a tiny
circle around Mia, our hands joining at her
elbows.

Sonya gave her a life blessing: *Now your
life is blessed, rich and full in every direction.
You are now connected to the truth of your
being, you can never be lost or stolen again.*

And I gave her a mother's blessing. My
voice shook as I said: *I love you and have
loved you since this day twenty-two years ago
when you came through me, onto the earth.*
She has my grandmother's laugh, my father's eyes. I leaned in to kiss her and her
hair grazed my neck and I brimmed with

gratitude for her blazing nearness to me.

Her face was flushed. She smiled shyly at us and I wished we could stay in that magical moment, on top of that hill, protecting my daughter forever in the womb of our arms.

90
MIA

When we got home from Sonya's, there was crepe paper and balloons.

I never had a homemade birthday cake before. Ayi didn't bake. Lucy always ordered cakes from a fancy bakery on the East Side. They looked perfect and tasted good, too, but it was awesome having a homemade cake. This cake was lopsided, icing pink with pomegranate juice and animal crackers in a parade all around the sides to remind me, Chloe said, of the Central Park Zoo, which I'd told her was one of my favorite places to go as a kid. I loved to go sit in a dark room and watch polar bears behind glass doing water ballet, and Chloe said that even though she's never been there, now it is her favorite place, too.

How different this birthday is than last year. My friends gave me a blowout party for twenty-one. We started in Middlebury and ended up in New York, watching the sunrise over Coney Island. I feel a tug, remembering them. They wouldn't recognize me now. I don't recognize myself.

Where is the girl who always knew what she was about? I made to-do lists when I was in kindergarten, even ones for the cat. I asked for a Filofax for my twelfth birthday. I had five-year plans when I was a teenager. Where is that girl so sure of herself? I don't know.

After I cut the cake, presents. Chloe gave me a Magic 8 Ball. Connor and Thatch gave me funny yoga socks. Grant gave me a wooden box that he made and inside was Marilyn's gift: photos taken when I was a newborn, pictures I'd never seen before, snapshots of a tiny baby wrapped in a striped blanket and a little knit hat. Staring at that baby, I swallowed back tears, knowing what was about to happen to her.

91
LUCY

April 4. Today is a national holiday here. Not because of Mia's birthday, of course. It's the Qing Ming festival, Chinese Day of the Dead.

I imagine Mia celebrating her real birthday for the first time and I feel the breath knocked clean out of me. Other years, I'd celebrate this day without her knowing it, taking her out for a prebirthday dinner, or letting her have one of her presents early.

Wendy and her family are out of the house, having gone to sweep the graves of their ancestors and to bring them gifts. They left carrying bowls of bananas and litchis, kumquats, and pears. Lin brought a bottle of maotai and millions in paper money. He told me that in the old days, people used to bring real gold. But there were too many grave robberies. Now, people burn gold paper instead.

The air-quality app is orange today, which

means the air in Shanghai is clean enough to open the windows. As I pull back ancient wood sashes, spring breezes blow in, clearing the air of smoke from the joss, little sticks of incense. They're burning in front of a little altar to Wendy's parents and grandparents set up atop a dining room chest.

How can I repay Wendy and her family for their generosity to me? Here, in their country, I have nothing to offer. I burn a dollar on their altar, between sticks of incense, murmuring my thanks.

Sad songs of mourning float in from the street, the volume rising and falling, from families on their dutiful way to the graves. I, too, mourn someone lost, overcome with desire for the company of my daughter. How glad I am to find myself alone in the house, to be able to pace the rooms and sob with abandon, instead of having to muffle my cries in a pillow as I do when thoughts of what I have done, of what I have lost, trouble me so that I can't sleep at night.

I find a square of golden paper on the floor. Lin must have dropped it on his way out the door. I put it into an ashtray and take it to my room — Lin's room — and sit before a photo of Mia, in a silver oval frame. It used to sit on top of our piano. I use one of his lighters to set fire to the paper, watching it light up her smile, then relegate her to darkness as it burns down to nothing, as I mourn, along with millions, the loss of my loved one.

92
LUCY

Once, years ago, I came upon Wendy standing at the living room window, looking out. I asked if something was wrong. She turned to me with tears in her eyes. "I am not a Chinese anymore," she said. "I am also not an American person. I'm a no-country woman."

That is what I am, in this place of refuge. A no-country woman. I'm lucky, of course, to have a refuge. But how would it feel to spend the rest of my life here? I can't work without papers. But even if I had them, what work could I get, not being able to speak the language? I'm studying with a tutor, but I don't expect I'll ever master it. One of the few words I thought I knew in Chinese was the word for "light." It was Mia's first word. *Dengdeng*, Wendy taught her to say, pointing to track lights in the ceiling. But my tutor tells me *dengdeng* isn't the word for "light." The word for "light" is *deng. Dengdeng* is baby talk, like calling a horse "horsie." Word repetition is used only by children. I'll always sound like a child here, with childish thoughts, an imbecile.

I am sweeping the front stoop with an ancient straw broom and a breeze undoes my work with a drift of cherry blossom petals. Beside the stoop is a bush with a frenzy of yellow foliage growing out of it, wild as Mia's hair used to look coming out of the shower, before she'd take her wide-toothed comb to it. How oppressed I sometimes felt by that hair, by her desire to leave it unmanaged, her refusal to brush it, claiming that brushing ruins the ends. She'd read that somewhere, a claim that seemed preposterous to me, who was raised to believe in the habit of brushing one hundred strokes every day. How much stock I put in her neat appearance, which, to me, meant a glossy sheet falling sleekly down the back of her uniform blouse. Now I see that her desire to leave her hair untamed was a harmless attempt to claim individuality. I'm sorry I discouraged it. I'm sorry, I breathe useless apology into the wind. Mistakes I made as a mother. Regrets. Mia's days were proscribed: playdates and practices and after-school activities fit together as tightly as puzzle pieces. There were no unplanned spaces in which a mind could idle. I should have allowed her boredom. I should have been less indulgent, more vigilant. I should have spent more time with her after Wendy left. Would Marilyn have done better? I can't let my mind go there.

I can't get a job.

I can't make friends among expats who would surely see me for only the worst thing I have done.

My visa is good for seven more months. And then what? What will happen to me?

The falling blossoms make a pink path and I imagine following it, setting out on a road to oblivion.

93
MIA

Today, Marilyn asked me about Lucy.

She was kneeling on little pads she
strapped to her knees, not looking up from
the row of arugula she was picking for dinner. I was filling a basket with cherry
tomatoes. Gardening is new to me and I
still haven't stopped being amazed by being
able to walk into your backyard and pick
out a meal.

"Was she a good mother?" Marilyn wanted
to know.

Marilyn never asked about Lucy this
directly before and I never wanted to talk
about her to anyone here. Especially Marilyn. Why would she want to talk about my
having another mom. I can't call Marilyn
"Mom." I try not to call her anything.

When I didn't know what to say, she stood
up with her basket and I watched her kneel-
ers go back and forth on her legs as she
came to help me with the tomatoes.

Lucy wasn't a "homey" mother like Marilyn was, who made us purple juice for breakfast every day, surprisingly tasty, waking us with the roar of a mixer spotting the wall tiles with colorful specks of kale, beets, carrots, who only served us bread she'd made herself, who kept a huge freezer in the garage stocked with homemade snacks in frosty Ziplocs. The only things in our little freezer in New York were pints of Häagen-Dazs and blue ice-wraps left over from my high school sports injuries.

Lucy hadn't been there to greet me after school with snacks and questions about my day — Ayi had done that. She hadn't cooked except when Ayi wasn't there, and then we usually had takeout. Lucy didn't spend anywhere near the time being a mother that Marilyn did. So I said what seemed true, and what I knew Marilyn wanted to hear. "She wasn't as good a mother as you."

But as soon as I said it, my stomach lit with flashes of memory: the smell of Lucy's shirt as I sat behind her, on a bike seat, passing runners in Central Park, the thrill I felt as one of them high-fived me; making homemade Play-Doh with her at the stove when she let me stir and add drops of color; her hands covered in glue as she stayed up all night with me in fifth grade, fixing my map of Egypt out of papier-mâché; her excitement when I got the part of Tom in Tom Sawyer, regretting she couldn't be there opening night, but then she flew home early from a meeting in London, surprising me in the front row. She'd bring me on shoots for commercials where I did my homework in a director's chair, everyone going out of their way to be nice to me, because she was the boss. Once, I saw Sarah Jessica Parker in an elevator; *Sex and the City* was shooting on a different floor and Lucy spoke up and introduced me, as if I were somebody.

Marilyn's eyes were shaded by the big straw hat she wears to shield her face from wrinkles, but when she adjusted it, I could see tears. I saw I'd said the wrong thing. She didn't want to hear that my childhood hadn't been perfect.

"But I loved growing up in New York," I added. "I liked going to museums on school field trips and musicals on Broadway and *The Nutcracker* at Christmas and have school recess in Central Park and a sleep-over birthday party at the Plaza once, like Eloise." Suddenly I got an ache in my stomach. I missed it all. I missed my mom. I missed sitting on opposite sofas, watching *Gilmore Girls* with her. I missed my bed, I missed my room, I missed things I didn't expect, like the smell of our house, which is a place I can never go back to. It would make me too sad.

"Mommy, look!" Chloe's voice rang out from the other side of the yard, where she was jumping on the trampoline they call a rebounder. Each of us was supposed to use it a half hour a day to transport nutrients through our system, to drain our tissues of toxins.

But Marilyn didn't look. Her arms were going around me in a hug. I smelled the sweet peppermint Dr. Bronner's we all used instead of gels or soaps that have aluminum in them.

Usually, when Marilyn hugged me, I relaxed into her arms, but this time something in me resisted.

"Mommy, look!" Chloe called again, bounding higher this time. There was no way she could hurt herself, the trampoline was shielded by a protective wall of netting.

"I'm looking," I called to Chloe, but I knew my attention wasn't what Chloe wanted.

94
MARILYN

Mia's not getting enough rest. Chloe wakes up sometimes and sees her reading her iPad in bed. I tell Mia that screen light depresses her melatonin, but she doesn't listen.

When she was born, after the scare in the delivery room, they put her into my arms and I didn't recognize her. She was long and thin and dark. Not the plump, pink-cheeked baby I'd imagined was floating inside me. At first, she didn't seem related to me. She seemed like a stranger. But after a few days, that stranger evolved into Natalie — and I came to understand her and her wants and needs almost better than I did my own. So I thought that maybe my daughter's coming back to me was like this. Someday soon I'd understand all of her again because she was once a physical part of me.

I put lavender drops on her pillow, but she still can't sleep.

95

LUCY

The Blind People's Massage Parlor. Wendy says a massage will realign my chi. She says massages are medicinal here, good for the health. The massage parlor isn't a spa, it's more like a clinic. No scented candles or fluffy white robes or sweating pitchers of cucumber water. Outside the entrance, two old ladies stretch out on vinyl Barcaloungers, reading newspapers, while white-coated men on stools rub their purpled, gnarly feet.

Inside, in the massage section, shower curtains separate paper-covered mattresses that are flat as cutting boards, and almost as hard. How different from massage rooms I am used to, humming with soft music and white-noise machines. Under low-watt bare bulbs, I take off my shirt and pants and fold them on a plastic stool and nest my face in a hole flowering with paper towels. Soon foreign fingers are divining my ills, the silence broken only by the rustle of the curtains, a distant cough or a groan. The *slap, slap, slap* indicating that a session is over.

The hands work over my shoulders, kneading the muscles on either side of my spine, relieving me of the weight I am carrying, granting blissful distraction, temporary respite from the weight of my bones.

I am a child again. It is a dream so real I feel I am standing in the old bedroom I shared with my sister, Cheryl. Cheryl isn't there. The door to our closet is open and I notice that the closet is a lot bigger than I'd realized. It is big as a field — in fact it *is* a field, and standing in the middle of it is a horse. I run through the tall grass to pet his coat gleaming like honey. He doesn't have a saddle and I run my hand over his bumpy back and wish I knew how to ride him. The horse nuzzles me in a way that seems an invitation to mount him, and once astride, I see that riding is a simple matter. All I have to do is hold on to the ropelike strands of his mane. The horse moves swiftly, but his back doesn't sway. We keep up a good clip across the field, which ends in a row of houses. When we get to the houses, the horse doesn't stop. He runs right through them. We whoosh through living rooms, dining rooms, down narrow hallways, and out back kitchen doors. The horse is surprisingly adept at avoiding furniture, but he breaks his stride for a narrow spiral staircase. We stop. There is my mother, still alive, coming downstairs, young enough to be wearing makeup first thing in the morning. Right behind her is my father with all of his hair. He'd left us as soon as he lost it, when I was five. There they are, so young and attractive, and I hold my breath, hoping the horse will keep us in shadows so they won't see us. It is of great importance that they don't see us. But the horse bolts out from under me and I see it isn't a horse at all. It is Mia, running from me, her golden hair flying. I scream to her but I have no voice.

I wake, embarrassed to discover that I am sobbing. At first, I am relieved to remember that the masseur can't see me. But of course, he must have felt vibrations racking my back.

96
LUCY

Wendy took me to a wedding today. The bride was her cousin's niece, a relationship for which the Chinese have a word, as there seems to be a word for every relation here, no matter how distant — except for a daughter you raised who is no longer your daughter. There is no word in any language for that.

I wore a dress I'd brought from home. I put it on for the first time since I've been in China and was happily surprised at how loosely it fell over my hips. I don't have a scale, but I suspect I have lost the ten pounds I've been trying to get rid of for years. Partly due to the illness, of course. But also because I eat healthier here — vegetables fresh from the market, tiny portions of meat. In Wendy's home, meat is eaten sparingly, added for flavor, not as a dish in itself, unless the meal is for celebration of something. I think back to the days when she cooked for us, in my kitchen. Our appetite for full chickens, legs of lamb, must have appalled her.

The wedding was beautiful. The ceremony was outdoors and the bride wore white, an unconventional choice because red is the traditional color here for bridal wear, white being the traditional signifier of death. White was reserved for funerals until recently, when the "one-child" generation was sent abroad to be educated and started bringing home Western ways.

When Mia was growing up, we'd sometimes plan her wedding together. She'd loved to look at dresses in magazines when she was little. Now, when it comes time to plan her wedding, I won't be there.

I was the only Westerner in attendance. But the language of food is universal, and all of us around the embroidered cloth tables communed in our enjoyment of the elaborate feast: five kinds of fish and roast pig and dragon shrimp (lobster) and chicken cooked in red oil to symbolize prosperity for the new couple.

We toasted them with maotai in little brass cups. Maotai is strong! At first, it tastes sweet, but going down it feels like you're swallowing jet fuel. I was tipsy after a few toasts, and so, I could tell, was Wendy, who

I've never seen take a drink of even wine before. We both needed the loo and we made our way toward the door, but the line was long and we waited together on a red velvet sofa.

Suddenly, for some reason, it seemed like the right moment to speak. Perhaps my courage was bolstered by the maotai, or the fortifying presence of a noisy crowd. Wendy sat there laughing at a little niece twirling around and around in her ring-girl dress (Chinese have ring girls; boys are entrusted only to carry flowers), but she stopped laughing when she saw my serious face.

"I have something important to tell you," I said.

She fixed me with an inviting expression and I remember thinking that after I spoke, I might never see her look kindly at me again.

I told my story, and when I had run out of words, she leaned forward, taking my hand in hers, pressing my palms with her steadying thumbs.

"How is Mia?" she asked.

"I don't know," I said. "She won't talk to me."

Wendy's eyes grew wet. She looked down at our entwined hands. We didn't say anything for a while. Then, she said she had something to tell me, too.

97
WENDY

This story I never tell any person. But tonight, I tell Lucy.

In 1979, I gave birth to a daughter. Lin was three years old then. In my country, a new rule became law in 1978: One Family, One Baby. Babies were rationed, like eggs and rice. More babies were allowed families who lived in the countryside, but we lived in Shanghai, so our rule is One Baby. Lin is One Baby. If we have Two Babies, we will lose our good status. We must pay many fines. When I was pregnant, people come to my home. Nurses, doctors, even my own mother talk to me, talk to me, saying I need to give up my baby. They want me to take medicine, make baby die before it is born. They say number two baby is not good for Lin, not good for us. But I want to keep my baby, and so does Feng. We think maybe this rule will change.

Many things are changing in China at this

time. For years, no one was allowed to sell any wares. Then, one morning, I am biking to work and I see a man by the side of the road selling cabbages. If the man is still there when I ride back, I think this means big change coming for China. That afternoon, the man was still there. So, we think maybe this means that the One Baby rule can change, too. But it doesn't.

When my baby is born, Feng works in another province and cannot come home. My baby is a girl. I am so happy to have a daughter. I name her Jin, that means "gold," because she is precious like gold to me.

I stay in the hospital ten days, this is normal in China at that time. When I am in hospital, I get a visit from the local police. A man comes with a big plastic satchel to collect my fine. The fine is so high the number scares me. But I say I will pay. Come back, I tell him. My husband will come with the money.

That night, very quietly, I leave the hospital with my baby. She is a good baby, she never make cry. I love this baby but I know I cannot keep her. I cannot ruin the good lives of my husband and son. I put her in a basket, wrap her in soft blanket. I tie a string around her wrist with a gold ring from my grandmother. I want who gets her to know she comes from a good family.

Chinese people say you have to use up all your energy to go forward, otherwise you cannot get there. I use up all my energy to make my feet take my baby to the foreigner hotel. Before we get there, I sit on a bench with Jin and feed her until she falls asleep. I don't want her to see what I have to do. When she is sleeping, I carry her basket to the front of the hotel. I put her basket down on the top step in front of a big wooden door. I wait nearby, behind a tree, looking out to see who will find her. Everything in my stomach is up, not down.

Finally, a tall man opens the door and I cry out because he is not looking and I am afraid he might step on her. But he sees her. He looks down at her, then up at where I am hiding. I am afraid he sees me, even though this is impossible. Finally, he stops looking and picks up the basket and goes back through the heavy door and I never see my daughter again.

I write Feng that our baby died in the hospital.

Every day I take care of Mia, I think about my daughter and hope she gets a good life like her. When I come to New York, I see many Chinese girls are adopted and sometimes I wonder if Jin is near.

If Jin knows I give her away, she thinks she has a bad mother. But really, she has a mother who loves her.

Mia has a mother who loves her, too. Lucy did a bad thing. But this is one bad thing against twenty-one years of good things. Lucy must think of this. Mia, too.

98

LUCY

July 4. Independence Day. I have my own apartment. Wendy and Feng helped me find it. It isn't fancy. It isn't big. Just two rooms, furnished, each about the size of my kitchen in New York. It's owned by Feng's cousin who is working in Xian. He had to apply to rent to a foreigner. The floors and walls are cement and everything was covered with coal dust when I got here. I spent a cathartic few days on my hands and knees, scrubbing.

The kitchen is stocked with spices, and the first day I attempted to cook, I mistook the sugar for salt and ruined the vegetables. The Chinese store their salt in big tins, their sugar in tiny jars. Everything is upside down here.

I made dinner for Wendy and her family last night, to thank them. It was a simple meal, but here even a simple meal can be hard to prepare. My stove isn't a real stove, it's a tin box with two burners that sits, ter-rifyingly, on top of a wooden table. You open a flap on the box and light the gas and close the box quickly before the table catches fire. There is no oven.

I wanted to serve something American, but not *too* American, which I feared might be off-putting to Feng and Lin, who have eaten Chinese food every day of their lives. I decided on spaghetti. It's a dish that even I, with minimum cooking skills, could execute with a modicum of confidence. (For daily sustenance, I rely on local eateries, which abound.)

Spaghetti isn't technically an American dish, but it's a menu item often found on American tables. I knew they'd like noodles. Noodles was a frequent dish at their table during the months I was living with them.

The apartment came with a bike, a sturdy three-speed Flying Pigeon, and that morn-ing I pedaled twenty blocks to Carrefour to purchase real butter and imported Parme-san cheese and Ronzoni No. 8, not Chinese noodles, which are thicker and have a wheatier taste. Then to the French quarter to buy a baguette to transform into buttery garlic bread. Then to the vegetable market for tomatoes. The tomatoes here are huge and bright red and the best I've ever tasted.

I try not to think of the fertilizer that helps grow them: night soil, euphemism for waste collected at night from the public toilets.

Finally, I went to the reliable meat market where I know, from Wendy, you can trust the ground beef. I knew to bring my own plastic bag. The first time I shopped there, I didn't know any better and they gave me the bloody mass in a plastic bag fine as tissue, which ripped, of course, on the way home. A little white dog on the sidewalk lapped it up, horrifying its owner, a young woman in high heels shouldering a Louis Vuitton bag, who tugged on its leash, trying to pull it away. The dog wore pearls — some owners dress up their poodles here — and seeing the little mutt-matron go at raw meat with primal enthusiasm was a sight I'll not soon forget.

Wendy has visited my apartment since I moved in, but Feng and Lin hadn't and they seemed to delight in seeing the cousin's apartment "Americanized."

"So much light," Lin said, apparently impressed by my lamps from IKEA.

Yes, I went to IKEA. I made myself go. It's the best place in Shanghai to buy Western furnishings at a good price. I'd thought the store would look different, but IKEA here is the same big box it is in New

401

Jersey, painted the same bright blue and yellow, a startling contrast to the gray concrete buildings and beams supporting the highway behind it, so that when I got out of the cab, having peeled brown notes into the driver's white-gloved hand, the site triggered a rush of memory and I didn't think I could go in. But the turquoise car was already a dot in the distance.

I stood on the sidewalk, trying to get control of my breath. Don't be ridiculous, I told myself. I needed things for the apartment I could get only here, where signs were assured of being in English. Besides, it was hot. It wasn't yet noon, but the sun was already bearing down on the back of my neck. The relief of industrial air-conditioning was just steps away.

My heart started palpitating as soon as I walked through the doors and I was suddenly afraid that some sophisticated detector, some global, all-seeing robot was embedded in the ceiling, would train his infrared eyes on me, reach down and seize me. But after I'd walked a few aisles, my common sense prevailed and I proceeded to shop, untormented by paranoid apprehensions.

The merchandise was the same as I remembered: colorful building blocks of furniture, open storage units, melamine closets, and chrome forests of lamps, but one thing was different. The room displays, the little stage sets of domestic tranquillity of which I'd once been so enamored, were occupied by customers sprawling all over the furniture. People sat at dining room tables, reading newspapers, or took naps on beds, getting under the covers. Whole families spread out on sectionals, watching films on their phones or letting kids bounce on coffee tables. Two middle-aged women dozed on opposite ends of a sofa, snoring loudly, heads resting comfortably on the pillowed backrest. A couple interested in the price of it had to gingerly move a hand to reveal the tag.

I came upon a baby asleep on a daybed, atop a sheep-pattern quilt. She looked to be about six months old. Her fine black hair was gathered into two narrow tails that stood straight up at the top of her head and were secured by pink ribbons. Her cheeks had deepened to red the way babies' cheeks do when they're asleep for a while. She was on her back, arms and legs flung wide, and across her middle, an embroidered floral handkerchief rose and fell, which the mother must have improvised for a blanket.

I lit with anger at the mother for recklessly

trusting her baby to the mercy of strangers.
I lingered by the bedside, compelled to keep
discreet watch over her, pretending to focus
on cube shelving and modular tables instead
of the heartbreaking tenderness of that
handkerchief rising and falling, showing me
the monstrousness of what I had done. Now
I would never be capable of it. Because I
have a child. I know what the stakes are.

Yet — I couldn't wish I hadn't done it
either. I'd never regret my years of loving
Mia, being loved by her.

When a harried-looking woman in her
thirties approached the bed and bent over
the baby, I knew by the proprietary way she
picked her up, still sleeping, and gently laid
her against her shoulder, that she was the
mother. It was as if they were two halves
coming together, and I was queasy with the
knowledge of what I had inflicted on a pair
such as these, when I'd been oblivious to all
but the ache of my own empty arms.

I couldn't shop that day. I made my way
through living dioramas and out of the store
and figured out how to shop IKEA by
phone, pressing 3 for English, so it was
weeks before lamps and chairs and wall-size
framed prints were on their way to my
apartment, teetering on the back of deliv-
erymen's bicycles.

Dinner conversation was mainly between Wendy and me. Feng speaks no English and Lin's English is wanting, though Wendy brags that he studied it and passed every test with superior grades.

"We learn for test, not for talk," Lin explained, shrugging.

Lin glazed his noodles with a thin layer of meat sauce, until I urged him to take more. Chinese manners can make people too restrained.

How much does Lin know about me? Has Wendy told him? Has she shared my story with Feng?

I watch their faces, but there are no clues in their eyes as we talk about weather — hot! — and the food — delicious! Our topics are limited, without shared vocabulary. I find myself agreeing, at Wendy's urging, to meet Lin on Sundays, his day off, for English conversation practice. I'm glad. I'm in need of company and grateful for the chance to glimpse through his native eyes the country where I may be exiled for the rest of my life.

99
Lin

Dinner at the American Ayi's house tonight. So many lights! What does one lady need so many lights for? I counted six lights in the apartment — table lights, wall lights, even a bed light. Such extravagance. At home, we have only one light in each room. I think Lucy must have regretted this scarcity while living with us.

Unfortunately, her extravagance did not extend to our meal. Only three dishes, not the many dishes one expects to be set out for guests. One of the dishes was spoiled with the addition of cheese. How can Americans like cheese? How can they think old, curdled cow's milk is a delicacy?

But I am polite. Not only because she is my mother's old boss, but because I feel sorry for her. She has lost face in her country, to which she is never allowed to return. My mother didn't share this information with me. I found many interesting announcements in English on the Internet. She stole a baby who is now a woman and has returned to her place with her rightful mother. Her punishment — if she will be lucky — is permanent exile to our country, a place where she will always be *lao wai:* outside person.

100
LUCY

Hot, hot, hot. Over one hundred degrees. The portable air conditioner, which I paid a small fortune to have delivered and installed, rattles and groans, protesting as if it is a small animal trapped in the window. It is almost as useless. The air that wheedles from it is barely cooler than the air in the apartment. But I haven't the language — or energy — to make the fuss required to return it.

Instead, I try to cool myself with tea. I have learned Chinese wisdom: hot drinks — not icy ones — relieve heat in the body. Red Tea Bloom — Wendy gave it to me — comes in what looks like little balls of rubber bands. I drop one into a cup and pour in boiling water and wait a few minutes until the ball expands into what looks like a cactus plant with a pink flower on top.

I'm sweating, but not only because of the heat. My special visa is good for a year,

408

which seemed an interminable time when I got it last February. But already six months have gone by. My ticket to freedom is only good for six more. What will happen to me when it runs out? As I understand from a lawyer here, China won't extend my visa. Without a visa, Wendy says, the Public Security Bureau (keeper of all manner of statistics, including my glove size and results of a lung test!) will come after me. The day after my visa expires, a security officer is apt to knock on my door. And what will he do? Pull me out by my hair? Toss my belongings out the window, onto the sidewalk five floors below? I picture my bras and panties flying through sooty air, landing on the moon roof of whatever luxury car is parked on the sidewalk below. Buying an expensive car in Shanghai seems to come with the right to park it wherever you please.

Here, I have no connections to anyone with sway. In New York, I felt myself for years to be separated by only a few degrees from someone who could help me with any problem. A client's brother-in-law, a colleague's best friend, the parent of a school chum of Mia's — all proved helpful in situations that at one time seemed dire: pull with the right dental surgeon, an investment question, a college recommendation letter.

Of course, no connection, no matter how powerful, could be contacted to help me out of the problem that landed me here.

I've never felt so alone, so disconnected from any seat of power, from any who have a say in what happens to me. Wendy and her family are my only "ins" here, and while they have been helpful to the extent that they can, her family — an academic family, her parents once taught at the prestigious Jiao Tong University — lost its cachet during the Cultural Revolution, and while with difficulty and persistence they managed to reclaim family real estate: the narrow house where they now live in a historic *longtong* district — they've never been able to reclaim the network of powerful connections they once enjoyed.

What will become of me? Mia. My Mia. I can't even be sure of what she looks like anymore. Is she fatter, thinner? Has she cut her hair? Is she tanned by the California sun? There was no photo of her in the *Psychology Today* magazine I found on a table in the lobby of a Hilton Hotel where I go to buy American toothpaste. The article referred to me as Mia's "sociological mother." I stared for a long time at those words on the page, reading them over and over, grateful to be recognized as any kind of mother at all.

In my mind, Mia is all the ages she was: the three-year-old tottering around in my pumps, plastic bag slung over her shoulder, going to "work"; the little girl chatting merrily with every doorman; the ten-year-old, tall for her age, longing to be elfin; the thirteen-year-old who still sits on my lap, trying to distract me from the computer; the sullen fifteen-year-old blasting music from the CD player behind her locked door; the poised young woman at our dining room table, poring over practice law school admission tests.

I envision her more and more at a distance, as if I am on one boat and she is on another, water rising between us, pushing us farther and farther apart. I get up to boil water and there is a heaviness in my stomach, so that I feel I must drag it after me across the room.

101
Mia

Grant is teaching me how to drive. He is patient and a much better teacher than I had for driver's ed in New York. Quinton was a part-time bouncer at a bar, who was always bored or smoking or apologizing for not paying attention because he'd been up all night with his girlfriend who caught him hooking up with his other girlfriend again. Once, on Riverside, he made me pull over so he could steal rims off a parked car! He justified it by saying the size rims his car needed was really rare; he'd been looking for a long time. The funny thing was, he was the driving instructor all the private school moms requested. They had no idea. It was a good driving school and he must have charmed the first mom, who recommended him to everyone else's. I never learned enough to pass the test.

I didn't care about driving then, but I do now, because if I stay here, I'll need a job and all the good jobs are up in San Francisco. I could take the Caltrain to get up there, but as soon as the money from *People* comes in, I'll buy a used car to get back and forth.

I want to stop taking money from Lucy. My allowance is still automatically deposited. I thought her bank accounts would be frozen, but the detective said it's not like *Law & Order,* DAs don't hand out freeze orders like donuts. Lucy didn't take a ransom. Her money isn't related to illegal activity, so it's hers.

I want to start working, not only to earn money, but because I need to get out of the house. I can't stay in the house all the time, even though Marilyn (she wants me to call her "Mom," but I can't) would like that. She's happiest when we're all under one roof, when we're all holding hands around the table, saying grace before dinner, or playing "family band" in the living room — everybody in the family plays an instrument except me. Marilyn plays the piano, Chloe the flute, Connor and Thatch play guitar, Grant plays the harmonica. The only thing I know how to do is clap. I hated piano lessons. Lucy should have made me stick with them and not let me quit. She was the grown-up. She shouldn't have listened to a kid.

I know it sounds corny, but there is something really nice and warming about playing music with my new family because they do it sincerely. Irony can be tiresome when what you really need is a hug. But I wonder when I'll get tired of it. It's like a different planet here, from where I grew up. Manhattan is irony's world headquarters.

102
Lucy

I met Lin at our usual spot for language exchange yesterday, our Sunday date at the Golden Palace Dumpling House, a local eatery, a hole-in-the-wall despite its grand name. Stout older women in white coats and caps serve steaming bowls of dumplings plump with pork or beef or greens or whatever one's pleasure, dumplings so delectable that Lin says diners come from far districts for them. I've convinced him to stop calling me "Ayi." I explained that American women like to be called by their names, not referred to, incorrectly, as somebody's aunt.

I am sure, now, that Lin knows my secret. He assiduously avoids asking me questions in the workbook having to do with whether or not I have children. What does he think of me? Am I a criminal in his eyes?

Oh, for the language to explain myself to him. But what would I say?

Instead, we do a module about the weather. I tell him no one in the United States really talks like his workbook. No one says, "Today precipitation exceeds the norm." They say, I tell him, "It's raining cats and dogs." He smiles, trying to picture this and I picture it with him: a torrent of pets, meowing and yelping midair, paws out to brace themselves before hitting the ground.

103
Mia

Today is my 212th day with my birth family. I've kept track. It's my new life and I keep track of how long I am living it.

Last night, like we always do, we sat at the wooden kitchen table that Grant made. It's a single piece of redwood; he is proud that it's all one piece, instead of pieces that had to be fit together. Once he pointed out to me discoloration at its side, near the bevel, proud of that, too, because a flaw is proof that something is real.

The table is covered every night by a cloth that protects it, but also obscures its beauty. The cloth is usually vintage and floral, from Marilyn's collection of them from her mother, and it's Chloe's job to put it on every night, and sometimes, as roses or peonies or carnations come fluttering down on that table, I admire the quality of the cloth and the light that comes through it from the big kitchen window. It's western light, which is a shade of light very different than you see back East. The light here at five o'clock is strong yellow, even in the fall, when light goes away in Vermont and is almost always too weak in Manhattan to exert itself beyond the front room of our apartment.

Our apartment in Manhattan. I've received several calls from the managing agent asking about our plans for it, but I haven't called back. I don't know what to say.

Last night, Marilyn made something called Vegan chop suey, thinking to please me by serving Chinese. She hadn't let me help with dinner, like I usually do. She'd wanted to surprise me, to celebrate my getting my license. I didn't have the heart to tell her that chop suey isn't Chinese. It's something dreamed up by Americans, like fortune cookies.

104
MARILYN

I took Mia to the beach today and saw that she has a tiny tattoo on her lower back. Seeing it made me feel punched in the stomach.

How could Lucy have allowed Mia to mar herself in that way? It looks like a squiggle. She says it's a leaf. She says she did it without Lucy's permission. She snuck downtown with a friend after school one day instead of going home after volleyball practice. She was fifteen. Fifteen! How could tattooing a fifteen-year-old even be legal? Mia said the laws are for anesthesia. Kids don't get anesthesia.

Didn't it hurt? I asked her. She said it did. Her friend and she held each other's hands during the procedure. I think of the last time I bathed her, pulling a washcloth over the small of her back, not enough aware of its immaculate perfection.

I make a mental note to talk to the boys, to warn them of the dangers of infusing your skin with permanent toxins.

I ask her not to show it off to the kids.

Mia says Chloe has already seen it. But she told her it was only henna.

We are lying on sand, without towels, letting the healing earth draw out stress and poisons. This part of the practice is usually mind-clearing but my mind is anything but clear.

I sit up. Mia turns on her back.

The top and bottom of her bikini don't match. I guess this is a New York fashion.

What did Lucy say when she saw it, I ask. The sand is a great detoxifier, especially here at the edge of the ocean, the womb of the earth. I'm glad the tattoo is pressed into it.

Mia said that Lucy was angry at her for sneaking downtown but she wasn't grounded because Lucy said, "It's your body, not mine."

That's not how a real mother thinks! A true mother can't ever distance herself from a body that began in her own.

Sand covers her navel. I resist the urge to brush it away, to clear the sacred place of our first connection.

105
Mia

I got a job! I'm an education assistant at the San Francisco Zoo. I found it on craigslist. Relationships with animals are so underestimated. Just because they can't talk doesn't mean they're incapable of connection. I think not being able to talk makes the connection stronger. Creatures that don't talk are very sensitive to emotions. You can see it in their eyes, they can tell when they're unloved.

Chloe understands, even though they don't have pets because Thatch is allergic. She told me, "It's like we have magical powers, but we don't notice because to us the powers seem totally normal, but to other animals, they seem fantastic!"

When I came home from work the first day, Marilyn met me at the door and hugged me like I'd been gone a year. She's trying to cram twenty-two years of love into me all at once. Sometimes I get the feeling who she loves isn't me. It's someone she's been inventing in her head since 1990.

Here is what I miss: being normal.

I miss Lucy leaning against the counter or pouring coffee while I cut fruit. I say, "Do you want some of this mango?" and she says, "No, I'm okay." And then, "Well, I'll just have a piece." And so I cut off a slice and give it to her and she says "mmmmm" and her eyes widen. Maybe I sing an impromptu mango song. I miss her hands.

Tonight I ate mango that came in a fruit basket Aunt Cheryl sent. I'd been saving it and it tasted good, sweeter than the hard ones we used to get in New York, but it made me miss one of those anyway.

I have my birth mother. But I miss my mom.

106
MIA

Thatch asked me tonight: Is your kidnapper going to jail? It still hurts when I hear them call Lucy that.

Marilyn has told the FBI she'll testify for the prosecution, but I haven't agreed.

Part of me is angry at Lucy and will never forgive her. But Sonya says that feelings are complicated. You can be angry at someone and still love them a lot.

How can I send the mom who raised me to some horrible place she'd probably be in for the rest of her life, where she can't talk to anyone, except through glass.

I'll never forget her rescuing me from what felt like jail. Lucy always wanted to go to sleepaway camp when she was little. I was just eight, and wasn't sure I wanted to go, but Lucy thought I should give it a try. I did try, for a week, but when I called her sobbing, homesick, she dropped everything to drive six hours to get me. The car she had rented was a convertible. We drove home through the night, hair blowing in my eyes as I reclined the front seat, looking up at the stars. I remember seeing a shooting star and breathing in the cool air and feeling free as that star streaking unexpectedly out of its place in the universe.

I can't ever just forget about her. She is always there, like a phantom limb.

107
MARILYN

I was taking laundry upstairs and saw Mia sitting on the bed, her back to the doorway, and I walked into the room to talk to her. When I got closer, I saw she had a Chinese silk box in her lap. I knew what it was. I heard from Chloe that Mia keeps a memory box of things to look at when she gets sad. As I set down the basket on Chloe's bed, Mia put the top back on the box but I asked if she wouldn't mind showing it to me. She was reluctant, but I sat down on the bedspread next to her and I said I was grateful that she was sharing things from her life. There's so much of her life I want to know about — all of it. I want to hug her all the time, hug her hard, the reality of her. I half expect she'll disappear again.

She showed me her collection: a jar of sand from Coney Island, a Chinese flash card, a plastic ring, a wristband from a place named Polyester's, a curl from her first haircut, tied with pink ribbon. I couldn't help thinking of where Tom and I were when she got that haircut, what hell we must have been going through.

There was a Polaroid picture of her as a toddler under a Christmas tree. I asked her to tell me about the picture. Was this her house? Someone else's? But she turned away from me, shaking her head, and I saw a tear plop into the box.

I offered to add something to the box for her. I had her newborn bracelet from when she was in the hospital. Did she want that?

"Me being an infant is *your* memory, not mine," Mia said softly, closing the box.

Sometimes I wonder if she says things to deliberately hurt me.

108
Mia

Marilyn and Grant met with a lawyer tonight and I took the kids to Plant Heaven for dinner. It's easy to think of them as my siblings, but I still can't think of their parents as mine.

Chloe's Plant Burger came with a little plastic egg that opened and inside was a toy. It reminded me of a Tamagotchi.

"Remember Tamagotchis?" I asked the boys, but of course they didn't. It made me feel old.

And then I told them a story I'd forgotten, from when I was little. They — especially Chloe — loved hearing stories about growing up in New York.

It was a rainy Saturday, I said, back on the Upper West Side. I was about eight, doing errands with Lucy. There was a pet store in our neighborhood. I loved to go there to play with the puppies and kittens in the window, or go to the back of the store to talk to the birds who were silent and sad; their feathers were dull. I'd try to cheer them up through the bars of their cages, saying I would take them home if I could. I'd beg Lucy to let me, tell her how much better it would be for them to live with us than squished up in their cages. I'd say Pumpkin needed company, but she wouldn't listen.

The pet store also sold little toys. Tamagotchis were a craze.

Tamagotchis were little plastic egg-shaped pets on a key chain. Everyone had them, including me. They were cyber-animals you had to pay attention to 24/7: feeding them, playing with them, making them nap, and if you didn't care for them right, they beeped or played little electric melodies to remind you. Ayi had bought me the dinosaur in Chinatown. Lucy had given me the rabbit for Easter. I bought a frog with my allowance. Schools banned them because of the noises they made, so you had to keep them in your backpack and run to your locker to take care of them between classes.

"So many school rules." Chloe shook her head.

The new Tamagotchi was Nano Baby. Nobody had one yet, except a classmate whose father had brought one back from

Japan. But now here they were in our neighborhood pet store! I begged Lucy to buy one. "For your birthday," she said, but April was months away.

As she was talking to Mrs. Kim at the counter, I unhooked a package from the display. Someone had already pried open the plastic bubble. The Nano Baby fell easily into my hands. It was so beautiful.

"Time to go," called Lucy, waiting for me by the door.

"Good-bye for now," I told the Nano Baby, and started to push it back into its bubble. It fell. I bent down to pick it up, but it wasn't on the floor. It wasn't anywhere! I got down on my knees and felt around and around the dirty linoleum but nothing was on it, even when I felt under the metal display case.

"Mia!" Lucy was getting impatient and not knowing what else to do, I stood up to join her, and as soon as I started walking I realized where the Tamagotchi was — in my rain boot! I felt it hanging on to my ankle. Should I take off my boot and give back the toy I hadn't paid for? Or should I keep walking as if nothing had happened?

I couldn't come to a decision. My feet just kept walking. My brain was jumping inside my head as I passed Mrs. Kim at the register. She invited me to reach into a jar of wrapped candies like she always did, but I didn't. I hurried past her and out of the store, worried that my boot might start pinging or dinging or singing a song and give me away, which it did as soon as we walked into our apartment. Lucy saw me taking it out of my boot and made me put my coat on again and she walked me back to the store and made me return it to Mrs. Kim and apologize to her. I could never go to that store again. I told Ayi I didn't like the smell in there anymore. A few months later, they went out of business and I always worried I had something to do with it.

"You were Lucy's Tamagotchi," Connor said, squirting pomegranate ketchup onto his notdog.

Why hadn't I made that connection before? It was obvious.

"Too bad you couldn't make Lucy return you," Connor said.

But I was glad Lucy hadn't. Which made me feel sorry for Marilyn.

109
GRANT

People think a kidnapped baby comes home and that's the end of the story. Everyone gets to live happy. But that's not how it works.

I don't tell Marilyn this, but I worry about what Mia is doing to our family. Chloe's all right, but the boys are confused. Mia is smart, but she has no life skills. No one's taught her the basics of how to live in this world. She came to us not even knowing how to drive.

I took her to my workshop the other day, wanting to show her a few things, how to hold a hammer, how to steady a saw — things she'll need to know when she's on her own. It's not that she wasn't interested. She just didn't have any facility for it. Maybe too much time has gone by for her to pick up those skills.

Marilyn keeps reaching out to her, but you can't force a fit. Go slow, I say. Give her time. I tell her about the job I'm working out in Hillsborough now. It's an old house, built in 1853. Post and beam. Miter joints. You see how exacting master carpenters were back then. They didn't have laser levels, but their work is almost always perfectly plumb. Most of the house, the post and beams fit together, dead accurate. In the part of the house I'm working on, though, the posts and beams pulled away from each other. Earthquake, probably. We're using rope to pull them back together, but they'll never fit as snug as they originally did. They've been separated too long.

110

MARILYN

We talked to the prosecutors today. In the car on the way home, I explained to Mia why Lucy needs to go to jail. She needs time to think about all that she did.

"Jail isn't a monastery where she can sit and contemplate things!" Mia said. Her tone was more harsh than I expected. Clearly, she had thought about this.

"It's not just the law that says she deserves prison," I continued. "It's the law of what's right in the universe. She needs to face the consequences of what she has done. Kidnapping a baby didn't just affect you. It affected other people."

I turned from the wheel to look at her, but Mia kept her eyes straight ahead on the road.

"You can't imagine the terror of losing a child, wondering where you were, worrying about you constantly, for years."

"If you cared about me so much, how

come you left me alone in a shopping cart?" It was as if she had slapped me.

My eyes filled with tears. I couldn't blink them away. I thought about pulling over because I almost couldn't see to drive anymore. But it was the first real conversation I was having with Mia. Some people can't share their feelings unless they're not looking at you.

"Leaving you was a mistake," I said quietly. "A mistake I paid for every day for twenty-one years. Lucy has to pay for her mistake, too. That's what is fair."

"Life isn't fair," Mia murmured, still staring ahead.

"That's why laws have to be," I said. "I understand you don't want the person who raised you to go to prison. But the law says that's what kidnappers deserve."

"My mom isn't a kidnapper," Mia said quietly.

"What?"

"I'm the only baby she ever took. It's not like she's planning to do it again."

"That's not the point," I said. Argument filled my brain, bigger and bigger, like an inflating balloon. "If Lucy doesn't serve time, that's like saying that taking a baby doesn't matter. Her kidnapping you was the worst thing that ever happened to me and your father. It changed our lives. It ripped us apart."

"So you need to put her in jail to get your revenge?"

"Restitution!" I said as we passed a police car on the meridian and suddenly I put my foot on the brake, realizing I was going way over the speed limit.

111
LUCY

As Lin and I were meeting for language exchange and dumplings yesterday, a friend of his came into the shop. Lin introduced me and shifted on the bench to make room for him at our table. His name — his American name — was Spock. He'd grown up reading *Star Trek* comic books in Chinese.

Spock's English was better, far better than Lin's, and we began talking in English and there came an odd brightness into his eyes as he asked where I was from, what I was doing here. Alarms went off in me, but when I looked to Lin, he was calmly spearing dumplings and so I assured myself that no harm could come of his friend's determination to practice his English. I told him I was in China on business, which is what I always say to people who ask.

Spock and I continued talking: about weather, American pop stars (Miley Cyrus), television shows — a favorite here is *Friends,* title translated as *Six People Walking Together.* At one point, Spock took up his iPhone and tapped into it, and almost as soon as he set it down, it began buzzing and beeping, moving itself across the table, and he caught it just before it fell to the floor slick with spilled broth and spit.

I was too nervous to finish my dumplings. I said I remembered something, I had to leave. But the bill took a long time, and when we exited the shop, I heard my name. "Lucy? Lucy Wakefield?" I turned around and there was a woman flashing a press card, thrusting a phone in my face, asking me questions one after another. "What made you kidnap a baby? Will China send you back to the States?"

Spock slunk away and Lin took off his jacket and put it over my head, steering me toward the street and into a taxi. As we approached the car door, and I ducked under Lin's arm to get inside, his jacket slid off, exposing my face and the phone rose in front of it again.

"Do you have anything to say to the girl you held captive for twenty-one years?"

I stopped and turned suddenly. "Yes," I said, leaning into the screen in her hand.

"Katcheratchma."

And then Lin pulled me into the taxi and we drove away.

112
LIN

I regret I told Wang Xueling about Lucy.
Wang is son of my mother's friend. I think I
can trust him. I did not know he would sell
the informations to Dragon TV. But, I
should know. Wang's wife is in Arizona. She
went there so their baby can be a United
States citizen. Their son was born, but she
doesn't come home yet. Wang is always having to send her money.

113
MIA

I saw Lucy for the first time since last February. On my phone. Connor forwarded a video he got from a kid at school. The footage was from some show in China. A reporter caught my mom coming out of a restaurant. Poor Lucy. Her face is drawn and she looked wild-eyed and scared. I felt sorry for her. The footage was subtitled in Chinese, and I wondered how they translated the only word she said, a word that nobody understands but me.

I was glad I was alone, which I hardly ever am in this house. Grant was at work, the boys were at school, and Marilyn had taken Chloe to harp lessons. I sat on the bed in the room I share with her, watching the clip over and over on my phone, hugging the big yellow bear Chloe keeps on her pillow, crying for my mom, as if I were ten years old, too.

114
MIA

I called Ayi this morning. Her number was still in my phone. She'd written it on a postcard almost all covered by stamps. I'd always meant to call her.

I told Marilyn I needed the car to get something. But really, what I needed was privacy. I drove to the shopping center and sat in the parking lot. It was 8:30 in the morning, 11:30 at night in Shanghai. I knew Ayi would still be up unless her habits had changed. She didn't like to go to bed before midnight. I hoped she still had the same number. So many numbers to connect me to her! I let it ring and ring. The rings were strange. First, they were too long, then too short, and just as I was about to give up, I heard a man say *Wei?* The Chinese word for "hello."

"Is this *Ba*?" I asked, thinking it was Ayi's husband. *Shi Mia!* I said. "It's Mia!"

I was amazed that Chinese words I hadn't

spoken in years all came tumbling into my head.

There was a long silence and I thought we'd been cut off.

Then, "This is Lin, the son of Wanling," a voice said, and I realized the man was the boy I hadn't talked to in years, not since Ayi put me on the phone to say hello to him once or twice when I was little.

Lin! Ni hao, I said, meaning to start a conversation with him, hoping his English was better than my Chinese.

But no one was there. There was a clatter in the background, and conversation.

Ayi said, *Ren si le?* "Who died?" And I realized that Lin hadn't, for some reason, told his mother it was me, that she thought it was some faraway relative calling late at night with terrible news.

Suddenly Ayi's voice on the phone was so clear, it was as if she were standing beside me.

Wei? Wei? Wei?

My throat filled and I couldn't speak for a moment. When I said my name, she made a happy sound then began talking rapidly in Chinese. All those words I thought I had forgotten. We talked for an hour, until my battery was about to run out and we made a date to talk and I drove home and, pulling into the garage, I decided not to tell Marilyn, though I didn't know why.

115
MIA

I've been doing research. The lawyers I interned with in January gave me the name of a criminal firm and lawyers there have been Skyping pro bono with me.

I do the calls on breaks at the zoo. I sit in the café, where cell service is best, at a window watching spider monkeys play in trees on an island made to look like a forest.

Today I talk to a lawyer named Adele. We talk about something called the Comprehensive Law Movement. She's Skyping from her office, and seeing the tops of skyscrapers in the window behind her makes me miss the city. To me "the city" is and will always be New York.

"There's a new way to deal with crime," Adele is saying. She looks tired; there are bags under her eyes and I remember a funny thing Ms. Laniere once told us: because of earth's rotation, people on high floors travel a mile farther each day than people at sea level.

"Restorative Justice," Adele says. I know a little about this already. We learned about it in Struggles for Change class.

Adele thinks she can get a written guarantee from the State of New Jersey that if Lucy comes back and surrenders herself, the state will convict, but she won't serve any time.

My stomach jumps when she says this. Do I want Lucy back? Maybe I do. You can't love someone for twenty-one years and expect that love to just evaporate inside you. What she did was wrong. But she also raised me with her whole heart. She's a huge part of who I am. I don't want her to spend the rest of her life in a jail.

Adele is offscreen, getting another cup of coffee, but she is still talking.

"She'll have to meet face-to-face with the birth parents and you. She'll have to agree to do something to restore you and the community."

"And she won't go to prison?" I ask to be sure. "Even with a crime as bad as kidnapping?" It's hard to believe. I've watched every *Law & Order* — they used to shoot episodes in our building — and no defendant ever got off like this.

Adele is back, stirring her cup with a straw.

445

"The DA just wants this case off the books."

A few days later, I call the dean about going back to finish at Midd, to get my degree and go to law school, like I planned.

Maybe I'm the person I thought I was, after all.

116
Marilyn

Sonya says I have to make peace with the way things are. I have to come to a place of forgiveness. If I don't forgive, how will my life move on?

The woman who took my daughter also raised her with love. Like it or not, she is part of my daughter. Hurting her would be hurting my daughter. Mia has been through enough in her life. I don't want her to have to visit a prison. I want my daughter to walk in the light, as far away from that darkness as possible.

Maybe bringing Lucy face-to-face with the people she injured is a path to healing for all of us. Let her see the destruction. Let her be forced to confront the truth, instead of the lies she must have told herself all these years.

For Mia's sake, I agreed to ask them not to prosecute to the full extent of the law.

But the prosecutor warns that Tom must consent.

117
Tom

She ought to be put away.

She's a criminal. A felon. She has to serve time. She stole another person's life. She stole the lives of three people.

I'm not the same man I was when it happened. I'm doing entirely different work. I couldn't take my law degree to Costa Rica. I'm a businessman now. The woman I married is Costa Rican. I haven't been back to the States in years.

The way I see it is, bad things can't be reversed. Say, you get into an accident and lose an arm or a leg. It's not as if you can get that limb back by wishing. The fact is, I lost a child. It devastated me. It broke up my marriage. In the end, I adjusted. But it's still a monstrous crime.

The law says that when someone commits a crime — when you step forth and damage someone else's life, we need prosecution to deal with that. That person has to pay commensurate with the offense. She has to face consequences. If the state disregards this, if it lets her off scot-free — what are we saying as a society here — that taking away someone else's kid is no big deal?

118
MIA

Marilyn gave me my dad's number, to see if I could change his mind.

My dad. It still feels weird to say that. I Googled him before calling, so I'd have a face to think of while we were talking. She said he didn't do Facetime or Skype. He wasn't on Facebook but there were pictures of him at dinners and such. His smile is like mine. He's got dimples, too.

It took a long time for me to press the last couple of digits. My heart was in my throat. What if he didn't like me? What if I didn't like him? What if I'm not his idea of a daughter? He didn't have another daughter. He didn't have any other kids. Something in me was glad about that.

It took a lot of rings for him to answer.

"Hello," he said. He sounded tall.

"It's Mia." My tongue felt like it weighed a thousand pounds. Then I remembered he'd known me as Natalie. "Your daughter."

There was a silence so long at the other end that I thought maybe the call had dropped.

"Oh," he said. "Hi."

That's all? That's how he greets his long-lost daughter he hasn't seen in twenty-two years?

"Is this not a good time?" I asked. Maybe he was at work. But Marilyn said it was his home number.

"It's fine," he said. "How are you . . . Mia?"

I loved hearing my name in my father's voice.

"Fine," I said. "Well. Not really fine. A lot's been going on with me, as you've probably heard."

"How can I help?" he said. "Do you need money?"

"No," I said right away. "Is that what you think?" I felt insulted.

"I don't know what to think. I don't know what you're expecting."

His voice sounded choky. He was worried about his impression on me!

"I'm not expecting anything!" I tell him.

He wasn't like Marilyn, who had practice being a parent, who knew what to say, what a parent should sound like. He was awkward with this as I was afraid I would be.

"I'm a different man than I was when I was your father."

Was my father? Did that mean he thought he wasn't my father anymore? That made me sad. For the first time in my life, I wanted a father. It wouldn't be complicated. He'd be my only one.

"No worries, I don't remember that man," I said. "So you can totally be who you are. I don't expect you to be anything, really. And I get the same deal from you, okay?"

I heard a little breath. Maybe it was relief.

"Okay," he said. "That sounds like something a kid of mine would say."

And then we were talking, and when I hung up, we'd made a date in New York, and it was as if I'd never not had a father before.

119
MIA

We all decided that I should be the one to fly out and explain things to Lucy. I wanted to do that. I didn't want anyone else to do it, especially not a paralegal.

I want to see Lucy in person. I want to see Ayi.

I got my first passport. With my real birth certificate. But first, I had to go to Social Security and change my legal name to my real one, Mia Wakefield.

I bought a ticket for December 21, the date nobody in California wants to travel because it's predicted to be the end of the world. Doomsday. Planet collision. Foretold by ancient Maya. Marilyn says she doesn't think it will happen, yet she is stocking the basement with flashlights and batteries, water bottles and granola bars. Store-bought, with preservatives, breaking her rule against them, which is necessary, she says, in case it's a long haul.

I don't worry about this date. My end of the world has already happened.

120
CHERYL

I called Mia to invite her for Christmas and to Jake's engagement party, which will be the day after. It was nice to hear her voice. It's been a long time. I knew she probably wouldn't come, that she'd be celebrating the holidays with her new family in California. But I wanted her to feel included.

She surprised me by telling me her plan to go to China and bring Lucy home. She said she wanted to reassure me that Lucy wouldn't go to jail. As she explained, I had to keep myself from sounding angry. Why was I angry?

I thought about it after we hung up.

Things have always come easily to Lucy. She got good grades without really trying. She was popular. She made the swim team. She got a scholarship to an Ivy League college. She got to leave home and get a glamorous job. When our mother got sick, I took care of her at the end. Lucy sent money, which helped, but I took on the brunt of her care so our mother wouldn't have to die in a hospital. Lucy has always been good at slipping off the noose of responsibility.

There was only one thing Lucy couldn't do that she wanted to do: have a baby. So she took someone else's. Try as I might, I can't forgive her for that. I can't pretend she never did what she did. She deceived our family for years. She deceived that poor girl who she deprived of her parents.

Restorative Justice? How could she restore what she took from those parents? She took their baby. She took their marriage. She took the lives they were meant to have.

Lucy is my sister. I'm sorry for her. But I can't forgive her. I'm sorry, but I can't.

I'm glad the district attorney didn't reach out to me.

121
MARILYN

We all take Mia to the airport. Grant parks the van as we escort her in, Thatch carrying her backpack she'll take on the plane, Connor shouldering her duffel, Chloe carrying the bags of treats that I packed her: almonds and kale chips, figs and rice cakes, so she won't have to fill up on what they serve on a plane.

The airport isn't crowded, because of the Doomsday scare. I woke up this morning, my heart weighted by the prospect of Mia's departure, but also full of gratitude for the uneventful dawn.

Mia has been with us for ten months, the amount of time she needed to begin to heal. Mia is a Horse. She needs to keep moving. Her sun is in Pluto, the planet of profound change, which pushes you toward your destination, unaware as you are of what that fate is.

This morning Grant asked me if I was

sorry to lose her all over again. The answer is no. I am not losing Mia. She began in my body. She will always be part of me, no matter where she is in this world. Even when we were separated, I felt her with me. I've learned that loss is part of life; it reminds us to appreciate what we have now.

I will never stop being grateful for her return. Do I wish her return had been earlier? Of course I do. But I've stopped arguing with the universe. I've stopped arguing with Mia.

Yesterday, we planted a tree. All six of us gathered in the backyard. Wherever Mia travels, wherever she goes, the tree will be here, representing her roots in our family. It's a weeping willow. I made that choice. Because part of me will always be weeping for what I have missed. And yet willow energy is healing, too, helping the spirit move through sadness to joy.

I try to imagine what it will be like, months from now, face-to-face again with the woman who took her, this time knowing what she did, in some room somewhere dictated by the court of New Jersey. They'll ask me what I think restoration should be. Restoration! Nothing can restore the years I lost with my daughter.

But I will forgive the woman who took her.

I've thought a lot about what I will say. I will take her hands in mine and look in her eyes and thank her for raising my daughter to be the beautiful person she is. I hope I can do that. When you forgive, the prisoner you set free is yourself.

We wait with Mia as she stands in line for China Eastern, passport ready, luggage unlocked. I wonder when we will see her again. She'll spend Christmas in China. Then go back to Vermont to finish up her last semester. Will she come visit in the spring, as she says she will? She's invited us to her graduation in May.

There's some problem with Mia's luggage, I see her gesturing to an attendant. I go over to help. The bag is overweight. Mia bends down, unzips the duffel, rummages around, brings out some things, including the little 8 Ball Chloe gave her for her birthday.

"Keep it safe for me," she tells Chloe, then zips the bag again. The attendant places the bag onto a conveyor belt behind her and it disappears.

One by one, we say good-bye to her. Thatch, Connor, Chloe. I wonder when I'll see my four children together again. Grant gives her a bear hug. I saw him slip bills into her backpack, earlier, while it stood by the front door. When it's my turn to hug her, her face is wet. I tell her I have something for her and pull out the tiny red, silken box from my pocket.

"I'm already overweight," she says, wiping her cheeks.

"No, you're thin as a rail." I smile. This was true when she came here. But I'm pleased that she's not quite as angular anymore. I'm sending her off healthier, nourished.

She opens the box.

"Two necklaces? Did you make them?"

I nod, picking up one of the delicate silver strands, then the other. Hanging from each is a tiny red half-moon. The two moons come together, forming a heart. I put one around her neck, the other around mine.

"When we're together, our hearts are one," I say.

We hug for a long time. I am conscious that soon she'll be in a different country, hugging the woman who stole her, who, without a thought on a summer day, changed all of our destinies.

But I have to let go of remembering that. I have to let go.

"I love you," I say.

Mia nods as we pull apart.

"I love you, too, Mother." She bends to pick up her carry-on, not looking at me. Something catches at my throat. She has never called me "Mother" before.

I watch her as she drifts away, toward the long line for security. She is the daughter of my past who stopped growing at four months; and also the daughter of my present, whose past I'm slowly getting to know. Both are equally precious to me.

"She's gone, c'mon," say the boys, the kids following Grant, who's already striding away, in the direction of parking.

But I stand there, watching the place where she was.

122
LUCY

In the greeting hall of the Shanghai Airport, red LED letters above me announce in both Chinese and English that Mia's plane has landed. I feel current in the linoleum, so highly polished it shines like marble — as if it has acquired an electric charge. For the first time in almost a year, Mia's feet and mine are touching the same part of the earth.

I wait for her in a sea of searchers, almost crushed by others seething forward in a crowd straining against railings that hold us back from frosted-glass doors marked *Arrivals*. Cabbies and drivers in uniform are in front, leaning over the railing, holding signs scrawled on cardboard, most in Chinese characters. Others carry signs, too, and I duck to prevent the corner of one of them from nicking my eye. Security police, men and women in blue shirts with epaulets and black caps with gleaming visors, wave us back again and again. When some eager greeter succeeds in thrusting himself past the rail, a guard speaks harshly, pushing the offender back with white gloves, not gently, putting him back to his, to our, designated place. Whatever you do in China, wherever you are, there's a crush of others beside you, doing it, too.

I wait for what seems like forever for Mia. I am standing at Gate 18, which Wendy advised was the best place to wait for people flying international. It's opposite the arrivals gate. Both Wendy and Lin offered to drive me here, to pick Mia up with me, but I insisted on taking a cab. I want to greet Mia alone, have her all to myself for at least the forty minutes it will take the cab to get to Wendy's house, where she will stay, where we will feast on a banquet that she's been preparing for days.

It makes me happy to picture Mia with her. I see Mia helping Wendy make dumplings, Mia's favorite dish from childhood. I see how quick Wendy's hands are, and Mia's, too, flouring the dough, cutting out triangles that Wendy flours and wraps around filling — some vegetable, some pork — then flutes the sides with pinches between thumb and forefinger, quick, quick, quick all the way around. I can almost hear

Mia ransacking Wendy's memory for recipes: Three-Day Noodles, Seven-Egg Stew. And I fast-forward the vision, seeing Mia in the future, cooking the dishes for her own children, *xi fan* for them when they are ill, and how sad it makes me that I will not be there to see them grow up.

Sometimes I feel so heavy with remorse, I can't move.

Finally, the frosted doors open and people around me jostle for a better position, to ensure that they can see and be seen by the ones they are waiting for. I am pushed farther back in the crowd. I don't fight my way forward. I can wait. I've waited this long.

123
MIA

I wait and wait. Huge pieces of luggage bang down the shiny slide. Boxes tied with fraying ropes, suitcases that are shrink-wrapped, black roller bags almost as big as refrigerators. But none are my duffel.

Finally, no one is standing by the carousel but me. I see that nothing new is coming down the slide. I walk toward a window marked *Questions* in English.

When I get to the window I am surprised at how much Chinese I know, how the words I need are flowing back into me. All this time, they must have been sleeping inside me, and even though I've never been in China, I feel, somehow, as if I am coming home.

When I was little, I used to be afraid my mother would die. If she died, who would take care of me? Ayi said she'd bring me to China and I'd grow up there. I couldn't imagine it. Now I was here.

The clerk asks for my nationality. *Mei guo ren,* I say. "Beautiful country person."

"Who are you?" he asks in English, meaning what is my name.

I'm trying to figure that out, I want to tell him.

I am not Marilyn's baby (I feel for her delicate heart, safe in my shirt pocket). I am not Lucy's daughter. I am Mia.

They can't find my luggage. My duffel is lost. My clothes and my gifts to Ayi — the face cream and vitamins she asked for, cigars for Feng, peanut butter for Lin — are in Singapore or Bangkok or Hanoi, they're not sure, and as I stand there filling out forms — so many forms! — I realize that I don't feel upset. In fact, I feel lighter, freer than I've felt in a long time. Maybe the luggage will make its way to Ayi's home. But whether or not it does — to my surprise, it doesn't matter.

I lift my backpack and slip it over my shoulders and walk toward the exit doors, passing a wall covered in metal, and I stop to fix my hair in its reflection. I peel a hair elastic from the rainbow of them on my wrist, and gather my hair into it, smoothing it back from my face, getting ready to see my mom.

124
LUCY

One by one, travelers who aren't Mia emerge through the doors, looking disheveled and weary, most hidden by suitcases big as mastodons they try to keep upright on shiny carts, so weighting the carts that they are hard to maneuver.

Once through the glass doors, the travelers must choose: left or right. It is as if they are celebrities. The crowd roars in welcome, hands and signs bobbing, trying to get their attention. Most stop and squint, trying to discern the presence of someone waiting for them. Once past the rail, travelers fall into embraces, so many encirclements of people holding each other, some screaming or crying, others silently hanging on, and I wonder how coolly or warmly Mia will greet me.

The crowd starts to thin. Where is she? Did she miss the plane? Change her mind about coming? Was she detained by authorities because of me?

The glass doors open and I see, in the distance beyond them, a silhouette too small to recognize, yet I know it is her.

It is as if an ocean is breaking inside my chest.

Of course she has come. I needn't have worried. But I can't help worrying. I am her mother.

ACKNOWLEDGMENTS

Thanks
To Kate Johnson, my agent, enabler, and highest reader.

To Kathy Sagan, for acquiring this novel, and to Natasha Simons for invaluable editorial guidance. To Meagan Harris, Liz Psaltis, and Diana Velasquez for getting the word out. And to everyone behind this at Gallery Books. Thank you.

To Abigail Thomas, who midwifed this narrative in short-story form. To Karen Braziller, whose guidance and encouragement helped grow it into a novel. To the generous readers their workshops afforded, especially Jill Bauerle, Daphne Beal, Simone Bloch, Sarah Broom, Heather Cross, Elyssa East, Elizabeth Ehrlich, Kira von Eichel, Marcelle Harrison, Elizabeth Kadestky, Karen Crumley Keats, Dana Kinstler, Sharyn Kohlberg, Madge McKeithen, Sarah Micklem, Kathleen O'Donnell, Oona Patrick,

Beth Passaro, Laurie Shapiro, and Liz Welch.

For reads of drafts in multitudinous forms: Ann Arensberg, Amy Axler, Valerie Borchardt, Anja Konig, Jane Otto, Carol Paik, Katherine Ross, Margaret Ross. Special thanks to Maggie Abruzese whose insights helped profoundly in character development.

For input on topics explored in this novel: Chris Allen, Patricia Allen, Marianna Connolly, Barbara Demick, Lee Gould, Charles Keil, Cathy Klein, Mara Klein, Cindy Kumamoto, Mary Shannon Little, Ellen Mahoney, Betsy Maury, Ruadh McGuire, Theresa Klein Richter, Donald K. Ross, and Kathleen Voldstad. Special thanks to Katherine Kane, whose command of alternative medicine played a critical role in this story's development.

To my fellow students and teachers at the New School MFA Program, especially Jonathan Dee, Mary Gaitskill, Luis Jaramillo, and David Lehman.

To the New York State Summer Writers Institute, especially Bob and Peg Boyers and Frank Bidart.

To Bill Roorbach, for earliest encouragement.

To Clint van Zandt, for introducing me to

the concept of restorative justice.

To James Hitchcock and David Lauruhn for invaluable corrections.

To Robin Wilkerson, for outside information.

To Peter Becket, who helped spare me from grammatical oversights. Similar thanks to Margaret Klein and to Judith and Ray McGuire, whose supportive friendship meant a lot on this journey.

This novel owes debts of detail to authors, editors, and publishers of the following:

All Souls, Christine Schutt (Mariner Books)

The Child in Time, Ian McEwan (Rosetta-Books)

Daddy Love, Joyce Carol Oates (Mysterious Press)

The Deep End of the Ocean, Jacquelyn Mitchard (Penguin Books)

The Face on the Milk Carton, Caroline B. Cooney (Laurel Leaf)

Finding Me, Michelle Knight (Weinstein Books)

Ithaka, Sarah Saffian (Delta)

Kidnapped, Paula S. Fass (Oxford University Press)

The Light Between Oceans, M. L. Stedman (Scribner)

Remember Me Like This, Bret Anthony

Johnson (Random House)

Schroder, Amity Gaige (Twelve, Hachette Books)

Two Years in the Melting Pot, Liu Zongren (China Books & Periodicals)

Wanting a Child, edited by Jill Bialosky and Helen Schulman (Farrar, Straus and Giroux)

White Oleander, Janet Fitch (Little, Brown and Company)

"In France, A Baby Switch and a Lesson in Maternal Love," Maïa de la Baume, *The New York Times*

"Kidnapped at Birth," Robert Kolker, *New York Magazine*

"The Mixed-Up Brothers of Bogotá," Susan Dominus, *The New York Times Magazine*

"The Real Lolita," Sarah Weinman, *Hazlitt Magazine*

"South African Teen Stolen as Infant Found After Befriending Sister," Robin Dixon, *Los Angeles Times*

Deepest thanks to my family: Donald, for unwavering support and good humor, which makes everything possible. To Katherine, Margaret, and to my parents and brothers and sisters and their spouses and children. How grateful I am to be a part of your club.

READING GROUP GUIDE: WHAT WAS MINE

Have you ever done something in the heat of the moment that you could not undo? Lucy Wakefield never thought she would commit a crime, but when she finds a baby alone in a shopping cart, she is overcome by long-held desire for a baby, and in one life-altering, incomprehensible decision, she kidnaps a beautiful baby girl. For over two decades, she manages to keep this secret and raise Mia as her adopted daughter. But Mia's birth mother never gave up hope that she was alive and her unshakable conviction eventually helps bring the secret to light. When Mia discovers the devastating truth of her origins, she's overwhelmed by confusion and anger. Who is she? Who is her mother? And who is the woman she's called her mother all these years?

A tale of loss and grief, identity and reflection, hope and acceptance, *What Was Mine* is ultimately a story about the meaning of motherhood and the ripple effect of a split-second decision that alters so many lives.

DISCUSSION QUESTIONS

1. The title of the book, *What Was Mine,* gets at the themes of ownership and belonging. Discuss how that theme relates to the three main characters: Lucy, Marilyn, and Mia. What was theirs? What did they each lose throughout the story?

2. What is the effect of knowing from the beginning of the story that Lucy eventually gets caught?

3. In Lucy's mind, aside from her one egregious act, she is a normal person — a good person, even. Is it possible for someone good and normal to stray so far from the path of what's right and then simply return to it? Is it possible for a good person to do a bad thing, or are some acts so egregious as to define one as a bad person?

4. Marilyn's character is portrayed as almost a different person before and after her daughter's kidnapping. Discuss the ways in which she changes after going through this traumatic event.

5. "So much of who you are has to do with

your mother." Do you agree with this statement? Who is a mother to Mia in this story? How do each of her mother figures help shape who Mia is? Do you think Mia would have been a different person if she had lived her life as Marilyn's daughter and had not been taken by Lucy? How is Mia's identity rocked when her concept of her "mother" is turned upside down?

6. Mia and Marilyn try to forgive Lucy for what she did, but others like Tom and even Lucy's own sister, Cheryl, are not able to. Discuss the theme of forgiveness in the story. Why do you think two of the people most directly affected are the most willing to try to forgive? Have you ever been asked to forgive someone for something you thought was unforgivable?

7. Throughout the story, Lucy's intentions don't always line up with her actions. Even as she was kidnapping Mia, she was in denial about what she was doing, intending to give the baby back somehow. When she then almost lost Mia in a store, she "made promises to the universe" to set things right which she wouldn't keep. She says she meant to tell Mia when she got older. "Part of me thought that if I waited long enough, if I used just the right words, perhaps she'd

be able to understand." Do you think Lucy ever really intended to tell Mia the truth — or was she lying to herself about that, too? Do you think Mia's reaction to the fact of her kidnapping would have been different if Lucy had told her herself when Mia was older?

8. After Mia discovers the truth about what happened to her, she has a hard time referring to either Lucy or Marilyn as "mother." Discuss what the word "mother" means to you. What makes a mother a mother? Is it the person who birthed you, whose genes you share, who raised you — and what if these don't describe the same person? How do Mia's feelings toward both of the women who think of themselves as her mother change over the next ten months?

9. When Lucy confesses her crime to Wendy, Wendy is kind and understanding, as she has a secret of her own to confess. Why do you think Wendy's secret makes her sympathetic to Lucy? How do you think her secret compares with Lucy's?

10. If the kidnapping hadn't happened, Marilyn presumably would have chosen to remain employed and Mia would have been raised by a woman who, like Lucy, works

outside the home. Compare the images presented in the book of different mothering styles and decisions that led to various choices. What do these differences in styles represent for Mia?

11. Marilyn and Tom both managed to eventually move on and make new lives for themselves after the kidnapping. Cheryl wonders how Lucy could ever "restore what she took from those parents? She took their baby. She took their marriage. She took the lives they were meant to have." How do you think Marilyn and Tom would reconcile the regret of losing the lives they were meant to have with embracing the seemingly happy lives they ended up with?

12. Does the fact that Lucy raised Mia with love excuse her actions? What does "restorative justice" mean in this case? How do you think she deserves to be punished for her crime?

ENHANCE YOUR BOOK CLUB

Does Wendy's cooking have you craving Chinese? Try your hand at some homemade dumplings to serve during your book club meeting (chinesefood.about.com/od/dim sumdumplings/r/jiaozi.htm) — or order takeout!

In California, Marilyn gets really into things like yoga, meditation, palm reading, and astrological charts. You can find lots of free astrological charts online. For an indepth reading of your birth chart, try this one: http://www.chaosastrology.net/freeastrology reports.cfm. How accurate do you think your chart is? Highlight some fun parts to share with your book club.

You can read about real kidnapping stories similar to Mia's by searching online for the kidnappings of Carlina White and Zephany Nurse, who were both raised in other families and found their birth parents years later. How do they compare to Mia's story?

Fascinated by Wendy's story of giving up her daughter? Read more about the history of China's one child policy by visiting http:// www.britannica.com/EBchecked/topic/1710 568/one-child-policy.

ABOUT THE AUTHOR

Helen Klein Ross is a poet and novelist whose work has appeared in *The New Yorker, The Los Angeles Times, The New York Times,* and in *The Iowa Review* where it won the 2014 Iowa Review award in poetry. She graduated from Cornell University and received an MFA from The New School. Helen lives with her husband in New York City and Salisbury, CT.